HEART

∼ OF THE ∼

IMPALER

HEART
OF THE
IMPALER

ALEXANDER DELACROIX

New York

*For Emeline Parr, who was kind to me when
I was far from home and encouraged me when
I was badly in need of encouragement.*

A Swoon Reads Book
An imprint of Feiwel and Friends and Macmillan Publishing Group, LLC
120 Broadway, New York, NY 10271

Our books may be purchased in bulk for promotional, educational,
or business use. Please contact your local bookseller or the Macmillan Corporate
and Premium Sales Department at (800) 221-7945 ext. 5442 or by e-mail
at MacmillanSpecialMarkets@macmillan.com.

Library of Congress Cataloging-in-Publication Data is available.

ISBN 978-1-250-75616-9 (hardcover) / ISBN 978-1-250-75615-2 (ebook)

Book design by Michelle Gengaro-Kokmen

First edition, 2021

1 3 5 7 9 10 8 6 4 2
fiercereads.com

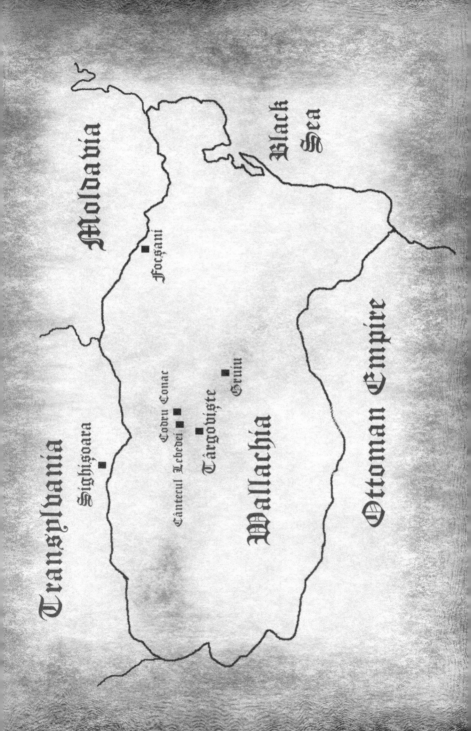

CHAPTER ONE

Târgovişte, Winter 1442

THE SUN HADN'T SET, BUT THE MOON HOVERED OVER THE CUR-
tea Domnească like a curious orange eye. It seemed almost as
interested in the two boys' antics as Ilona and the rest of their
all-female audience. The boys unsheathed their Magyar long-
swords, wiped the blades on their shirttails, and swiped the
weapons experimentally through the air. Both paused to cast
sidelong glances at the watching girls. The boyars' daughters
obliged their hopes with flirtatious laughter.

Ilona watched the girls lean close and whisper to one another
behind their hands. They were as duplicitous as the courtiers
in Transylvania and twice as vicious. Ilona's family had been
guests of Vlad Dracul's court for only a few short weeks, but
in that time she'd learned to carefully guard her thoughts and
her words.

Something tugged at her embroidered sleeve. Ilona wiped the scowl off her face and looked down at her younger sister.

"Which one is the *voivode*'s son?" Gizela asked.

"The shorter one."

"What's his name?"

"Honestly, Gizi, we've been here for weeks. He's the one who's named after his father. Vlad. Vlad Dracula."

Gizela giggled. "Dracula. That means 'little devil.' I think I'll marry him. I want to be a prince's wife."

"If you want to be a prince's wife, you'll have to marry someone else."

Gizela frowned. "Why?"

"Because the voivode's eldest son—Mircea—is next in line for Wallachia's throne."

"Then I'll marry *him*."

"He's eighteen. I don't think he's interested in seven-year-olds."

Gizela thrust out her lower lip and petulantly crossed her arms. "I'm nearly eight and very mature for my age!"

Ilona laughed, which drew the attention of the boyars' daughters and the sword-wielding boys. Vlad clearly decided Ilona's laughter was for him; he grinned and bowed, his wavy hair falling over his eyes.

He wasn't heart-stoppingly handsome, Ilona thought, but he wasn't unattractive either. And he was funny. The other day she had watched from a corner as he mocked the boyars behind their backs. He had mastered Grand Boyar Golescu's scowl and Boyar Văcărescu's pompous strut. He didn't fear any of them, although perhaps he should have.

Vlad Dracul II was a powerful voivode, Wallachia's princely

warlord, but the boyars were powerful landowners with soldiers and alliances of their own. Dracul only maintained power by keeping a slim majority of the aristocracy on his side.

Up to this point, Ilona had only exchanged a few words with Vlad in passing, so she didn't know why she blushed now at his unexpected attention.

Vlad's tall, quiet companion stared too, but when Ilona looked back, he quickly lowered his gaze. He was Vlad's cousin Andrei. The boyars' daughters had been whispering his and Vlad's names ever since they entered the courtyard. Two of the three girls now stared daggers at Ilona.

Despite what they might have thought, Ilona wasn't seeking Vlad's attention—she had no interest in climbing the social ladder. But when he addressed his audience, his gaze lingered on her.

"Andrei and I are training to be knights," he said. "We've already fought Wallachia's enemies at the border, and the next time they dare to set their worthless feet on our soil, we'll be there to stop them again. Isn't that right, Andrei?"

He clapped a hand on Andrei's shoulder, and Andrei nodded.

"I'm already a member of Sigismund's Order of the Dragon," Vlad said. "I've been preparing my entire life to lead Wallachia's armies."

The boyars' daughters responded with appropriate nods and smiles. Vlad beamed and Andrei blushed.

"These are sharpened," Vlad said, brandishing his sword. "One false move and Andrei or I could lose a hand."

A pretty girl with a long braid falling down her back pretended to swoon into one of her companions' arms. It earned another coveted grin from Vlad. Ilona bit her lower lip. The pretty girl was Golescu's daughter. Grand Boyar Golescu was possibly the most powerful boyar in Wallachia. This, in and of itself, made his daughter particularly dangerous.

"Are you ready?" Vlad asked, returning his attention to Andrei.

Andrei didn't seem as enthusiastic as Vlad, but he mumbled an acknowledgment. Vlad moved into a ready stance. Neither boy wore protective armor; both had stripped off their fur-lined coats and now shivered in their linen tunics.

This exhibition was foolish. An adult would put an immediate end to it, but all the adults were in the banquet hall. Ilona knew she should say something, but fear of how the other girls would react kept her quiet. She was already enough of an outsider here at court.

The boys bowed and crossed their blades.

"*Începe!*" Vlad shouted. His sword met Andrei's, and a metallic clang rippled off the courtyard walls. Vlad—clearly the more aggressive—lunged at his cousin, forcing Andrei to hastily swat Vlad's blade aside. Undeterred, Vlad came at him again. And again. And again . . . It took Andrei seven tries to finally catch Vlad's blade against his own spade-ended cross guard.

"Good one," Vlad grunted.

Andrei nodded. He shrugged Vlad's ringing weapon aside, and the mock battle resumed. Strike. Block. Strike.

Ilona again considered creeping back to the banquet hall to find her father, but self-doubt held her in place. Vlad and Andrei were skilled. Maybe they did this often. Maybe they knew how to handle a sword without harming each other. Vlad was better, but it was a friendly match. Nobody was going to get hurt.

Despite her worry, the longer she watched, the more impressed Ilona became. Vlad played swords the way Ilona's father played rithmomachy—a mathematical board game similar to chess, but far more complex. Like Ilona's father, Vlad used just the right amount of strategy and reckless aggression to intimidate his opponent. It was working on Andrei. Step by step, Vlad forced his cousin backward.

And then Andrei surprised everyone. He struck Vlad's swooping blade with a heavy blow that nearly sent it flying; Vlad fought to maintain his grasp. One of the boyars' daughters cheered, and Vlad's jaw tightened.

Ilona saw a change in Vlad's eyes. They grew darker. His swordplay became less restrained.

Gizela clapped. "This is exciting! Who do you think will win?"

Ilona pushed her sister behind her. It was time to go for help. She stepped toward the nearest corridor, but she was too late. Andrei slipped on a patch of icy snow and Vlad's razor-edged blade carved a crimson path down the left side of his face.

Blood.

Everywhere.

The boyars' daughters shrieked, Andrei dropped his weapon, and Vlad staggered backward with a horrified look on his face.

Ilona didn't remember moving, wasn't sure how she ended up between Andrei and Vlad, but sticky blood oozed between Ilona's fingers where she pressed her handkerchief against Andrei's face.

Andrei stared at her. Behind her, Vlad stammered, "I . . . I . . ."

She looked at Vlad. He looked away.

"WHAT'S GOING ON OUT HERE?"

The words thundered off the courtyard walls. Vlad dropped his sword, and Ilona jumped and turned her head toward the voice.

A fierce man with a drooping mustache swooped toward her and Andrei. The man wore a red velvet cap and an ermine-fringed coat. A dragon-shaped medallion bounced against his chest.

Vlad's father. Vlad Dracul the Second, Prince of Wallachia.

The voivode forcefully pulled Ilona's hand away from Andrei's face and examined the damage inflicted by the younger Vlad's sword. Ilona crept back to Gizela, reaching for her sister's hand, but drew back when she saw the blood on her own.

The voivode turned away from Andrei. He saw the dropped swords and kicked them across the cobbled courtyard.

"I asked what's going on here."

His words were for Vlad, but Vlad didn't answer.

The voivode glared at Andrei. "Find Raluca. Tell her to clean that up."

Andrei nodded and wiped the back of one hand across his face, which only made his wound look worse. He ducked past the voivode and disappeared down a corridor.

Dracul turned his attention back to his son. "Is this what I pay that tutor a small fortune for? Train you to strut like a cockerel in a henhouse to impress a few empty-headed girls?"

His hand flew out, and Ilona bit back a startled cry as his open palm met the side of Vlad's face. The slap rang across the courtyard. Vlad staggered but didn't make a sound.

"Come with me!"

The son fell into obedient step behind the father, and the voivode's bodyguards closed in around them as they exited the courtyard. The silence that followed was uncomfortable, but not as uncomfortable as what came next.

"You're Nicholas Csáki's granddaughters."

Ilona turned. The girl with the braid stared at her, arms crossed, a smirk on her face.

"We are."

"He was vajda of Transylvania."

"Yes."

"And your uncle Ladislaus ruled after him."

"You know a great deal about our family. I can't claim the same about yours."

The braided girl smiled. "I make it my business to know everything about any family that thinks it's good enough to worm its way into the voivode's court, but even in Wallachia the Csáki name is famous. Famous for suffering history's most humiliating defeat."

Gizela stiffened and frowned, mirroring Ilona's own actions. The braided girl saw this and sneered.

"Your family was shamed during the Peasant Revolt. You're the laughingstock of all Transylvania."

One of the girl's companions—a tall, gaunt girl with too-angular features and too-shrewd eyes—snickered at the vicious comment.

"We're richer and more important than any of you," Gizela said hotly. "You don't know what you're talking about!"

Ilona bumped Gizela with her elbow, and her sister glared at her.

"Ow, Ilona! What was that for?"

"Ilona?" the braided girl said. "What a pretty name! I'm Daciana. This is my cousin, Sorina."

She gestured toward her tall, unattractive companion. Her other companion, a round-faced, hazel-eyed girl, cleared her throat.

"And this is Magdalena."

The third girl had friendlier features than the others and looked uncomfortable about what was happening, but she couldn't feel anywhere near as uncomfortable as Ilona did.

"It's such a pleasure to meet all of you," Ilona said, forcing her words through clenched teeth. "But as stimulating as this conversation is, Gizela and I must be going."

"Of course," Daciana said. "Naturally you wish to be at the banquet to get a good seat for the big announcement."

"What announcement?"

"Oh, my! You don't know!" Daciana turned to her companions. "The poor dear! She doesn't know!"

"What announcement?" Ilona repeated, clenching her teeth again.

Daciana's smug smile grew larger. "Tut, tut. I wouldn't want to ruin the surprise."

"You're just jealous!" Gizela said. "Jealous that Vlad likes Ilona more than he likes you!"

That comment struck a nerve. "Jealous?" Daciana spat. "Jealous of a pair of paupers who wouldn't have a crust of bread on their plates if not for the voivode's charity? Your family was flung out of Transylvania like a chamber pot emptied into a gutter. Thrown out like slop to a swine!"

Gizela glared and Ilona pressed her lips tightly together as

Daciana and Sorina flipped their hair and strode away. Magdalena hesitantly followed. Ilona remained rooted to the spot until the boyars' daughters and their mocking laughter faded.

"Don't pay them any attention," Gizela said. A fierce look darkened her seven-year-old face. "They're just jealous because they're not as pretty or as smart as you."

"You're the smart, pretty one, *madárka*. Smart and pretty like Mother."

It was still painful to mention their mother, but the compliment brought a smile to Gizela's face. Ilona smoothed back her sister's long dark hair. Unlike Ilona, who looked far too much like their father, Gizela possessed their mother's grace and beauty. Perhaps that was why Gizela had always been Father's favorite.

"Do you think they'll have chimney cakes at the voivode's banquet?" Gizela asked.

"I hope so. It seems like forever since I've eaten a good *kürtőskalács*."

"Last Christmas, Mama let me have as many as I wanted."

Ilona felt a stab in her heart. That was enough talk about their dead mother.

"Come on, madárka. We need to find Father."

She straightened her black skirt and realized her hand was still sticky with Andrei's blood. She would have to do something about that before they returned to the voivode's great hall. Father would never forgive her if she disgraced him by showing up unpresentable.

Alliances. To him, everything was about forming alliances. First impressions—especially bad ones—could undo his efforts to restore his lost honor by making a place for himself in Wallachia. To that end, Ilona's father could be downright ruthless.

Like Daciana. Ilona already hated that girl! Daciana knew about alliances, and if Ilona was going to survive in Dracul's court, she would need to form a few alliances of her own. It was what her mother would have done. The question was, who would Ilona ally herself with, and how would she do it?

In Wallachia, as in Transylvania, survival depended on such choices.

CHAPTER TWO

THE UNEXPECTED SHOVE FROM BEHIND NEARLY SENT VLAD TO the floor. He regained his balance and spun to face his attacker.

"I hear you're once again working hard to disgrace our family name," Mircea said with a smirk.

Vlad scowled at his older brother. "At least I have to work at it," he snarled. "All *you* had to do was be born."

Mircea dismissed Vlad's comment with a guttural laugh. "You're so pathetic. A real man doesn't need to cut off someone's face to get a woman to pay attention to him."

Vlad balled one hand into a fist.

"Are you thinking about punching me?" Mircea said. "Go on then, and see what happens."

Vlad already knew what would happen. He would show up at the voivode's banquet with a black eye and a bloody nose. Mircea was a full head taller than Vlad and twice as brawny, but it wouldn't always be that way. Eventually Vlad would catch up, and when that happened . . .

"Why don't you go find a mirror to admire yourself in," Vlad retorted. "If self-obsession is all it takes to rule a kingdom, you'll become the greatest voivode Wallachia has ever known."

Mircea took a threatening step toward Vlad and chortled when his brother involuntarily shuffled back.

"So says the spare who will *never* rule Wallachia." Mircea shoved Vlad again. "Run along to your room, little brother, and comb your hair. You look like a flock of pigeons tried to nest on your head."

Mircea swaggered away. Vlad started to brush his fingers through his hair, then angrily dropped his hand to his side. He glared at the back of Mircea's head until his self-absorbed sibling disappeared around the corner. One day Vlad *would* rule Wallachia. He was far more deserving of it than his *neispravit* older brother.

And of course he could get a woman's attention without trying; Ilona had noticed him, after all. She'd noticed him on her very first day at the Curtea Domnească.

Vlad relaxed his clenched fists and daydreamed about her a moment. She was fearless. Today in the courtyard when the other girls screamed and covered their eyes, Ilona walked calmly to Andrei's side. Vlad almost wished he'd been the one who'd received the ugly sword wound; he couldn't help but wonder what it would feel like to have her hand pressed softly against *his* face.

He shivered. Strong. Brave. Beautiful. He needed to get to know her better.

He smiled until he thought about Andrei again. He still felt guilty about hurting him. He could think of a thousand ways he'd like to hurt Mircea, but not Andrei. He and Andrei were more than cousins. They were best friends. They were allies.

The echo of heavy boots alerted Vlad that somebody was coming. A moment later, a palace guard stepped out of one of the side corridors and bowed.

"Your Highness, His Excellency the Voivode requires your immediate presence at his personal chambers. He is about to make an important announcement and wants the entire royal family present."

Vlad nodded. "I'll be there in a moment."

"He would like Prince Andrei there as well."

"I'll find him," Vlad said. "Tell my father we're both coming."

The guard bowed again and marched back in the direction he had just appeared from.

An important announcement . . . Vlad knew tonight's banquet must be about something more than a friendly meal with the local boyars. Friendly! It almost made him laugh out loud even to think the word. The boyars were anything but friendly. As a group they wielded enough power to make the voivode's life difficult at best.

Vlad hoped the announcement would be something to thwart the boyars and their backstabbing schemes. When Vlad was voivode, he would do something about them. He would make sure Wallachia's throne got the respect it deserved.

"This is going to hurt worse than the sword."

Raluca held up a needle and a long strand of thread. Andrei hooked his fingers under the chair, winced, and clenched his teeth.

"If you do that, you're going to make it worse."

"Don't you have some kind of herb to make it not hurt?"

"No. Now hold still. If the voivode doesn't call the doctors to bleed you, you might live to try some other stupid thing."

Raluca wasn't the most consoling type, but she did know how to take care of battle wounds. She fixed Mircea up the time he took a scimitar to the shoulder. He barely had a scar after the wound healed.

"Stop squirming."

"I'm trying."

"If you're going to play like a man, I expect you to take your pain like one."

Despite his resolve to appear manly, Andrei yelped when the needle pierced his swollen cheek.

"I warned you it would hurt."

The thread tugged uncomfortably, making Andrei's oozing wound burn, and the needle stung like an angry bee. But he held back tears. Sometimes he could forget pain—like the throbbing after one of the voivode's beatings—if he closed his eyes and thought of something pleasant.

Like that Transylvanian girl. There was a pleasant thought. He didn't know many courtiers who would dirty their hands with another person's blood, but she'd come to his aid without a second thought. She had gentle hands.

Unlike Raluca's.

"Ow!"

"There," Raluca said, setting the needle aside. "All done. Hold this over it, but don't do anything to mess up my sewing. I won't do it for you again. After this you'll have to deal with it on your own."

She smeared a sticky herbal paste over the stitched wound, covered it with a square of muslin cloth, and put Andrei's hand over it. Andrei gingerly pressed the cloth against his throbbing cheek.

"You're lucky you didn't lose an eye. Or your entire head."

"I know."

"I risked my life to bring you to Wallachia. Do you know that? Your mother *sacrificed* hers. How do you think she would feel if she knew you were making reckless decisions?"

"She would be unhappy." Andrei hung his head. "She would be ashamed."

Raluca observed him a moment, decided his remorse was sincere, and patted his knee.

"You're a fine young man, Andrei Muşat. Most of the time. But you and Vlad need to change your ways before you fall into the kind of harm stitches can't fix."

She shook her head. "That Vlad . . . There's another boy who is badly in need of a mother. Heaven knows the voivode gives him far less love than he deserves."

"Vlad and I will stay out of trouble," Andrei said. "I promise."

"Put on some clean clothes in case the voivode calls you down to his fancy banquet. I'll take this"—she retrieved Andrei's blood-smeared shirt from the floor—"and see if Danica can salvage it."

Raluca ruffled Andrei's hair, gave his wound one last look, and exited the room. Andrei remained on the edge of his bed, staring at the wall.

She was right. He and Vlad needed to take fewer risks, but Vlad was persuasive. Andrei had never been able to say no to Vlad's misadventures. Even knowing Vlad's schemes perpetually ended in disaster, he always gave in.

"There you are."

Vlad's voice made Andrei jump.

His cousin entered the room, staring at Andrei's face.

"I . . . I'm sorry. I . . ."

"It was an accident," Andrei said. "You didn't mean to do it."

"I know, but . . ." Vlad edged closer to get a better look. "Ow . . . That's going to leave a scar. A *big* scar."

He saw the expression on Andrei's face and grew remorseful again.

"But it will be an amazing scar. It will make you look intimidating."

"You think?"

Vlad nodded. He was trying to appear convinced, but the twitch at the corner of his eye gave his true feelings away.

They stared uncomfortably at the floor.

"She's interesting, isn't she?"

"Huh?"

"Ilona Csáki," Vlad clarified.

Andrei didn't answer, but warmth spread through him again as he recollected the sensation of her soft fingers touching his face.

Vlad was staring at the ceiling now. "She couldn't stop looking at me. Did you notice?"

"I was too busy bleeding," Andrei grumbled.

"What?"

"Nothing. You're right. She only had eyes for you."

Vlad grinned. "She's brave. She's smart. I need to get to know her."

Andrei clenched his hands into fists but quickly loosened them when Vlad looked back down at him.

"The voivode sent me to bring you to the banquet," Vlad

said. "Apparently he has something important to say and wants *everybody* there."

"I need a clean shirt."

"I'll get it for you."

Vlad wasn't usually this helpful. He glanced at Andrei's face again before hurrying to the big wardrobe. When he returned, he helped Andrei pull a long-sleeved tunic over his head.

"I really am sorry about what happened."

"It was an accident. It's all right."

"Does it hurt bad?"

Andrei shrugged. "Not as bad as at first."

They stepped out into the corridor, and Vlad changed the subject. "Earlier today, I overheard something I wasn't supposed to hear. The voivode is giving Codru Conac to Ilona's father. His family will be occupying the manor immediately. I think the announcement has something to do with that."

"That would explain why Ilona's family suddenly showed up at the Curtea Domnească," Andrei said. "But the voivode doesn't give anything away for free. What do you think he's getting out of it?"

Vlad shrugged. "I don't know. Information about Transylvania's armies. Secrets Csáki's former allies wouldn't want the voivode to know. Whatever it is, I'm glad he came to Wallachia with his family. His oldest daughter isn't like the other girls around here. She hasn't been tainted by boyar politics."

"You've barely even talked to her," Andrei said. "Just a few words of greeting here and there. How do you know she's different?"

Vlad glared. "I just know. And I think we should visit

Codru Conac after Csáki's family moves into the manor. Ilona will need friends at court. We can be those friends."

Andrei squirmed. "Will the voivode let us do that?"

"Why wouldn't he?" Vlad asked.

"I don't know how soon I'll be able to travel. My face—"

"What? Do you plan to sit on it while you ride?"

"No," Andrei said, annoyed by Vlad's joke, "but . . ."

He couldn't bring himself to give the real reason for his hesitance to be near Ilona. Vlad would laugh at him, but Andrei would bet Vlad would feel the same if it were *his* face that had been marred.

"We'd better hurry," Vlad said, walking faster. "The voivode's going to grow impatient. I don't want to anger him twice in one day."

Andrei hastened his own steps. Vlad was right. Angering the voivode was never a good idea. It was time to forget about his pain and humiliation.

The banquet hall was dark, narrow, and drafty. A fire roared at the hall's iron-grated hearth, but the flames did little to drive away the damp chill. Candle-laden chandeliers dimly illuminated the room, and moonlight cast weak color through the hall's stained-glass windows. The hall's lancet windows vaguely reminded Ilona of the ones in the old church at Sighișoara. She used to pray there with her mother every Sunday . . . until Mother got sick. Ilona swallowed the tight lump in her throat and forced her mother's image from her mind.

Unlike in the church's windows, here there were no prophets or benevolent saints to stare down at Ilona. Instead, a scowling prince lifted a curved sword while leading a cavalry charge against sinister-looking enemy soldiers. Ilona shifted her attention elsewhere. Servants now bustled in to fill the split-timber tables with pots and trays. Lamb stew, mushroom-stuffed carp, garlicky sausages, grilled fish in savory pickle sauce . . .

Ilona's stomach rumbled. She wasn't the only one starving; Gizela's eyes were round and wide. Her little sister scooted forward to examine a newly arrived dish—sugar-dusted *scovergi*, golden-brown and still glistening with hot oil.

She and Gizela hadn't experienced a feast like this since . . . since . . . Ilona shook her head. She couldn't remember how long it had been. Maybe this move to Wallachia wasn't an entirely bad thing. Maybe Ilona's father had been right to bring the family here.

Father . . . Ilona was supposed to be looking for him. She spotted him in a corner, half surrounded by fur-clad men in tall plumed hats. One of them—a short, round fellow with frizzy hair and a bushy mustache—laughed at something Ilona's father said and thumped him on the back.

"You're hilarious, Csáki! I didn't know it was possible to be Transylvanian and still have a sense of humor."

Her father smiled. He was handsome—and charming when he wanted to be. He had a knack for gaining people's trust. That was probably why the voivode invited him to Wallachia.

"Rumor has it," the frizz-haired man announced, "that our voivode has given you three of his best villages north of Târgovişte."

Ilona's father nodded. "My new property is an hour's ride northwest of here. The voivode has generously bequeathed me a small manor near the foothills."

The frizz-haired man grinned. "You're near the Mănăstirea Dealu, then. That makes us neighbors. My properties are also there."

Her father asked the man about the monastery. Ilona didn't hear the answer because a voice behind her made her jump.

"New property. What does a penniless, disgraced foreigner possess that he could trade to a voivode for lands and a title?"

Ilona turned slowly toward Daciana. As with their first encounter, Daciana wasn't alone. This time there were even more girls in her entourage.

"He didn't bring much with him, after all. Just a few trunks of clothing. And your sister. And you. Which of those do you think he offered to the voivode to become a boyar?"

Something cold crept up Ilona's spine. Frantic bells rang in the back of her mind. She tried to come up with a snappy response, but Daciana's friends laughed and sneered at her, and the unfriendly group walked away before Ilona's numbed lips could move to make words.

One girl, however, stayed behind, and she spoke to Ilona without making eye contact.

"Your father and mine seem to enjoy each other's company."

"What?"

"That's my father speaking to your father. I think they're enjoying each other's company."

Ilona looked at her father and the jolly boyar. "Yes . . . Yes, they are."

"I'm Magdalena. We met a little while ago. In the courtyard."

Magdalena attempted a shy smile.

"It's a pleasure to meet you, Magdalena."

"Call me Magda. That's what most people call me."

"It's a pleasure to meet you, Magda." Daciana and her viciousness still hung between them awkwardly. Ilona searched for a way to excuse herself but couldn't think of a way to do it without seeming rude.

"I apologize for Daciana," Magda whispered, apparently reading Ilona's mind. "Her father is a *grand* boyar. She thinks that makes her superior." Magda lowered her voice so it was barely audible. "That's him over there. Dragoș Golescu."

Daciana's father stood near the great hall's double doors. Ilona had already seen him several times before. He was a tall, broad-shouldered man with threatening eyes. Like the other boyars, he wore a fur-trimmed coat and an over-tall hat. Unlike the others', his lower face bristled with thick, dark whiskers. It made him look like a bear.

"My father hates him," Magda continued. "Golescu comes from old boyar blood, and he uses that status to intimidate the rest of the boyar council into doing whatever he wants. But Papa says your family comes from old blood, too. He hopes your father's influence will weaken Golescu's."

Ilona didn't have a chance to respond; the sounds of booted feet echoed in from the corridor. A group of armed men appeared, followed by the voivode and his family. Another group of soldiers marched in directly behind them.

The voivode's guards didn't look Wallachian. Ilona remembered her father saying something about the voivode hiring mercenaries. Foreigners were loyal to the prince who paid them rather than to a local boyar patron.

The boyars removed their tall hats. Their wives smoothed

out their skirts, and men and women bowed in unison. The voivode strode across the hall to a high-backed chair and seated himself at the main banquet table.

Two scowling guards positioned themselves behind Dracul's chair while the others placed themselves in strategic spots around the room. The voivode took no chances with his safety. Ilona supposed she would be equally cautious if she occupied a throne.

"Sit," Dracul commanded, and his guests hurriedly found their places. Ilona hadn't attended many banquets, but she was trained in court etiquette and was fairly certain it was customary—even in Wallachia—for a prince to announce his arrival before striding into a room.

Ilona's father noticed that she and Gizela were still standing at the back of the hall, and he impatiently motioned to them. She'd forgotten about Gizela. Her little sister was still walking around the tables, eyeing the steaming trays.

"Gizi!" Ilona whispered.

Gizela hurried to her side. Their seats were a few places removed from the voivode and his family. Andrei was seated next to Vlad, his head ducked, a blood-pinked rag held to his face. Ilona glanced down at her hand. There had been no time to properly clean it. She'd scrubbed it with a clump of snow, but Andrei's blood still rimmed her fingernails and darkened the creases in her palm. Using her skirt, she wiped at her hand again. The voivode's wife—the *cneajna*—smiled at her, and Ilona attempted to smile back.

Dracul's wife was the princess Vasilisa. She was young and beautiful—too young to be Vlad or Mircea's mother. There were rumors that Prince Dracul had sent his first wife back to her parents so he could marry Vasilisa and forge an alliance with Moldavia's royal family.

That's what it meant to be a woman in a world ruled by men. Sold. Traded like livestock. Used and eventually cast away.

The warning itched again at the back of Ilona's head. What had her father traded for lands and a title?

The voivode cleared his throat. The crowd's lingering whispers scurried into the shadows.

"I've invited you here, friends, boyars, clergy," the voivode began, "to make several important announcements."

Something about the way he uttered the words "friends," "boyars," and "clergy" made them sound menacing rather than friendly. Ilona remembered the way the voivode struck his own son. She shuddered.

"First, I have invited you to celebrate with me as I bestow the title of grand boyar upon my longtime friend Anton Csáki."

Silence. Ilona didn't have to understand boyar ranking to realize a promotion of this magnitude was uncommon. Especially for an outsider—a Transylvanian—who had resided in Wallachia for only a few weeks.

Grand boyar. It was the same title Daciana's father held. Ilona risked a glance toward Dragoş Golescu. His jaw was tight, his face livid. Daciana sat beside him, fixing Ilona with an icy stare. Ilona looked away.

The obligatory applause finally came, but it was slow, and the enthusiasm was forced. Neither the voivode nor Ilona's father acted as if he noticed or cared.

"As a grand boyar," Dracul said, "Anton Csáki will command Wallachia's second and third infantries. He will oversee the defense of our northern borders . . ."

Northern borders? The borders with Transylvania and Moldavia? Why those and not the frontier separating Wallachia from the Ottoman Empire? Maybe the warning tingle at the back of Ilona's neck was wrong. Maybe the voivode had only wanted her father's knowledge of Transylvania's armies and political affairs.

"This is an important event," the voivode continued, "but not my only reason for bringing you here. I also wish to announce another happy event—the betrothal of my son Mircea to our newest grand boyar's eldest daughter."

Ilona's body went numb. She hid both hands under the table to keep the other guests from seeing them shake. There was more applause, this time unforced. One of the boyars reached across from his table to thump Mircea heartily on the back. The woman seated directly across from Ilona beamed and offered her congratulations. The voivode motioned for Mircea and Ilona to rise.

Ilona sat like a lump of granite. She sat so long, her father finally prodded her with his elbow. Ilona recoiled from his touch. *He* was the one who had done this to her.

The numbness in her limbs slowly dissipated, replaced by frightened anger. She could barely bring herself to look at Mircea as she moved mechanically around the table to join him.

Ilona was only faintly cognizant of her part in the betrothal rituals that ensued. She and Mircea took turns sipping from the same wine-filled cup. Ilona felt the gold betrothal ring's chill as Mircea slipped it onto her right third finger. She flinched when the smooth metal touched her flesh as if it burned. She didn't even look at Mircea until his father and hers picked up a feathered quill to sign the betrothal contract.

Mircea was visibly unimpressed with Ilona. He looked her up and down, frowned, and quickly turned his attention to the exposed cleavage of a boyar's buxom daughter.

Ilona wasn't impressed with him either. He was unattractive. His nose was too flat and too wide, and he was built like a bull. He looked almost as intelligent as one, too.

One year from this evening. That was the wedding date spelled out on the contract. Ilona turned sixteen in a month. The wedding would happen shortly before her seventeenth birthday. Just thinking about it made her feel nauseous. It was fortunate she hadn't eaten anything, because she might have embarrassed her father by doing something unsightly all over the freshly inked parchment.

Trust in God's tender mercy.

That's what her mother would have told her. But if God were merciful, He would have prevented this from happening.

"I have one final announcement," the voivode said after Mircea and Ilona returned to their seats. "You all know I recently made a trip to Adrianople to meet with the sultan. While I was there, I signed a treaty with him."

Nervous murmurs skittered through the hall. The sultan, Murad II. Leader of the powerful Ottoman Empire. But that wasn't Ilona's concern. She had bigger worries. In front of all these people, her father had sold her to Vlad Dracul and his son.

"The sultan has promised me protection against my enemies," the voivode continued, his cold gaze sweeping the room. He smiled. "Enjoy your feast."

No one would enjoy it now. Least of all Ilona.

CHAPTER THREE

Vᴌᴀᴅ sᴌᴀᴍᴍᴇᴅ ʜɪs ᴅᴏᴏʀ, ᴋɪᴄᴋᴇᴅ ᴀ ʙᴏᴏᴛ ᴀᴄʀᴏss ᴛʜᴇ ʀᴏᴏᴍ, and whipped his hand over a tabletop. Random objects clattered to the floor. A belt buckle. An unlit candle. A decorative dagger in a bejeweled sheath. Vlad kicked them all aside and paced the room.

Not only did Mircea get the throne, he would also get the girl Vlad was interested in. It was completely unfair!

Ilona deserved better than Mircea. Much better! She deserved someone who would be devoted to her. Someone who would worship her. Someone like Vlad.

Vlad went to his shuttered window, flung it open, and stared out into the frosty night. The evening's announcement shouldn't bother him like this. He didn't *know* Ilona, and yet he felt a magnetic attraction toward her that made him want to know everything about her. Now he would never get that chance.

Mircea was too much like the voivode. He used people to get what he wanted, and when they wore out their usefulness, he threw them away. Just like the voivode had done to Vlad's mother. Vlad would never forgive his father for that. He still cried in his sleep when he relived it in nightmares, once more feeling the trauma of being ripped from his sobbing mother's arms.

A week after her departure, he had a new stepmother. Vlad no longer remembered his real mother's face, but he remembered her love. Vasilisa didn't love him. Other than herself, the only person the voivode's Moldavian princess loved was her darling little Radu.

Vlad snorted angrily, kicked another object, and watched it ricochet off a wall. He needed someone to talk to, and there was only one person who could sympathize with his frustrations. Sometimes Vlad felt like Andrei understood him better than he understood himself.

He reshuttered his window and returned to the hallway. He didn't bother knocking when he reached Andrei's room, just walked right in.

Andrei was seated on his bed, one hand pressed lightly against his stitched, swollen face. Vlad winced, but he had already apologized, and he now had other things to discuss.

"We have to stop Mircea. We can't let him marry her."

Andrei stared at Vlad, a slight frown creasing his face.

"He shouldn't get to have Ilona," Vlad continued. "He shouldn't get to be married to her. He'll be a terrible voivode and an even worse husband."

Andrei played with his shirt cuff. "Maybe she's happy about it. Most boyar girls would be thrilled to be betrothed to a future voivode. *Any* future voivode."

Vlad glared at his cousin. "She's not happy about it! Didn't you see her? She looked like she wanted to die!"

"So we're going to rescue her from Mircea?"

"Yes!"

"How?"

"I . . . I don't know. That's why I came in here to talk to you."

Andrei fidgeted again with his sleeve. "We could sit down and write your father a letter. We could explain why forcing her to marry Mircea is a really bad idea."

Vlad scowled. "Seriously? That's the best you can come up with?"

He walked to Andrei's window and took a small wooden figurine off the sill, an intricately carved bird. A swan. Vlad remembered Andrei saying something about how it once belonged to his mother. Agitated, Vlad tossed it from palm to palm.

"What else do you have?"

"Nothing. I gave my idea. It's your turn now."

"All right," Vlad said. "Here's my idea. Maybe we should poison Mircea. You know, a little at a time. Slowly. So everyone thinks he has a mysterious sickness."

Andrei blanched.

"I'm kidding!" Vlad said. "I couldn't kill a member of my own family."

Although plenty of other princes had done it.

Andrei's uncles, Iliaş and Stephen, did it. They killed Andrei's father in order to secure Moldavia's throne for themselves. That was why Andrei now lived under the voivode's protection at the Curtea Domnească. That was why he was now, and ever would be, an orphan.

"Your turn," Vlad said. "Give me a better idea."

"I can't. I don't have any."

And that was the problem. There was nothing either of them could actually do.

Vlad stopped bouncing the swan and returned it to the windowsill. Andrei stared at the carved object as Vlad walked away from it.

"You look terrible," Vlad said. "You should get some rest."

Andrei nodded. "I'm exhausted."

Their brief conversation had accomplished nothing, and now Vlad felt stupid. If Andrei hadn't known it before, he probably now guessed that Vlad was infatuated with Ilona Csáki.

"I'm going to bed, too. *Noapte bună.*"

"Good night," Andrei repeated back.

Vlad went out and shut the door behind him.

He was being stupid. *Olyan hülye!* So stupid, to care so much about the fate of a girl he barely knew!

But he was going to become better acquainted with her, he decided. He was going to learn everything he possibly could.

There was no end to the upheaval in her life. First her family fell from grace, then her mother grew ill and died. Soon after, they departed Transylvania, which brought her to where she was now.

Sold. Like a prized cow. To the House of Drăculeşti.

She had never wanted to be married. Especially not to a self-absorbed pig like Mircea.

She hadn't been at Wallachia's royal court long, but it was long enough to watch Mircea bully the servants, make lewd comments to the maids, and swagger around like the world should bow before him. Her only consolation was that she had one year to live away from Dracul's Princely Court, time to search for some escape from this mess.

Escape . . . It was probably as impossible as it sounded.

Ilona's stomach hurt. It had hurt since the voivode made his terrible announcement. It was cinched into tight knots that refused to loosen. She had felt hopelessness and despair like this once before: when she watched the surgeons bleed her mother, and her mother descended deeper and deeper into the sickness that eventually took her.

Ilona's father blamed *her* for that sickness; his wife nearly died the night she gave birth to Ilona, and her health had never fully recovered after that. Ilona felt guilty for it, even though she knew it wasn't truly her fault. She felt guilty every day, and now she carried that guilt within her along with the dark weight of an unwanted betrothal.

Even at this late hour, torches still flickered on the Curtea Domnească's walls. The voivode's castle guards looked at Ilona and bowed when she walked past them, but they didn't speak. She was glad for that; she didn't want to talk to anyone. She wanted to remain cold, alone, empty, and silent.

Her feet somehow led her to the secluded courtyard where she'd witnessed Vlad and Andrei's ill-fated "duel." The courtyard provided the solitude she had been searching for. She sat on a stone bench. It was definitely silent here. She was certainly cold.

But she wasn't alone.

Something shifted in the shadows and she jumped up. "Who's there?" she cried.

"I'm sorry, I didn't mean to startle you," a young man replied from the darkness. "When I heard you coming, I should have warned you I was out here."

She only recognized him by his tall silhouette as he stepped away from the courtyard wall, not by his voice. He was usually Vlad's silent shadow; Vlad was the sociable one.

"Andrei . . . Hello."

"*Bună seara,*" Andrei said. "Good evening."

Ilona attempted a smile even though there were no smiles left in her. "What a surprise to see you out here. In the dark."

She blushed. It was a stupid comment. She, after all, was also standing out here in the darkness.

"I . . . couldn't sleep."

"Me either," Ilona said.

She searched for something else to say. "How is your face feeling? Does it hurt much?"

Andrei shifted to turn the left side of his face away from her.

"It won't stop throbbing, but Raluca says I'm lucky. It could have been worse."

"Raluca? She's in charge of the kitchen?"

"And the servants. And pretty much everything else. She looks out for me. She stitched up my face."

"She did a good job. I saw you in the great hall. I think it will heal well."

Andrei looked uncomfortable. Now *he* was searching for something to say.

"Congratulations on your betrothal."

She felt the knots in her stomach tighten again. "Thank you."

"Are you afraid?"

"What?"

Even in the darkness there was no mistaking the mortified

look on Andrei's face. "What I mean is . . . You probably weren't planning on this. You looked as surprised as everyone else."

"No." She stared at her feet. "It was unexpected. I had . . . other plans for my future."

"What were your plans?"

She looked up at him, and he studiously avoided her gaze.

"I'm sorry," he said. "That's none of my business—"

"I like science. Especially studying birds."

She didn't know why she told him this. It was embarrassing. Women didn't devote their lives to studying birds. They did needlework, maybe learned to play the harp or the lute, did the bidding of men.

Andrei, however, didn't laugh, scoff, or have any of the other reactions she would expect from a man. Instead he sat beside her—at a gentlemanly distance—seeming . . . interested.

"I've never known anyone who studied birds," he said. "What have you learned?"

"Lots of things. How to identify birds by their calls. How their plumage changes from season to season. The different shapes of their wings. The differences between their nests. When my mother was alive, she encouraged my interest. She introduced me to Aristotle's *Historia Animalium*." Ilona remembered something and laughed. "My language tutor thought I loved Latin grammar. He didn't realize I was obsessed with it because it was helping me read Aristotle's text."

She stopped speaking, suddenly self-conscious. She had never revealed these things to anyone but her mother. Not only that, but for a few moments at least she had forgotten the misery that drew her to the courtyard tonight.

"I'm probably boring you with my stories," she said.

Andrei shook his head. "Maybe you can teach me about birds sometime. There are lots of birds in the forest around Codru Conac. When Vlad and I come to visit, you can tell me more."

"You're planning to visit? You and Vlad?"

Andrei opened and closed his mouth, then avoided her gaze again. It took a moment before he collected himself enough to answer her question.

"Vlad thinks it would be a good idea for us to . . . um . . . spend time with you to . . . to help you prepare for life at the Curtea Domnească. Court politics can be a little . . . tricky."

Ilona nodded. "Yes . . . Daciana Golescu already did her best to make me aware of that."

Andrei grimaced. The grimace turned into a wince, and he touched the stitched side of his face. He was still turning the injury away from Ilona.

"Daciana isn't the nicest of girls," he said. "I'm sorry you had to make her acquaintance."

"There are girls like her in Transylvania," Ilona replied. "It's not the first time I've dealt with someone like her and probably not the last. Unfortunately, there are girls like her everywhere."

Andrei nodded and grimaced again, but this time he was more careful with his facial expressions.

"You're from Moldavia," Ilona said, changing the subject. "That's what I've heard, at least."

"Yes."

"So how is it that you ended up here in Wallachia with Vlad and his family?"

"My parents were murdered."

For a moment Ilona didn't know what to say. "Oh," she mumbled. Perhaps she should apologize for her question, but he continued before she could find the right words.

"I barely remember them. I was a little boy when it happened. Raluca—she was my mother's lady-in-waiting—she brought me to the Curtea Domnească. She says my father's brother Iliaş poisoned my father so he could get Moldavia's throne. He killed my mother, too. If Raluca hadn't escaped with me when she did, I would have been next."

He said it in an unemotional way, like a memorized fact, but Ilona saw turmoil in his guarded brown eyes.

"I'm sorry," she whispered. "That's horrible."

Andrei shrugged. Ilona allowed her fingertips to stray across the space between them to sympathetically touch the back of his hand. He flinched but didn't pull away.

"It's cold out here," Andrei whispered. "We should probably go back inside before we both freeze to death."

Ilona looked at the sky. "I think I'll stay a little longer."

"All right . . ." Andrei hesitated, probably wondering if it was unchivalrous of him to leave her in the cold and darkness alone, but she smiled to reassure him.

"Good night, Andrei."

"Good night," he said.

He waited a few more moments before disappearing into a torchlit corridor. Ilona watched him go, realizing she no longer felt cold or empty inside. Maybe she had formed her first alliance. Maybe Andrei would become a friend.

CHAPTER FOUR

They didn't have much in the way of possessions to take with them. Besides the clothing on their backs, there was one cedar trunk per family member. There had been little time to gather much of anything before their hasty departure from Sighişoara. Possessions became somewhat less important when an unfriendly ruler rose to power and you were in danger because of your family name.

The voivode's servants had almost finished tying the trunks to the backs of three skittish mules. Ilona's husband-to-be wasn't here to see her off—she was grateful for that—but the voivode was conversing with her father, and two more members of the House of Drăculeşti showed up to give their regards.

"Leaving already?" Vlad asked Ilona as he sauntered up to her. "You haven't been at court long enough for us to have a decent conversation."

He grinned, and it was hard not to feel drawn toward his easygoing personality.

Andrei was with him, silently avoiding direct eye contact, but smiling furtively when she stared long enough to force him to look up. It was hard to imagine this was the same boy who had held such a friendly conversation with her last night, albeit a short one. It was hard to believe she was leaving Prince Dracul's court as suddenly as she had come.

"I certainly wasn't expecting to leave like this," she said. "I thought there would at least be a few days' warning."

"But I'm sure you're happy to have a place to call home," Vlad said. "Until next year, at least . . . when this palace becomes your permanent home."

One sentence. That's all it took to send a flood of unhappy emotions coursing through her again.

"Yes," she whispered. "Until next year."

Vlad noticed the change in her mood, and his mood darkened with hers.

"I apologize for my older brother," he said. "He's a late riser. It would take an Ottoman invasion to get him out of bed this early in the morning. But that's no excuse. He should be here. *I* would be here if I were betrothed to you."

"You are here," Ilona pointed out.

Vlad grinned.

"And Andrei told me you plan to visit me. To help prepare me for life at court."

Vlad glanced at her father and his. The two men were engrossed in their own conversation, not paying any attention to the boys, Ilona, or Gizela.

Gizela . . . Ilona looked around. Where *was* Gizela?

"We'll come for a visit after you've had time to settle in at Codru Conac," Vlad said.

"Yes," Ilona said, distracted. "That would be wonderful."

Father would be angry if it came time to leave and Gizi was missing. He would blame Ilona for it. Gizela had been right beside her moments before Vlad and Andrei showed up. Ilona glanced toward the gatehouse, looked around the courtyard again. Her sister had vanished.

"Have you lost something?" Vlad asked.

"My sister. I thought she was here ready to go."

"She went back into the palace with Radu," Andrei said.

"Radu?"

"My annoying little brother," Vlad said, one eyebrow twitching. "She's probably gone with him to the scullery. All Radu does is eat pastries and follow his mommy around. Come on. We'll help you find them."

Ilona cast a nervous look at her father and the voivode before nodding and following Vlad back into the castle. Andrei fell in step behind them.

"Have you eaten yet?" Vlad asked. "You should eat or at least get something to drink before you leave for Codru Conac. It's almost an hour's ride."

"I'll be all right," Ilona said. "I just need to find Gizela and bring her back so we don't make my father wait."

Vlad nodded. "The voivode doesn't like waiting either. I understand."

The voivode . . . It was odd to hear Vlad refer to his father as "the voivode" rather than simply "my father." She wondered if there was a reason for it.

"This way," Vlad said.

They traversed a long, windowless corridor. Ilona soon heard pots clanking, and she smelled heavenly odors.

"Are you sure you don't want something to eat?" Vlad asked. "Raluca is a marvelous cook."

Ilona shook her head. Despite how her mouth watered and her stomach rumbled, she needed to get back. Her father wasn't a patient man.

Vlad strode into the scullery. Ilona peeked in after him.

"Raluca," Vlad said. "Have you seen Radu?"

Raluca wiped her forehead with the back of one hand, leaving a streak of flour behind. Two scullery maids stood at a table behind her, kneading dough. Ilona knew she supervised the palace staff, but Raluca looked nothing like Ilona expected. She was tall and aristocratic. Every inch the regal lady-in-waiting Andrei told Ilona she was, even in a peasant's apron.

"Radu hasn't asked for breakfast yet. You might want to check for him at the kennel. One of the voivode's Vizslas birthed a litter of puppies this morning."

Vlad rolled his eyes. "Of course! Playing with puppies!"

Raluca glanced at Ilona, then looked at Vlad and Andrei. Her eyebrows lifted a little, but she refrained from voicing her curiosity.

"Thank you," Vlad said, and then they were moving again, down the same corridor and out the back of the palace.

Fortunately, the kennel wasn't far. It was small by nobility's standards, but elaborate. A stone wall surrounded a row of brick doghouses with thatched roofs. Fresh straw covered the kennel yard and several tail-wagging hounds bounded up to the gate as they approached.

"There they are," Vlad said, opening the gate and pushing the dogs aside.

Ilona hesitated outside the kennel.

"It's all right, they're friendly," Andrei said. "They won't bite."

Ilona nodded, but she still didn't move.

It took her only a moment to spot Radu and Gizela. Both were on their knees, shoulder to shoulder, at the nearest doghouse's dark opening.

"They're so cute!" Gizela said. "I wish I could have one!"

"I'll ask my mother. The voivode gives her anything she asks for."

Radu was about Gizela's age, perhaps a little younger. He had Vasilisa's slender build, long lashes, and high-boned cheeks.

"Gizi!" Ilona called out, suddenly annoyed.

One of the dogs responded to her voice and pushed past Andrei, sniffing around her skirt. She took two steps backward, and Andrei grabbed the hound's silver collar to pull it back.

"Gizela!" Ilona said again. "Come here at once, we're ready to leave! Father is going to be furious!"

At the moment, the one who sounded furious was Ilona. Gizela stood up, and two of the rust-colored hounds danced around her, pink tongues lolling, lips curved back in canine smiles. Gizela held a squirming ball of golden-red fur in her arms.

"Look, Ilona! A newborn puppy!"

"I see it. Now put it down and come with me."

Vlad gently lifted the puppy out of Gizela's arms and returned it to the brick doghouse. He glared at Radu. "Look what you've done. You're going to get Ilona and her sister in trouble."

"Radu says he's going to get the voivode to give me a puppy," Gizela said as she came through the gate.

"You're not getting a puppy," Ilona said. "What you're

getting is a new home—which we're leaving for any minute now. Come with me."

"You can't say I can't have a puppy," Gizela answered, sulking. "You're not my mother!"

Ilona bit her lower lip and said nothing until her temper was in check.

"Mother would have said no, too," she replied, "and so will Father. We can talk about this another time."

She grasped her sister's hand and led her toward the palace, too embarrassed by her own outburst to look back and see if Vlad or Andrei was watching her. She didn't usually snap at her sister like this, but life hadn't been easy lately. She'd thought it got as bad as it ever could when her mother died, but the voivode's banquet proved it could always get worse.

"If your father gets upset," Vlad whispered in her ear, "I'll let him know this was Radu's fault."

Ilona blinked. She hadn't realized Vlad was walking so close to her.

"It will be all right," she said. "It's not Radu's fault. My father and yours had business to discuss anyway. He probably hasn't even noticed Gizela and I are missing."

And if he did, it wouldn't matter whose fault it was because he would still blame Ilona. That was how it had always been.

"Thank you for helping me find her," she said to Vlad. She nodded at Andrei, too.

"You can look to us for help anytime," Vlad said. "After all, you're now a member of the Dracul family. We'll always be here for you."

CHAPTER FIVE

THE PAIN GREW WORSE AT NIGHT—SO BAD ANDREI COULDN'T sleep. Raluca checked his wound every morning, providing poultices to draw infection out, but a week had passed and it didn't seem to be healing.

He tossed and turned, twisted and rolled, until the bedsheets knotted themselves around his body. After several hours of this, he finally abandoned his bed and stumbled to the door. Maybe he could wake Raluca and ask for willow bark tea or another poultice to ease the pain. *Any*thing.

He unlatched his door, stepped groggily into the corridor, and nearly tripped over something sprawled across the floor. He stumbled to one side, placing a hand against the wall for balance, and slipped on something wet.

Blood. He was standing in a black pool of blood.

"Ah!"

Orange torchlight flickered over the slain sentry's corpse.

Andrei knew this man: he was one of the voivode's most trusted personal guards.

Andrei's stomach lurched. His head spun as he backed away from the body.

The corridor was empty, the palace silent. He wanted to scream, but his throat was too tight. Stooping close to the corpse, Andrei examined the jagged slash the killer had left across the dead man's neck.

Caught by surprise.

Caught from behind.

Andrei glanced up and down the corridor. Nothing moved except for the shadows cast by the torches' flickering flames.

The murdered guard's sword remained untouched in its scabbard. Andrei stooped again and slowly drew it out.

Part of him wanted to return to his room, lock the door, and cower in the shadows, but the voivode's family was in danger. They were the only family Andrei had. It was his duty to protect them.

Trembling so badly he could barely maintain his balance, Andrei crept toward the voivode's bedchamber. There were always two guards posted outside the prince's door. Andrei could alert them to the danger, and *they* could search for the killer. Tonight, however, only one guard remained at his post, and he didn't notice Andrei because he was on his knees twisting something in the locked door's keyhole.

Andrei froze. The guard turned the key until it made a small click. His sword was propped against the doorframe— still streaked with his murdered companion's blood. The guard reached for the weapon as he nudged the door open.

Andrei cleared his throat.

Actually, it was more of a frightened gurgling noise, but it was enough to get the man's attention.

The soldier spun. He and Andrei stared at each other. Andrei knew this man, too. His name was Horst, a Saxon who had worked in the palace for only a few months.

Horst saw Andrei shiver, watched the borrowed sword bob unsteadily in Andrei's hands. He was twice Andrei's size and ten times more experienced. Andrei stumbled backward as the hulking man raised his blood-streaked weapon to attack.

Horst's blade came at Andrei's stomach. Andrei pivoted and blocked. The next blow came for his skull but hit the wall instead. The Saxon cursed. He cursed again when Andrei's blade sliced his forearm, but he was a trained mercenary and he was quick. Andrei staggered and fell to one knee under the jarring weight of a counterblow.

Andrei's blade rang like a bell. He had been ready for the Saxon's sword, but he wasn't expecting the man's fist. It caught him in the temple and knocked him to the floor. His sword spun across the tile. Horst's blade arced down, and Andrei rolled, sparks flying past his face.

Somehow he reclaimed his lost sword before Horst could strike again, but Andrei was now backed against a wall. The big Saxon approached. He sized up his target and prepared for the killing blow, but he hesitated when running footsteps echoed up the corridor.

More guards.

Or at least Andrei *hoped* it was more guards.

The traitor turned back toward the voivode's door, but a shadowy figure now stood between him and the dark room behind it. The warlord prince snarled. Horst lunged at Dracul, but his master parried the blow and thrust his own sword into Horst's shoulder. The Saxon cried out, dropped his weapon with a clatter, and the voivode pressed the tip of his blade against his would-be assassin's throat.

Vasilisa appeared in the doorway of the next room over—Radu's bedchamber door. The cneajna gasped when she saw what was happening, and she pulled her night robes tightly around her as six white-faced guards exploded onto the scene.

"My prince?" one of them said, panting.

The voivode held up a hand. "I can deal with this." He shifted, forcing the Saxon to his knees.

"You attempted to enter my room." Even shirtless and shoeless, the voivode was intimidating. "Tell me why."

The kneeling Saxon didn't answer. Instead, he sneered and spat at the voivode's feet.

The voivode twisted his blade until Horst's sneer transformed into a grimace.

"I have a prison keeper who has a talent for inflicting extreme pain. It's a small matter for him to make tight-lipped people talk."

Horst lifted his chin. "I do not fear you." Strangely, the Saxon accent he usually spoke with had vanished completely. His new accent sounded more Hungarian. "I live and die for the House of Dăneşti!"

"You will die soon enough, but first you will tell me where you obtained the key to my room."

"Death to the House of Drăculeşti!" the Saxon shouted. "Death to all who serve you!"

The voivode silenced the man with a quick slash across the throat. Vasilisa screamed, and a wide-eyed, white-faced Radu appeared at his mother's side. The voivode ignored both of them and pointed his sword at Andrei. Andrei flattened himself against the wall.

"What happened out here, Andrei? What did you see?"

"I was on my way to find Raluca. There . . . there was a body outside my chambers. I came to get your guards, and he . . . he was unlocking your door."

The voivode looked Andrei up and down. "You confronted my enemy. You fought to defend me. I won't forget it."

Andrei could suddenly breathe again, and the voivode aimed his attention at his soldiers.

"Search the palace. There were supposed to be two guards at my door. The other is missing."

"My prince . . ." The nearest soldier dropped to one knee, head bowed. "The body young Prince Andrei mentioned. It was Heinrich. He's dead."

The voivode nodded. "Double the guard and find someone to clean up this mess." He walked through the Saxon's pooling blood, leaving crimson tracks across the floor.

Before disappearing into his room, he paused to remove Horst's key from the lock, and he examined it a moment. Andrei stared at it too. It appeared to be intricately carved from wood. The voivode bent it until it snapped and hurled the pieces into a corner.

Enemies. In the heart of the voivode's palace. And one of them had carved a key that could open the voivode's door. But how could a copy be made without access to the real key? Only the voivode carried it. Even Vasilisa didn't have a key to the room. Andrei shivered and stared at the broken pieces.

Long ago his mother sent him here to protect him, but there

was no safety in the House of the Dragon. If enemies could access the voivode's room, nowhere was secure.

"You should have woken me up," Vlad grumbled. "Together we could have taken him."

"I didn't have time to think," Andrei said. "I found the dead man, I went to warn the voivode's guards, and Horst was already opening the door. There wasn't enough time to run to your room to wake you."

"At least you were smart enough to get the key. Let me look at it."

Andrei dropped the pieces onto Vlad's outstretched palm.

Vlad held each piece up to his sunlit window to examine it. He flexed the wood, rubbed it with his thumb, and peered closely at its carved teeth.

"I wonder what type of wood this is."

"Yew," Andrei said. "The same as my longbow. The voivode had to bend it hard to make it snap."

"Yew," Vlad repeated. "Whoever made this thing knew what he was doing. Easy to carve, but something that wouldn't easily break in the lock. What I don't understand is how they knew what shape to carve. You would have to be looking at the voivode's key to figure it out, and he keeps it on a chain around his neck under his shirt day and night."

Vlad held up the bow end of the key and traced it with his thumb again. It was almost oval, shaped like a squashed heart. He held up the barrel portion and examined its flat, squared bit. The bit was notched at the end with four teeth at the bottom.

"Maybe he forgot one day and wore it outside his shirt,"

Andrei offered. "Maybe one of his enemies saw it and carved a copy from memory."

"Is your memory that good? Is *anyone's* memory that good? A key has to match the lock's parts perfectly. That's the point of having a lock. You can't pick up any old key or carve any old shape and get it to work."

Vlad was right, which meant this was a mystery that would probably never be solved. That would bother Vlad. He didn't like problems without solutions.

"I'm keeping these," Vlad said.

Andrei knew he would. That's why Andrei had sketched the key's outline on a scrap of parchment before bringing it here.

"I wonder . . . if we fasten the pieces together, can *we* get into the voivode's room?"

"Are you crazy?" Andrei said.

"We wouldn't do it while he's here. We would wait for him to be away on one of his long trips."

"How do you expect to fasten it together? With pine resin? If you do it wrong, one half's going to get stuck in the lock for sure. The voivode will know you tried to get in."

"We'll get some yew and carve another one. We have a copy to compare our key to."

"Why would you even want to go into his room?"

"He keeps several bags of ducats in there. He would never notice if a few coins went missing."

An assassin had been roaming the voivode's household and all Vlad could think about was getting his hands on a few pieces of gold.

"He'll probably change the lock anyway," Vlad said, "so it's only hypothetical. What we really need to concentrate on is finding out how that traitor got this wooden key in the first place. He had to have help from someone in the palace. One of the *cameriste*, I'd bet."

Andrei saw what was coming next, and he didn't like it. "We're going to interrogate the housemaids?"

"Frighten them half to death if that's what it takes. One of them knows what happened. One of them can give us information that will lead us to our enemies."

"Don't you think the voivode is already working on that?"

"Maybe, but imagine how pleased he'll be with me—I mean *us*—if we figure it out first."

Always wanting the voivode's attention but never getting it. As of yet, Vlad hadn't found anything big enough to steal away the light that constantly shone on Mircea.

"If I were the voivode," Vlad said, "I wouldn't have cut his throat. Maybe cut out his tongue. Cut it *slowly*. A little more patience and the voivode could have gotten all the information he wanted."

"If you cut a man's tongue out," Andrei observed, "he can't answer your questions."

"He could write it on parchment."

"I don't think Saxon mercenaries read or write. Although . . . I'm beginning to wonder if he was really Saxon."

Vlad scowled. "It doesn't matter. He would have spilled everything before I was through with him. There are other ways to open men's mouths. Like sharpened stakes on riverbanks."

Andrei shuddered at the memory. Years ago he and Vlad had accompanied the voivode to the southern border. There they had seen the aftermath of the Ottoman Empire's favorite method of punishment. Andrei still had nightmares about the impaled Wallachian soldiers—saw their skewered corpses rotting on wooden poles. Andrei blinked the image away. Vlad liked to talk about gruesome punishments, but he would never seriously consider something so cruel.

"We're going to solve this mystery," Vlad said. "You and I. We'll find whoever is responsible for this and bring them to justice."

"*We're* going to be punished," Andrei said, "if we don't find Radu and get ourselves to our morning lessons."

"Lessons?" Vlad snorted. "What Lupescu does can hardly be considered lessons. He's older than dirt. He settled Wallachia with the Romans. Everything he teaches us is useless and outdated. I don't know why the voivode keeps wasting good ducats on him."

Their tutor was admittedly a little odd, but Andrei still liked him, and it was an exaggeration to claim that nothing he taught was useful, but it would do little good to argue with Vlad about it.

"Come on," Andrei said. "The sooner we get morning lessons over with, the sooner you can start frightening the maids."

Vlad buckled his belt, grabbed his coat, and examined the broken key one more time.

"We're going to find them," he vowed. "We're going to find them and make them pay."

The voivode's room was the most magnificent in the Curtea Domnească. The fireplace alone was so huge Vlad could almost stand in it without ducking his head. He was tempted to test that thought, but if he left sooty footprints, the voivode might trace them back to him. He was brave, but he wasn't stupid. That's why the voivode hadn't figured out half the mischief Vlad had gotten himself into. Like entering this room while Andrei and Radu rode ahead to morning lessons, so he could search for something . . . he wasn't sure what—*clues*—without Andrei attempting to talk him out of it.

The voivode's personal crest hung above the fireplace—an image of a circling dragon with its tail wrapped around its neck. Technically, it belonged to Sigismund, founder of the Order, but the voivode had claimed it for himself. One day Vlad would claim it, too.

Three tall windows dominated the bedchamber's east wall. Golden sunlight spilled through the glass panes to warm the bearskins on the floor. Bearskins covered the bed as well. The voivode's bed was shrouded by a canopy and was large enough to hold three grown men. Possibly four.

Vlad's eyes swept the room, taking it all in. Someday this would be his. When the voivode was no longer in the picture to favor Mircea, Vlad would toss his irritating older brother off Wallachia's throne.

Vlad circled the room until he came to a long oak table. A ceremonial sword rested atop it, the hilt a spiral of carved ivory. Its cross guard was a golden dragon. Vlad touched it, grinned, and checked the door to make sure he was still alone. Other than the throne, he coveted this sword more than anything else the voivode owned.

Stylized words ran down the sword's polished blade: *Societas Draconistarum.*

Society of the Dragonists.

In a different age—in an era when a happier voivode gave

attention to both his young sons—his father had regaled the boys with tales of an unexpected summons to Sigismund's imperial fortress at Nuremburg. It was there that Vlad Dracul II was inducted as a "first-class" member of the Order. It was there that he claimed the family name.

Vlad reverently lifted the sword and tested its weight in his hand. It felt good, as if it had been made for him.

Voices sounded in the corridor.

He put the sword back and hurried toward the door, but something caught his eye.

A second table. Smaller, lurking in a corner. And it was weighed down with bags of ducats.

The voivode liked to say that those who didn't watch over their property deserved to have it taken from them. When he said it, he was referring to thrones, lands, and titles. Vlad, however, figured it probably applied equally well to ducats. He darted to the table, snatched one of the smaller pouches, and tucked it under his belt.

He opened the door a crack and peered out, but he was too late; two women appeared at the end of the corridor. He eased the door shut and pressed his ear against it, listening to their footsteps and their conversation.

"The locksmith will be here later today. The cneajna wants the room cleaned before he arrives . . ."

One of the women was Raluca, Andrei's dead mother's former lady-in-waiting. Vlad liked Raluca. When she first arrived at the Curtea Domnească, she became Vasilisa's lady-in-waiting, but at some point she did something to anger the voivode and was demoted to overseeing the housemaids and kitchen staff. It was a demeaning punishment for a lady of noble birth, yet she remained at the Princely Court. This was probably because she—like Andrei—had nowhere else to go.

"Dust the furniture, sweep the floors, but don't touch anything else. Do you understand?"

"Yes, *doamna mea*."

"I'll be back shortly to check on your work."

Vlad searched for a hiding place and his eyes landed on the huge fireplace. Fortunately, the fire hadn't been stoked this morning, so only a few glowing coals warmed the hearth. He kicked those coals aside and pressed himself into the fireplace's sooty shadows.

The door opened and the housemaid stepped in. Vlad listened to her movements and held his breath as she walked directly past him. If she decided to look in his direction, she would see him, but at the moment she was far too interested in the rest of the voivode's room.

She leaned her broom against the bed and absently dusted a chair. She paused to touch the bed's hanging canopy and admire its fine fabric. She was new to the castle and obviously wouldn't last long—Vlad could see that already.

The woman's feathered duster stopped moving when she spotted the ducats in the corner. She glanced toward the bedchamber door before moving toward the bulging coin bags. Vlad edged forward to see past the inner hearth.

She removed a coin from a half-opened pouch and examined its shiny surface. Then she checked the door again and tucked the coin down the front of her blouse.

The door opened. Both Vlad and the housemaid jumped. The housemaid took a step away from the table, smiled at

Raluca, and dusted the frame of a portrait of the voivode. Her hand was shaking.

Raluca glanced at the voivode's coin table, studied the maid, and narrowed her eyes.

"Pedia needs extra help with the east bedchambers. Go and assist her while I finish here."

The maid swallowed nervously, nodded once, and headed for the door. Raluca watched her leave.

Vlad eased back into the shadows, and Raluca turned to stare at the money bags. She looked uneasy. She should be; if the voivode bothered to count them, he would realize someone had pilfered from his stash.

Vlad felt his own ill-gotten ducats press accusingly against his midsection. That was different, he told himself. One day he would become voivode. He was merely taking what would eventually be his anyway.

Raluca quickly completed the housemaid's unfinished job. Vlad waited several minutes after she departed before daring to leave his sooty hiding place.

Now he knew who he would interrogate first when he started asking questions about the assassination attempt.

CHAPTER SIX

V LAD WAS RIGHT ABOUT ONE THING. LUPESCU WAS OLD. PROB-
ably as old as the hills that rose above his fields. His name
meant "wolf's son," and there was definitely something gruff
and wolflike about him. Vlad thought the old wolf would live
forever, but Andrei worried the ancient boyar would drop dead
during one of their early morning sessions. Andrei and Vlad
would have to carry the bad news back to the voivode, and the
voivode would probably blame them for it.

Except today the voivode wasn't here to take his belt to
them. He had departed for Adrianople, and the moment he
was out of sight, Vlad finalized his plans for an unauthorized
visit to Codru Conac. Andrei wasn't sure how appropriate that
was considering that Ilona was Mircea's betrothed, but Vlad
had insisted it was the same thing as visiting a sister or a cousin.
She was family now. How could that be inappropriate?

Lupescu shuffled to the edge of the field, scratched his bris-
tly mustache, and inhaled the morning air.

"Ah! *Minunat!* Perfect conditions for what we're about to do."

He wheezed a moment, thumped his chest with a wrinkled fist, and coughed until bloody spittle covered his lips.

Andrei grimaced.

The old boyar had bad lungs, a bad back, and rheumatism in both knees. He got around with a gnarled walking stick, always gripped in his left hand because the right hand was missing three fingers. No one knew for sure what had happened to those fingers, but the most believable rumor claimed a much younger Lupescu lost them in battle to an Ottoman scimitar. If you asked Lupescu, he gave a different story each time: Bit off by a Transylvanian bear. Lost to hungry *strigoi*. Sometimes Andrei wondered if Lupescu even knew the real story.

"Battle-axes," the old wolf announced. "Today we practice with battle-axes. Such an excellent weapon for splitting steel helmets and punching holes through armor!"

"I prefer a good sword," Vlad muttered.

"Yes, yes, of course you do. Now what was I saying? Oh, yes. Battle-axes. We're going to split skulls today."

Radu, who had been trailing behind Vlad and Andrei, was no longer there. Andrei glanced around and saw Radu skipping to a nearby tree. The bodyguards left the older boys to their lessons and went to shadow the younger prince.

Lupescu didn't notice Radu's absence. He never did. Maybe if Andrei were seven instead of seventeen he, too, could play with twigs under a tree.

"Before we begin," Lupescu said, "put on your armor. No soldier goes willingly into battle without it. Superior armor gives us an edge over the accursed Ottomans and the meddling

Transylvanians. People who don't wear armor end up with injuries like this."

The old wolf gestured toward Andrei's stitched cheek, and Andrei's face grew warm. He heard Vlad muffle a snicker. Lupescu ignored them both and tottered over to his young page, growling something about gambesons and chain mail. The page jogged toward a small wagon, and Lupescu lowered his creaking body onto a tree stump.

"This is a waste of our time," Vlad muttered. "He thinks chain mail is proper armor! Everyone knows plate armor is lighter and better. Lupescu needs to die or wake up and join the fifteenth century."

Andrei glanced nervously in their mentor's direction.

"Don't worry," Vlad said. "He can't hear me. Even if he can, in two minutes he'll forget what I said."

He smirked, but Andrei kept his own mouth shut. Lupescu's page returned with their gambesons, and, while they laced up the quilted jackets, the page retrieved their chain mail. Lupescu watched the page help them into the heavy armor.

"Good, good . . . Helmets, too. And gauntlets. Definitely gauntlets. You need to protect your hands. I can't send you out against the sultan's best without something to deflect their arrows."

When Lupescu wasn't looking, Vlad surreptitiously tapped an index finger against his head. "Senile and crazy," he mouthed. Andrei pretended to be adjusting his mail to avoid acknowledging the comment.

Radu was no longer under the tree. He was now at Lupescu's manor house, chasing a small cat around a barrel. Radu would never survive a real battle—he couldn't stay focused long enough—but that didn't matter because Vasilisa would never let the voivode send Radu to war. Radu was soft and spoiled. His mother's pampering had left him vulnerable. If he ever inherited the throne, he would be assassinated within a week.

"Andrei," Lupescu said, snapping his fingers. "Pay attention. You're first. Mount up."

The page helped Andrei into his saddle, and his mare, Umbră, skittered nervously under the unaccustomed weight of the heavy chain mail. It took several moments to get her under control; then the skinny page handed Andrei an oak-hafted battle-ax.

"See those two stumps at the opposite end of the field?" Lupescu said.

The sun hadn't cleared the horizon, but there was enough illumination to make out two dark outlines.

"I see them."

"And see those gourds on top? Pretend they're soldiers' heads. Gallop across the battlefield and split a few janissary skulls."

There it was again. "Skulls" and "splitting." Lupescu was obsessed.

"One piece of advice before you begin," the wolf said, patting Umbră's neck. "Watch for counterattacks."

Counterattacks? Andrei stared at the old man, but Lupescu gestured for him to begin.

"Spring will reach those gourds before you do. Go!"

Andrei lowered his head and spurred his nervous horse forward, hefting the battle-ax.

He didn't see the archer until the peasant's padded arrow was already flying at his chest.

A surprise attack from a mounded haystack. Andrei didn't have Vlad's aggression or swordsmanship, but he did possess a natural talent with horses. He pulled Umbră into a sliding maneuver, and the arrow buzzed past his ear. Somewhere behind him Lupescu chortled, and Vlad shouted encouragement.

The archer loosed a second arrow and, more by luck than skill, Andrei deflected it with his ax blade. Even Lupescu's archer cheered as Andrei galloped onward toward the waiting targets.

Thwunk! The third arrow came out of nowhere, striking him just above the left shoulder blade. Even through protective layers of chain mail and padded gambeson, he felt the burn of bruised flesh.

"Not a killing wound!" Lupescu shouted. "Ride on! Ride on!"

Andrei glanced over his shoulder and saw that the archer had been waiting for him in one of the field's deep border furrows. *Danger everywhere.* His heart pounded so loudly it nearly drowned out Umbră's drumming hooves. He tapped his heels against the mare's ribs, and she galloped faster.

The stumps were about twenty feet apart. After Andrei split the first one, he would have to circle around and come back for the other. Andrei veered toward the center of the field, where another haystack, and probably another archer, waited.

"*Du-te*, Umbră!"

The mare leaped over the haystack, startling a waiting peasant. The man dropped his bow in his haste to jump out of the way.

"Bravo!" Lupescu applauded.

As Andrei expected, more archers waited for him in the woods, but he was a distant target. If he kept Umbră at a full gallop, it would be difficult to hit him. He swerved left to draw the archers' volley, swerved right and twirled the ax. When he swung, he not only split the gourd but sent its pieces hurtling in all directions.

One down. One more to go.

Five archers sprang from the brambles at the field's edge. They would pepper Andrei and Umbră with padded arrows before he reached the final target. Unless . . .

Andrei lifted the ax over his shoulder, gave a desperate war cry, and let it fly. The ax tumbled end over end before biting deep into the stump, cleanly halving the gourd.

The archers lowered their bows, Vlad crowed and clapped, and Umbră cantered back to the starting line.

"Good girl," Andrei said, patting her quivering neck. She was almost as jittery and breathless as he was.

"Excellent!" Lupescu exclaimed. "Excellent control. Excellent tactics. Now let's see what Vladislav can do."

Vlad stiffened. He hated being called by his full first name, but when the page brought his horse, his scowl transformed into a look of fierce determination. Andrei was sure he had no intention of being outdone, and if speed made any difference, he would have an advantage. His chestnut stallion, a destrier, was one of the finest warhorses silver and gold could buy. Invictus— his name was Latin for "undefeated"—stomped his large hooves and champed at his bit. The stallion was as eager as Vlad to meet Lupescu's challenge.

The page offered Vlad an ax, but he pushed it away.

"I want that one."

He pointed at an ax with a wicked spike at its top, a weapon designed for skewering as well as chopping. Andrei shifted nervously.

Two peasants placed fresh gourds on the distant tree stumps. Vlad turned his eyes on them like a wolf eyeing fat sheep. He scanned the bushes, examined the freshly piled haystacks, and narrowed his eyes at the newly turned furrows. He already knew what Andrei had faced and was making plans to deal with it.

"A few words of advice," Lupescu said.

"I don't need advice," Vlad replied haughtily. "A few peasants are no threat to me."

He kicked his heels into Invictus, and the stallion thundered forward. Lupescu sighed and shook his head.

Vlad's strategy was intimidation—that was always his style—and his first move was to charge at the nearest haystack. When the archer popped up and saw Vlad's lowered spike, the nervous fellow sent his arrow too far to the left.

Vlad gave his opponent no time to ready a second shot. The peasant, eyes still on the spike, dropped his bow and ran. Vlad followed. When he overtook his prey, he placed a boot between the man's shoulder blades and sent him sprawling.

Laughing, Vlad wheeled Invictus to the right and galloped toward the second archer's hiding place. This peasant—a boy no older than Andrei—didn't even try to loose an arrow; he sprinted in panic toward the field's edge.

Intent upon reaching his prey, Vlad didn't see the trap until it was too late. The fleeing peasant made it past the towering oak, but as Vlad bore down on him, the looped end of a rope snaked over Vlad's ax-wielding arm and pulled itself taut. Vlad flew from his saddle; when he hit the ground, Andrei heard the thud clear across the field.

Vlad lay motionless. Andrei ran forward, heart beating in his throat.

"Caution," Lupescu said, tottering along behind Andrei. "A knight needs caution as much as bravery. Young Vladislav is far too choleric."

Andrei wasn't sure what "choleric" meant, but he knew it wasn't a compliment.

He also realized it wasn't good that Vlad was now on his feet, glaring at the laughing man perched above him.

The rope was still tangled around Vlad's arm. The peasant still held its other end. Vlad yanked, and the startled peasant lost his balance and fell to the earth. The moment the man struck dirt, Vlad was on him.

His booted toe flew into the man's ribs. A gauntlet-covered fist smashed into his nose. Vlad stepped back to find his lost battle-ax and Andrei ran faster, waving his arms.

"No, Vlad! Stop!"

Vlad had his father's temper, but Andrei had never seen it manifest itself this violently. If he didn't reach Vlad quickly enough . . .

"Vlad!"

The added weight of Lupescu's chain mail slowed Andrei. It was slowing Vlad, too, but not well enough. Cold dread pulsed through Andrei's veins as Vlad took a first swing.

The peasant rolled, narrowly avoiding the blow, but Vlad raised the ax over his shoulder, ready for another try. Andrei stumbled over a furrow's raised edge, swung his arms to catch his balance, and watched helplessly as Vlad landed another chop.

Frozen chunks of dirt flew out from between the peasant's spread legs. Vlad's face was twisted with mindless fury.

The terrified man scooted backward. "Vă rog!" he cried. "Please! *Vă rog!*"

"*Vlad!*" Andrei shouted.

He would never reach his cousin in time, but something penetrated the dark fog clouding Vlad's mind.

Vlad dropped the ax. He stared at his hands a moment, then turned and staggered away.

By the time Andrei reached Vlad, his cousin was halfway across the field. Vlad's face was pale and his hands were shaking.

"Help me out of this mail," Vlad whispered.

Wordlessly, Andrei assisted him. When the heavy armor was out of the way, Vlad fumbled with his gambeson's laces and dropped the padded jacket to the earth.

"Is he all right?" Vlad asked.

Andrei looked back at the peasant. "Yes."

Vlad clenched and unclenched his fingers. "I don't know what came over me. I . . . I could have injured him. I almost . . ."

He stopped and shook his head. Neither of them needed him to finish that sentence.

"I have to leave," Vlad mumbled. "I need to get out of here."

"Where do you want to go?"

"We'll decide when we get there."

Vlad whistled for Invictus, and the big destrier trotted toward him.

"Get your horse, too."

"What about Radu?" Andrei asked.

"Let Lupescu babysit him. I'm not my brother's keeper."

"Our bodyguards . . ."

"We can outrun them."

Andrei cast a guilty glance toward the manor. Lupescu

hobbled toward him and Vlad. Radu sat on a barrel, stroking a captured cat.

"Don't worry about the old coot and the little *dăunător*. Call your horse. We're going to Codru Conac."

Codru Conac, her family's new manor house, stretched like a dying elephant over a dusty swath of earth. Its tusks—four stone turrets and three copper spires—held Târgoviște's wooded foothills at bay. The front entrance, lurking beneath a glowering Byzantine dome, was guarded by iron-banded double doors. Infinite arches frowned over narrow windows. Wooden outbuildings—stables, servant quarters, a small church—huddled around its hulking walls. It wasn't a welcoming place.

Ilona's upper-story room was about as hospitable as the rest of the manor—small, gray, and drafty. A four-poster bed with a faded yellow canopy crowded half the room, and a severe high-backed chair guarded the other. The floor's planks creaked, and the single lancet window allowed miserly shards of sunlight to pass through its frost-rippled panes. After several weeks in Wallachia, Ilona was still homesick for her old life in Transylvania. She missed Sighișoara's steep, narrow streets and pine-clad slopes. She missed her old, much smaller house. Most of all she missed her mother.

The new tutor hadn't arrived from Moldavia yet, and Father was out of the house early to meet with Mircea at the Curtea Domnească. This meant Ilona and Gizela could look forward to an unusual day free of supervision. Since Gizela was a late sleeper, Ilona had an hour, maybe two, to explore the manor's grounds on her own. An entire week at the manor and Ilona was yet to be allowed outdoors. Her father kept her and Gizela cooped up like ornamental birds in a cage.

Not this morning. Today he had left the manor without commanding Ilona to stay inside. Was it a sin to escape on this technicality? If it was, she would stop by the manor's abandoned church and confess her guilt before the icon of Christ. Surely He wouldn't condemn her for desiring a little freedom and a breath of fresh air.

Ilona searched for her clothing. Her kirtle and gown wilted over the high-backed chair's boxy armrests, but if she dressed in black again, the manor's hungry shadows would surely swallow her. Officially, the entire household was still in mourning, but Ilona was tired of wearing black. Her mother had hated black—she preferred softer, brighter colors like meadow green, sky blue, and dandelion yellow. She wouldn't have minded if Ilona discarded the black dress for a day.

Ilona unlatched the cedar trunk at the foot of her bed and lifted its lid. Her favorite gown was folded at the top. Ilona ran her fingers over it, feeling its soft fabric and thinking about better times. This gown was the deep green of fresh pine boughs, its rounded neckline and tight sleeves embroidered with silver stars and crescent moons. Ilona owned a matching silver belt to hold the skirt in at the waist. She felt freer just by clutching the familiar old clothing in her hands. When she pulled the dress on, it fit tighter through her chest and hips than she remembered, but it felt far better than the stifling black velvet her father forced her to wear day after long and dreary day.

Before she exited the bedroom, she removed three more

important items from her trunk: a quill, a bottle of ink, and her sketchbook. Mother had bought these for her. Father didn't know she possessed them.

Now she could go outside.

Codru Conac's halls were narrow, and its spiral stairwells were sticky with ebony shadows. Ilona stayed in the shadows, moving quickly. The manor house seemed abandoned until she reached the main floor.

In the kitchen, someone clanked pots and pans. It wouldn't be long before other servants were hard at work. For the moment, however, no one was near enough to observe Ilona as she unbarred the front door and slipped outside. The manor grounds were almost as forsaken as the house itself, but at least out here there were a few birds to greet Ilona with their cheerful chirps. Ilona threw back her head to inhale the frosty air. Her breath painted phantom images around her.

She should have put on something warmer before coming outside, but she wasn't going to turn back for a coat now. Her freedom was limited. She had to make the most of it while she could.

She hurried across the open courtyard, hugging herself for warmth, and stopped at the forest's edge to stare at its gray tangle of leafless trees.

Something rustled above her—a nuthatch hopping across a wild cherry tree's black bough. Mother had taught Ilona how to call birds. So much time had passed since she last played this game, but she licked her lips now and attempted a nuthatch's high-pitched whistle:

Tui-tui-tui!

The small bird scrabbled headfirst down the trunk and gave an answering call. Ilona smiled. This wasn't one of the artificial smiles her father made her wear for visiting dignitaries. This smile warmed her face. It was as if she was in the old garden with Mother again—as if her world hadn't been inalterably changed.

Father didn't think it proper for a woman to whistle, so she did it again just to spite him. The nuthatch ruffled its blue-gray feathers, tilted its overlarge head, opened its beak, and sang.

Ilona sat on the barkless trunk of a fallen tree, opened the sketchbook across her lap, and whistled at the bird again to get its attention.

Thwunk!

Ilona cried out and nearly dropped the quill and ink jar. The nuthatch raced away in a flurry of feathers. A crossbow bolt quivered in the tree a handbreadth away from where the bird had been sitting.

"Did you see that? Dead center at fifty paces! If I'd aimed for the bird instead of the knot above its head, I would have hit it."

Ilona turned toward the exuberant voice. Vlad Dracula strode casually toward her. He carried a crossbow in the crook of one arm. Andrei followed several paces behind. He had a crossbow, too, but when Ilona stared coldly at it, he hid it behind his arm.

"How do you like that for accuracy?" Vlad asked.

Ilona set her sketchbook and writing implements on the tree trunk and stood. It took her a moment to compose herself enough to speak. Even when her voice returned, it was impossible to prevent it from shaking with anger.

"Do you often use small, unsuspecting animals for target practice?"

"Anything that moves," Vlad replied. "Foxes, pheasants, small peasant children . . ."

A horrified look must have crossed her face, because he touched her arm and burst into laughter.

"It was just a bird," he said, "and I purposely missed it. If Andrei and I want to be ready to defend Wallachia, we need something to practice on."

He glanced toward the feathered bolt.

"That can be used again. Fetch it for me, Andrei, will you?"

Andrei frowned, but when he saw Ilona watching him, he ducked his head and moved around her to retrieve the bolt. As he slipped by, she examined the long gash on his face. It was puckered and purple and still looked painful, but it didn't look nearly as bad as it had a week ago.

Vlad stepped in front of her, blocking Andrei from her sight.

"You look good in green," he said, taking her hand. "It suits you better than black."

"I . . . um . . . Thank you," she finally managed.

"Does this mean your family is no longer in mourning?"

She carefully removed her hand from his. "I needed a break. I decided not to wear black today."

Andrei returned with the bolt. Vlad examined the projectile for a moment, then slipped it into the small quiver attached to his belt and returned his attention to Ilona.

"That's what brings Andrei and me here today," he said. "I needed a break too. So we're doing a little hunting in these hills. We left our horses in your stables. I hope that's all right."

"No . . . I . . . I mean, of course it's all right. Anytime you wish."

Vlad grinned again. He was handsome when he smiled.

"You don't have a coat," he said. "You must be freezing."

Ilona glanced down and saw she was unconsciously rubbing her arms.

"I forgot to wear one."

"Here."

He removed his own fur-trimmed coat and draped it around her shoulders. She started to protest, but he quickly cut her off.

"Do you want to watch us hunt? We're hoping to bring down a wild boar or a couple of pheasants. I can teach you how to shoot a crossbow. It'll be fun."

Ilona glanced at the manor house. How long did she have before Gizela or someone else came looking for her? There was also the uncomfortable fact that she was now betrothed. Was it appropriate to walk alone in the woods with two boys, neither of whom was her fiancé?

She worried only a moment before deciding she didn't care whether or not it was appropriate. Soon enough she would spend her days at a palace hearth doing needlework and engaging in meaningless conversation. If she was going to take risks to escape from her problems, she might as well make the day memorable.

"I suppose that would be all right," she said. "I mean . . . as long as we're not gone too long."

"I'll have you back before anyone even realizes you're missing," Vlad assured her with another charming smile.

The sun was doing its best to warm the trees. Darkening

circles expanded across frost-sparkled trunks and a light mist rose off the earth. Ilona followed Vlad and Andrei into the woods, her pulse ticking nervously. Winter's chill persisted in the shadows, and Ilona was grateful for Vlad's borrowed coat. He must be freezing, but he didn't show it. He was too intent on the hunt.

Ilona was glad for the coat for reasons besides the cold. It also protected her against scratchy privet, hawthorn, and elder branches as they pushed their way through the thick undergrowth.

What would Father think if he saw her now? She smiled at the thought.

Somewhere ahead, a high-pitched call and a burr of rapidly beating wings echoed through the woods.

"Sage grouse," Ilona whispered. "Male."

Vlad looked at her, surprised. Andrei smiled.

Vlad nudged Andrei's arm. "Give me your bow. Load mine in case I need a second shot."

Annoyance flickered in Andrei's brown eyes as he traded Vlad for the empty crossbow, but Vlad didn't notice because he was intently scanning the trees. The forest floor had a noticeable incline that grew rapidly steeper, collecting taller and taller trees as it rose upward. Hazelnut and wild apple gave way to towering oaks mixed with an occasional pine. Ilona's breathing grew labored. She wasn't used to trekking through rugged woodland, and she quickly fell behind.

Vlad wasn't aware of it, but Andrei fell back to match her pace.

"Is he always this intense?" she whispered.

Andrei nodded. He wasn't much of a conversationalist, but

he made up for it with lightning reflexes. Not paying enough attention, Ilona stumbled over an exposed root, and Andrei saved her from falling headfirst into a patch of bloodtwig. They stared at each other a moment. Vlad turned and saw them together, and Andrei immediately stepped back.

"Do you have that crossbow loaded yet?" Vlad asked.

"No."

"Do it, then."

Vlad watched Andrei a moment before grinning at Ilona.

"I said I'd show you how to shoot a crossbow. Do you want to try it now?"

She hesitated. "Your grouse might get away."

"It won't get away. Nothing I want ever gets away."

Ilona glanced at Andrei to see his reaction, but his back was now turned to her, his shoulders hunched as he strained to fit another bolt into the crossbow. Vlad strode down the slope and pressed the other crossbow into Ilona's hands.

It was heavier than Ilona expected. Her arms sagged, and she nearly dropped the weapon.

"Oops, careful!" Vlad said, helping to steady her. "We wouldn't want it going off and shooting you in the foot."

She lifted it gingerly, and Vlad put a hand against her back, gently guiding her farther up the hill.

"If you learn this right," he said, "you'll be surprised how easy it is. Here's a good spot." They stopped at an empty space between the trees. "Now we need a target. Do you see that big oak over there?"

Ilona nodded.

"We're going to try to hit that patch of orange lichen on its trunk."

He moved behind her, his arms unexpectedly circling her body. She stiffened until she realized he was merely attempting to position the crossbow in her hands.

"Hold the tiller over your shoulder," he said. "Good. That's it."

He stood close. Perhaps too close. She remembered she was betrothed and shouldn't allow this, but there was something pleasant about the warmth of Vlad's face so close to hers. She allowed his cheek to brush against hers, and a tremor quivered up her spine.

"Now hold this finger over the tickler. Squeeze it back when you're ready to shoot. Don't jerk it or you'll miss the target. Always remember to squeeze instead of pull."

Ilona rested her finger against the "tickler." What an odd choice of words for a mechanism that unleashed flying death.

"Next comes aiming. Put your thumb in this groove and look over your knuckle along the bolt."

Ilona's flesh tingled where his hand touched hers. Her breathing quickened. What was wrong with her? Why was she responding to his touch this way?

"I think I've got it now," she said, stepping out of his arms.

"Are you sure?" Vlad drew close to her again. "Maybe I should help with the first shot."

"I'm a quick learner. I can do it alone."

Vlad shrugged. A few paces behind, Andrei watched the entire exchange. His face was hard to read. As usual, he diverted his gaze the moment she looked at him.

"Remember," Vlad said. "Squeeze. Don't jerk. When I was first learning—"

Twang!

The yew bolt flew off the tiller in a golden blur. It hit the scaly splash of orange lichen with an echoing thud, and Ilona turned back to Vlad with a faint smile flickering across her lips.

"That was fun."

Vlad's mouth hung open.

"You've used a crossbow before," he said.

"No. This was my first time."

He gave her an uncertain half smile until he noticed Andrei watching again.

"Be a gentleman, Andrei. Get that bolt out of the tree for her."

"No," Ilona said. She pushed the crossbow into Vlad's hands. "I shot it. I'll get it."

The bolt was buried deep. Ilona grasped it with both hands and gave an experimental tug. The stubborn thing refused to budge, and, from the corner of her eye, she saw Vlad take a step toward her. Scowling, she tried again. Soft footfalls moved in her direction.

"I don't need help," she said. "I've almost got it."

She gritted her teeth and yanked even harder. Her strength, however, was no match for the tree's relentless grip. Slipping, she tumbled backward into a strong pair of waiting arms.

She looked up, expecting Vlad, but instead found Andrei's brown eyes. Her face flushed. He probably thought her the clumsiest thing he had ever seen. She opened her mouth to thank him, but Vlad pulled her away before she could form the words.

"Are you all right?"

"Thanks to Andrei."

"Yes . . . I don't know what we would do without him."

For a moment, it was silent.

"Want to shoot the crossbow again?"

"I should get back to the manor," Ilona said. "My sister, Gizela . . . She'll be upset if she wakes and I'm not there."

"You can't go yet," Vlad protested. "I won't let you go until you've seen the view from the hilltop. It will only take a minute. I promise."

She wasn't eager to return to the manor, don her black dress, and become a captive again. "I suppose I can spare a few more minutes."

"Minunat! I know a place where we can see for miles!"

Vlad dropped another empty crossbow into Andrei's arms. "Come on!"

Before Ilona could draw breath, Vlad had her hand and was towing her up the slope. Arms overloaded, Andrei quickly fell behind them.

As they ran, Ilona's skirt collected damp leaves, the earth slippery beneath her feet.

"Vlad . . . You're going too fast. I'm going to fall."

Vlad looked back and slowed his pace.

"*Köszönöm*," Ilona thanked him. "I mean . . . *mulțumesc*."

"*Szívesen*," Vlad said. "And *cu placere*. You can speak either Hungarian or Romanian to me. I'm fluent in both. I also know French, Italian, Latin, and a little Saxon."

"Six languages. You must have a good tutor."

Vlad scowled. "I suppose Lupescu has a few redeeming qualities. At least he knows his languages. You've been tutored in languages, too, I see. Your Romanian is flawless."

"My mother was Romana," Ilona said, her voice growing quieter. "We spoke Romanian when my father wasn't around."

Ilona glanced down the slope. Andrei was still nowhere in sight.

"Maybe we should stop here for a minute and let Andrei catch up."

Vlad waved off the suggestion. "He's probably down there picking dirt out of his fingernails. I don't know why he's lagging behind. He can move fast when he wants to."

Vlad chuckled. "You should have seen him today. We were training for battle. Peasants were shooting padded arrows at us. Andrei was amazing. If he and I ever fight together on a battlefield, I pity the enemy."

"You two seem like good friends."

"The best. I would trust Andrei with my life, and he would trust me with his. But enough about that. You have to get back and we're wasting time. Come on. We're almost at the top."

He still held her hand, and he tugged her into motion. The last part of the hill was the steepest and she needed Vlad's firm grip. Footing here was treacherous, and the hill split into several deep ravines. Ilona was grateful when the slope finally leveled out so she could place firm soil beneath her feet.

"This way," Vlad said, leading her between leaf drifts and thin gray trunks. Ilona was almost out of breath when he finally stopped. They stood where a toppled oak opened up a view of a broad, flat landscape. From here Ilona saw patchwork fields, Târgoviște's distant walls, and a winding blue ribbon—the Ialomița River.

"You were right," she said. "The view is breathtaking."

Vlad grinned. "If I'm ever voivode, I'll build a castle up here, and—"

He stopped, narrowed his eyes, and stared into the valley.

Following his gaze, Ilona saw movement to the southeast of Codru Conac. A winding line. A giant centipede. It took a moment before she could clearly see that the centipede's segments were horses and men.

"An army . . ."

"The Ottoman army," Vlad said.

Ilona's flesh prickled. "How do you know?"

"The banners . . . The flags . . ."

Invisible fingers traced frosty tracks up Ilona's back. "Are we being invaded?"

Vlad shook his head. "This must be the deal the voivode announced at the banquet."

"I don't understand."

"The protection Murad promised. The voivode must have agreed to let the Ottoman army cross Wallachian soil. They're on their way to Transylvania."

Transylvania. The icy fingers plunged deeper, closed around Ilona's heart, and froze it.

"But Transylvania is my homeland!"

Vlad grasped her hand and gave it a sympathetic squeeze.

"I'm sorry," he said. "The voivode has Transylvanian enemies who want to murder him and put a Dănescu on the throne. It's a matter of survival. He needs to be friends with the sultan today, and perhaps he'll be enemies with him tomorrow. You know how it works. My father's enemies tried to destroy your family, too."

Yes, she knew how royal politics worked, but the thought of foreign soldiers destroying Transylvania's cities made her shudder.

The terrifying procession marched closer and closer. Vlad and Ilona watched in silence, and Ilona began to make out individual soldiers. They wore red boots, balloon pants, conical helmets, and blue robes. Some of them came on horseback. Most marched on foot. Massive cannons reflected bronze sunlight.

"Janissaries," Vlad said, pointing at the blue-robed foot soldiers. "The sultan's personal army. Former Christians who converted to Islam."

A noise distracted him. It was Andrei coming out of the trees with a crossbow balanced on each shoulder.

"Look," Vlad said.

Andrei followed Vlad's pointing finger and almost dropped the bows.

Strange music—drums, bells, trumpets, a woodwind instrument with a high, piercing tone—rang in their ears.

"What's that noise?" Ilona asked.

"A *mehter*," Vlad replied. "A military band. The sultan's armies march to war by its music. And look over there."

Vlad pointed. Two groups of horsemen in brightly colored tabards trotted up the Ottoman line. Above one group a dragon-emblazoned banner fluttered. Above the other Ilona saw a square-ended cross.

"Mircea," Vlad muttered.

"My father," Ilona said.

Mircea Dracul and Anton Csáki with their cavalrymen, riding escort. Mircea, her future husband, riding with her father to send death to Transylvania.

"I need to return to the manor," Ilona said.

"Of course. Andrei and I will walk back with you." When she'd thought of ways to escape marriage to Mircea, Ilona had entertained the thought of stealing her father's horse, riding to her mother's family in Transylvania, and pleading with them for sanctuary. Now two clashing armies would soon stand between her and her homeland.

She clenched her teeth and said two silent prayers—one for herself, and one for Transylvania.

CHAPTER SEVEN

VLAD WATCHED ANDREI KNEEL TO UNBUCKLE UMBRĂ'S SADDLE, shaking his head. "Let the grooms unsaddle the horses, Andrei. That's what they're here for."

"It's been a while since I've given Umbră a good combing," Andrei said.

"The grooms are here for that as well."

"I know, but it gives me a chance to check her health and bond with her. She likes it when I give her attention." He fondly stroked the mare's velvety muzzle. "Don't you, girl?"

Vlad rolled his eyes. "She's just a horse. The only thing horses care about is if they get exercise and enough to eat."

"You still have a thing or two to learn about horses," Andrei replied.

"The only thing I need to know about a horse is how fast it is and how well it handles in battle. Come and find me when you get done *bonding* with your horse."

Andrei laughed and Vlad walked toward the stable doors.

"Don't forget to bring the crossbows when you come back to the palace," Vlad called back over his shoulder.

The weapons were still tied to his saddle. Andrei stood and walked around Umbră to retrieve them but froze when he saw they weren't there.

He felt a moment of panic. One thing the voivode had absolutely no tolerance for was a soldier—especially a prince—who didn't take good care of his weapons. If Andrei hadn't tied the carrying straps well enough . . . If they'd fallen on the trip home and gotten lost or damaged . . .

But then he remembered: he'd set them on a log near Codru Conac. He'd completely forgotten about them when he and Vlad were saying their farewells to Ilona.

He was still tired from the first trip, but he couldn't leave the bows.

"I guess you'll have to wait for that comb down," he said, patting Umbră's neck. "Do you mind taking me to Ilona's manor again?"

Umbră whickered and affectionately nudged him with her nose.

"I'll take that as a yes."

He considered telling Vlad to see if his cousin wanted to ride back with him. Vlad would probably jump at the excuse to be near Ilona again; he was clearly besotted with her. And if Mircea ever saw Vlad interacting with her, it would be obvious to him, too. That alone was reason enough not to invite him.

No, Andrei would go alone. There was no reason to bring Vlad. He would simply ride there, retrieve the crossbows, and ride back. If he did happen to see Ilona a second time . . .

He blinked and shook his head. Why was he even thinking about that?

"Let's go, Umbră. We'll make this a quick trip."

He led the mare out of the stables and swung into her saddle. Another image of Ilona flashed through his head. Ilona liked birds. She handled a crossbow after only one lesson. She tried to help Andrei when he did something stupid and got injured—

She was back in his head again no matter how hard he tried to push her out.

Now wasn't the time to be like Vlad and grow infatuated with her. She was betrothed to Mircea. There were plenty of other girls in Wallachia.

Târgoviște's hills reclined, gray and sleeping, to the north and the east. Andrei left the city and spurred Umbră toward them. He gave her the reins, and her muscled body rippled beneath him. He enjoyed this momentary sensation of freedom—this temporary escape from his uncle's court with all its ceremony, secrets, and restrictions.

The crossbows were exactly where Andrei had left them— through the trees where Ilona disappeared when he and Vlad saw her cross to the forest from the manor. There was also something else on the stump: a leather-bound book, a goose feather quill, and a corked ink bottle.

Andrei picked up the book. Its pages were filled with incredibly detailed sketches of myriad types of birds. A falcon on a leather glove. A sharp-eyed raven. A crested waxwing picking berries off a twig. Each sketch included a date and careful notes written in a graceful, flowing script.

She was a scientist *and* an artist. Was there anything Ilona couldn't do?

Andrei sat and slowly turned pages. It felt invasive, but he couldn't stop himself. There were hundreds of birds identified by their Hungarian and Romanian names. Many were also identified in French, Italian, and Latin. The last half of the sketchbook was empty—still waiting for Ilona to grace those pages with her beautiful drawings and observations.

Andrei couldn't leave it out here where it would be exposed to insects and weather. He would have to approach the manor to return it to her. He was rising to his feet to do just that when Umbră lifted her head, pricked up both ears, and turned to stare into the forest.

"What is it, girl?"

Twigs snapped. The muffled sounds of someone trying to be stealthy echoed in Andrei's ears. He searched the trees and spotted two figures. A man in black and a sorrel horse, appearing and disappearing between mossy trunks and low-hanging boughs. Neither of them seemed to have noticed Andrei or Umbră.

Umbră whickered softly. Andrei placed a silencing hand against her muzzle.

The movement through the trees stopped, and Andrei held his breath. The man in black was most likely a *haiduc*—a forest bandit. Andrei waited for what seemed an eternity before the stealthy noises continued on.

What now?

He probably ought to find out what the man was up to.

Andrei patted Umbră's muzzle. "Wait here."

Andrei was beginning to wish he'd brought Vlad with him; his cousin's natural bravado would have strengthened his courage.

The robber circled the manor, seemingly unaware that Andrei was following him. At the west side, the robber looped his horse's reins around a sapling before proceeding through the underbrush in a low crouch.

He was definitely up to no good. The haiduc dropped to one knee and balanced something across the other—a crossbow, already loaded. Andrei rested one hand on his sword's hilt. He wished he had his crossbow, but he'd left it with Vlad's back at the tree trunk next to Ilona's bird drawings.

What now? He might end up with a bolt through his skull if he confronted the thief head-on. Andrei dropped down and crawled behind a mildew-blackened tree stump to quietly catch his breath and think.

The robber had a clear view of the manor's upper-story windows. Andrei did, too, and he saw movement behind one of those windows' rippled glass panes.

Ilona. He recognized her long dark hair.

In one fluid motion, the outlaw lifted his crossbow to point it at the back of Ilona's head.

"No!"

Andrei charged toward the assassin and rammed his shoulder into the man's midsection. The sound of shattering glass filled the woods, a girl screamed, and Andrei's fists flailed blindly, striking again and again at the murderer's hard flesh.

Too slow.

Too late.

"This is risky business, Csáki. Very risky. Even the voivode's supporters are beginning to doubt. You can talk sense into him, convince him to switch alliances and join forces with Hunyadi before he has an uprising on his hands. If Wallachia attacks the sultan's armies from behind, we can bring the Ottomans to their knees and possibly undo the damage that's already been done."

Ilona's father shook his head, speared a piece of meat, chewed it slowly, and swallowed. "Murad would raise another army, and he would crush us. It would be unwise to betray him now."

"And allowing the sultan to attack Transylvania is wise?"

"I understand your worries, Virghiliu," Ilona's father said. "These are dangerous times. But the prince must do what's best for Wallachia . . . even if it isn't popular with the boyars."

"Popular!" Magda's father rubbed a hand across the perspiring bald spot on his head. "The voivode's actions are suicidal! Do you not realize this? Golescu, Văcărescu, Craiovescu . . . They're talking about raising a private army to throw him off the throne! This goes far beyond unpopular. If he loses the throne before we—"

He stopped speaking and glanced uncomfortably at Ilona, Gizela, and Magda.

Ilona's father looked pointedly at them. "This conversation is probably very boring to you girls," he said. "Ilona, why don't you and Gizela take Magdalena upstairs and entertain her there?"

Ilona glanced at her barely touched plate. The cook hadn't even finished bringing all the food from the kitchen, but the look on her father's face didn't invite disagreement.

"Come," Ilona whispered to Magda. "We'll eat later."

She motioned for Magda and Gizela to follow her, and they meekly exited the room.

"I apologize about my father," she said when they had

moved beyond his hearing. "He doesn't like Gizela and me listening in on his 'business' conversations."

"My father is the same way," Magda said. "'Run along, Magdalena. This conversation is for adult ears only.'"

Ilona laughed at Magda's imitation of Virghiliu Racoviţă's deep, loud voice. Hopefully he couldn't hear it through the great hall's closed doors.

"I'm still hungry," Gizela said, rubbing her stomach and looking cross. "All I got was two bites of *sparanghel cu smantana*, and I *hate* creamed asparagus!"

"It's all right, madárka. We'll stop by the kitchen and steal a loaf of bread."

Gizela shook her head. "I don't want to go there. Our new cook hates us. She'll curse us with her *deochi*, and we'll get sick like Mama and die."

Ilona frowned. "Our cook doesn't hate us. And the evil eye is a silly superstition. Don't talk that way, Gizela. If Father heard you repeating such rubbish—"

"She does hate us! She does give us the evil eye!"

Ilona would have continued the argument, but the cook herself appeared at the end of the hall. She carried a steaming serving pot in her thin white hands, and when she saw the girls in her path, the look she gave them was filled with loathing.

"All right," Ilona whispered. "No bread. We'll go to my room and talk."

"She's going to poison our food," Gizela whispered. "She came here to kill us."

"Shhh! Stop that!"

Magda giggled, and the cook glared at them. Ilona pushed Gizela toward the staircase, eager to be gone.

"My father hired extra guards to watch our manor," Magda said as they climbed the stairs. "Is your father doing the same?"

"Why do you need extra guards?"

"Because the voivode is aiding the Ottomans, and my father is one of the voivode's known supporters. Many Wallachians are angry. They might choose to take that anger out on my family."

"Do Wallachians fear the Ottoman Empire that much?" Ilona asked.

"Don't you?"

"As long as the voivode has a treaty with them, I don't see how Wallachians have any reason to fear."

"My father worries the voivode's treaty will weaken the House of Drăculești," Magda explained. "Many boyars would prefer a treaty with Transylvania, and they whisper about reinstating the House of Dănești."

They reached the top floor. Magda paused to catch her breath, and Ilona took advantage of the moment to add her own observation.

"Wallachia is a tempting target for all its neighbors. It's like a slab of meat in front of a lions' den. Maybe the voivode thinks the only way Wallachia can survive is to tempt the strongest lion with an even bigger piece of meat. I saw the Ottoman army . . . They had huge cannons and enough soldiers to fill the sea. I don't know how Transylvania—how anyone—can stand against them."

She wasn't sure why she defended the voivode's decision— she hated him for making it and hated her father for helping him with it—but the dread she felt upon viewing the Ottomans' vast forces still curled the edges of her stomach.

"You saw them?" Magda said. "You saw their army?"

"I watched them from the hilltop above Codru Conac."

"You climbed the hill? Without me?" Gizela stomped her foot and glared.

She should have known better than to say anything in front of Gizela. "You were sleeping. I didn't want to disturb you. And I wasn't planning on climbing the hill. Vlad talked me into it."

"Vlad Dracula?" Magda said. "The voivode's son?"

Another misspoken sentence.

"You were in the woods with him?" Magda asked. "Alone?"

"Not alone," Ilona said. "Andrei was with us."

"Alone with *two* boys!" Magda squealed in delight. "How did it happen? What were they doing at Codru Conac?"

Ilona glanced down the stairwell, put a finger against her lips, and waved Magda and Gizela into her bedroom. When they were inside, she shut the door and locked it.

"Nothing happened. It was completely innocent. Vlad and Andrei were hunting, and they saw me walking near the forest. Vlad wanted to show me a place up top where we could see for miles, so we climbed and that's when we saw the sultan's army had arrived."

Gizela looked envious. Magda grinned from ear to ear.

"So Vlad and Andrei just *happened* to be out hunting," Magda said, "and *by chance* they picked the woods near Codru Conac?"

"It's not what you think." Ilona backed up against the window. "I'm betrothed to Mircea. I'm not worth Vlad's effort. And Vlad told me he and Andrei hunt around here all the time."

"So you've seen them here before," Magda said.

"Well . . . No . . . But we haven't lived here very long."

Magda didn't look convinced.

"I'm sure you've seen them hunt near *your* manor," Ilona said hotly.

"Never. But I wouldn't mind if Andrei rode past every now and then. He has the most beautiful eyes."

Deep brown. The color of dark chestnuts.

Ilona blinked, startled that she could remember that detail. She was betrothed! She shouldn't be noticing other boys' eyes!

Magda said something else—something about Andrei—but Ilona didn't hear it over the sound of shattering glass. Glittery flakes of it drifted past her face. Tiny fragments sparkled like sharp diamonds all over her black dress.

She brushed shards out of her hair, and something warm trickled down her forehead. More glass fell from her hair. Something bright and sticky fell with it.

Blood.

She held her hand in front of her and watched crimson beads drip off her fingertips. Gizela's and Magda's screams echoed off the walls, but Ilona was too dazed to make a sound.

Something quivered in the bedroom door. A crossbow bolt. Black. Fletched with raptor feathers.

"Get down!" Magda cried. "Get down, Ilona!"

Everything moved in slow motion. Ilona's vision spun. Why was a crossbow bolt wedged in her door?

She didn't realize she was falling until her shoulder struck the carved bedpost. Her fingers left red streaks on her down-filled quilt as she slumped to the floor.

"Ilona!"

Magda's voice echoed as if Ilona were at the bottom of a deep, dark well. It was the last thing she heard before the darkness overwhelmed her.

Too slow.

Too late.

They tumbled to the earth, rolled, and landed in a tangled heap next to a tree. Andrei swung his fist into the assassin's face several times before the man's knee caught him in the groin. He might have been dead right then if not for the killer's haste to flee. High-pitched screams echoed through the manor's shattered window. Andrei couldn't tell if any belonged to Ilona.

The assassin's footsteps pounded away. Hoofbeats echoed. Unable to draw breath or pull himself to his feet, Andrei slumped against the cold, hard earth.

He needed to pursue the murderer, but it was all he could do to simply roll to his knees, coughing and wheezing. He cursed his wobbly legs for refusing to lift him. After a few moments, he managed to stand, but could only sway precariously while supporting his weight against a tree.

Ilona's window was mostly intact. Only one pane was missing, but it was the pane where her head had been.

Nausea twisted Andrei's stomach. His head swam, he took a few steps backward, and something tangled around his ankle. Balance broken, he fell sideways, arms flailing. The thing snaring him held on like a determined hunting dog. Andrei kicked in panic until the assassin's dropped crossbow flew off his foot.

Startled voices rang from the manor. Help was coming. He would point them in the direction of Ilona's attacker.

Ilona . . .

Andrei's throat tightened and his eyes stung. If she was dead . . .

He shook his head, refusing to complete that thought.

She was all right. She had to be. He stumbled toward the manor and heard a door creak open. Determined footsteps drummed in his direction. He staggered toward the footsteps, trying to find his voice, trying to figure out what to say.

"Over there!" a voice cried out.

Andrei lifted a hand in greeting, and an arrow nearly grazed his thumb.

He froze.

It wasn't until the second arrow flew that he realized what was happening.

They thought *he* was the assassin. They thought *he* was Ilona's attacker.

"Wait! Don't shoot! It wasn't me!"

"Put your hands up!" a voice with a Saxon accent shouted. "Stay where you are! Don't move!"

Andrei obliged.

Three burly soldiers charged toward him, twigs snapping under their feet. One of them grabbed Andrei by the arm and threw him to his knees.

"Tell His Lordship we have the assassin," the man barked, holding his sword across Andrei's throat. "Ask him if he wants him dead now or if he wants to question him first."

One of the man's companions nodded, turned, and jogged back toward the manor.

"It wasn't me," Andrei whispered.

The blade simply pressed closer to his throat.

CHAPTER EIGHT

ILONA'S FATHER WAS AN INTIMIDATING MAN. FORTUNATELY, Boyar Racoviţă was present for his interrogation. Racoviţă's friendly demeanor made it easier for Andrei to face Anton Csáki. Easier . . . but no less frightening.

"Tell me again about the assassin," Csáki said. "Did he have weapons other than the crossbow he dropped? Did you see anything about him that would help us identify him if you saw him again?"

Andrei shakily cleared his throat. He had already given every detail he could think of. He wasn't sure what more Csáki expected from him.

"I . . . I don't know. Like I said, his face was covered. I think he was about my height. Maybe a little shorter."

"My guards only saw you. Are you sure you weren't hunting in my forest and accidentally sent a bolt through my daughter's window?"

Andrei stared at Csáki, dumbfounded. When he recovered, his fear had given way to anger.

"I've told you exactly what happened! You've seen the assassin's bow and I've told you where you can find my own!"

"And Vlad Dracula can confirm your story?"

"Yes! We can ride to Târgoviște right now and he'll tell you everything."

Csáki's eyes narrowed. Andrei should have probably lowered his voice, but he was no longer concerned about offending the grand boyar. He didn't like being called a liar.

Virghiliu Racoviță, who had remained a silent observer until this point, now placed a hand on Csáki's arm.

"Look at the bolt we found in Ilona's room, then look at the bolts your guards took from Andrei's quiver."

He held the two projectiles up, side by side. Csáki examined them, his lips pulling downward into a deeper frown.

"Yes . . . ," he said finally. "They're different. The fletching is different, too."

"Did you see which direction the assassin ran after he shot the bolt?" Racoviță asked.

"He ran toward his horse."

"He had a horse?" Racoviță leaned forward in his seat. "That's important. What can you tell us about that?"

Andrei felt some of the tension leave his body. "It was a sorrel. It had white fetlocks, and there was a white stripe from its forehead to its muzzle. I would recognize it if I saw it again."

"A horse," Csáki scoffed. "You would recognize the horse but not the man?"

"The man's face was covered," Andrei said, growing irritated again. "And horses are as different from each other as people are."

"Don't underestimate our Prince Andrei when it comes to horses," Racoviţă said. "He's already made a reputation for himself. If he says he would recognize it, I believe him."

The shadow that had covered Csaki's features since Andrei's arrival softened and almost faded. "All we have to do, then," the grand boyar said, "is watch for suspected enemies with sorrel horses. That would eliminate two boyars. Possibly three." He stood and angrily paced in front of the fireplace.

"About Ilona . . . ," Andrei said. He had been wanting to ask this question since Csáki started interrogating him. "Is she all right?"

"Ilona? She'll survive." Csáki waved his hand dismissively. "The bolt grazed her head. Just a little surface wound. She'll forget about it by tomorrow."

Andrei and Boyar Racoviţă exchanged glances. Csáki didn't seem to notice how his lack of concern for his eldest daughter bewildered them.

"I warned you about the voivode's enemies," Racoviţă said. "Perhaps you'll now reconsider my recommendation to hire more guards. You wouldn't want anything like this to happen to your family again. I can only imagine what it must feel like to have almost lost your child."

"Yes, of course." Ilona's father returned to his seat and drummed his fingers on the armrest. "The welfare of one's children must always be a father's priority."

He stared into the fireplace. He was silent so long that Andrei ventured another comment.

"Out in the woods where I left my and Vlad's bows . . . I found something. Ilona's book of sketches. She'll probably be worried about it."

"Sketches? What sketches?"

"Her study of birds. The scientific notes and drawings she's made."

Csáki laughed. "Science? Women don't engage in science. You must be mistaken."

Andrei looked uncertainly between Csáki and Racoviță.

"Maybe it's not hers. You're probably right." But he *knew* it was hers. He would retrieve it and return it to Ilona later.

"If you don't mind," he said, "I need to get back to the Curtea Domnească."

"Allow me to send one of my men with you," Racoviță offered. "It's not safe these days to be traveling alone."

"I don't want to be a bother," Andrei said quickly. "I'm sure I'll be safe on my own."

Racoviță shook his head. "I insist! I could never forgive myself if harm came to you. We've already seen today that the voivode's enemies are at work."

With a hesitant nod, Andrei relented. Word of today's events—and of Andrei's involvement—would get back to the voivode. It was bad enough that Andrei left Târgoviște alone. It would be foolish to reject an offer of added protection now. He was certain the attempt on Ilona's life was linked to the attempt on the voivode's. Every member of the royal household—present or future—was likely at risk.

But the only thing that mattered today was that Ilona was still alive. Andrei felt deeply relieved. And he felt something else. He wasn't sure what it was, but it made him eager to see

Ilona again. And he would. After all, he still needed to return her sketchbook.

"You should have taken me with you! You shouldn't have gone alone!"

Vlad paced the room. He was angry, but not at Andrei. How dare anyone try to harm Ilona!

"I know," Andrei said, "but I only went to retrieve the crossbows. It wasn't like I planned on meeting an assassin in the forest."

Vlad shook his head, then surprised both himself and Andrei by bursting into laughter.

"You really have a gift, you know. A gift for stumbling onto nefarious plots. A gift for crossing paths with murderers."

"Believe me," Andrei whispered, "it's not a gift I've ever wished for."

"You say the assassin's face was covered?"

Andrei nodded.

"But you must have noticed other things about him. His height. His eye color."

"I don't know. It happened so fast. I didn't notice much more after his knee caught me in the groin."

Vlad winced. "Please tell me you at least got a few punches in before he ran away."

"I hit him in the face."

"Good. So we look for a man with a bruised face."

"What?"

Vlad laughed again. "We're going after him. We're going to find out who keeps sending these assassins. You and I are going to hunt him down and make him pay."

Andrei left the edge of his bed and backed a few steps away from Vlad. "Don't you think that job should be left to the royal guards? The voivode probably won't want us meddling in that."

Vlad waved Andrei's concerns away. "That's why we have to start today. If we find the boyar behind these attacks before the royal guards do, we'll be heroes. My father will finally give us the respect we deserve."

"You think a Wallachian boyar arranged to have Ilona killed? Both her and the voivode?"

"Of course I do. Golescu and all his cronies hate my father. They also hate Csáki: he's the voivode's greatest ally. Someone is trying to murder or intimidate anyone who openly supports the House of Drăculeşti. You and I are going to find proof of who it is. Or who they are. And, if we have to, we'll eliminate the threat ourselves."

Andrei squirmed. "Shouldn't we just tell the voivode everything we know—which isn't much—so he can investigate?"

Vlad harrumphed in disgust. "You understand nothing about politics, do you? Where boyars are involved, the voivode's hands are tied. He can't touch them or their property without risking a full-scale revolt."

"And you're saying *you and I* can search their homes without risking the same thing?"

"I'm saying someone has to find out what's going on and put a stop to it. We'll identify the traitor who gave the voivode's enemies that wooden key. We'll find the man who tried to kill my future wife."

"What?"

Vlad laughed uncomfortably. "A slip of the tongue," he said. "My future *sister-in-law*." He looked away and coughed into his fist. "No one does harm to my current or future family. Not without expecting the House of the Dragon to exact revenge."

He risked a glance at his cousin, but Andrei was now avoiding his gaze.

"Get your coat and crossbow," he said. "We're going for a ride."

"A ride? To where?"

"To look for a killer."

"Your father will be—"

"Out showing Mircea how to rule a kingdom he's not fit for. He'll never know we left."

Vlad tried to sound flippant, but he couldn't hide the bitterness in his voice. The voivode's favorite was Mircea. Vasilisa's was Radu. Vlad received little attention from either parent. This was as golden an opportunity as he would ever get to prove his worth.

Andrei stifled a sigh, but Vlad could see that he was already caving in.

"Lead the way," Andrei muttered.

Vlad thumped his cousin on the back. "Allies forever."

"Forever," Andrei agreed.

It was good to have at least one family member who understood him.

CHAPTER NINE

VLAD'S MYSTERIOUS DESTINATION LAY A SHORT RIDE SOUTH-ward near the banks of the Dâmbovița River. To the north and east, Golescu Manor faced open farmland, but the river's dense undergrowth provided some cover if they approached it from the west. Andrei's heart thumped nervously as he and Vlad followed a narrow trail between gray trunks and low shrubs. Neither of them spoke until Vlad reined in and stood in his stirrups.

"We'll leave our horses here," Vlad whispered, "and walk the rest of the way."

He dismounted, crept to a new vantage point, and surveyed the imposing manor.

"Load your bow in case something happens. We might have to fight our way out."

He said it jokingly, but Andrei got the feeling Vlad relished the idea of a fight.

It was a bad idea to come here. He shouldn't have been so quick to humor Vlad.

"I want to get closer. Follow me."

Golescu's fields touched the trees. Vlad dropped to his stomach and slithered like a snake through the scythed remains of last season's yellowed wheat stalks. Andrei followed until they reached waist-high grass and rose into low crouches.

"Who do you think Ilona finds more attractive? Mircea or me?"

"What?"

"Ilona. Who do you think she likes better?"

"I don't know."

He didn't want to discuss Ilona. Not with Vlad. It made him uncomfortable.

"If Mircea were to fall off a horse and break his neck . . . Or if someone poisoned him before the wedding took place . . . I'd be next in line for the throne."

"Poisoned?"

"You never know. He might be murdered before we reveal the traitors. His misfortune would be my gain."

Andrei stared at him openmouthed. Vlad met his gaze and chuckled.

"I'm kidding!" he whispered. "Don't be such a neispravit!" He turned his eyes back toward the manor and pointed. "Something's happening."

The manor's doors were open. Two men stepped into the courtyard. One was Golescu. Andrei didn't recognize the other, but he and Golescu appeared to be arguing about something.

"Look at his face!" Vlad hissed.

Andrei looked, and a cold tremor rattled his spine. The unfamiliar man's nose was lopsided. Swollen. Half his jawbone was purpled with fist-size bruises.

Vlad slowly lifted his crossbow.

"No!"

"Why shouldn't I? He tried to kill Ilona."

"We don't know that. It could have been another person."

Vlad glared at Andrei, but he refused to look away.

"Let's tell the voivode what we've found," Andrei said. "Let's let him deal with it."

"I've already told you, the voivode won't do anything. He can't. Golescu is the most powerful boyar on the council. If we don't bring justice, no one will."

Even though the air was cold, Andrei found that he was perspiring. "If you kill the assassin now," he said, "Golescu and his friends will hide his body and cover the whole thing up. We'll never prove that they were part of an assassination attempt."

Vlad lowered his bow. "You're right. We have to figure out who else was involved. We have to identify the traitor in the palace and link him—or her—with Golescu. After that, we'll deal with *him*."

Vlad jabbed an angry finger toward the assassin, and Andrei exhaled and nodded.

What had he gotten himself into?

Something rattled like hail against Gizela's window; Ilona sat bolt upright. Neither the noise nor Ilona's movement woke Gizela, but Ilona's heart pounded with terror as she considered what nearly happened the last time something struck one of the manor's windows.

Another series of light rattles echoed through the room. Someone was throwing gravel at the glass.

Her feet grew icy the moment her bare toes touched the floor.

Rattle! Rattle! Rattle!

She held her breath as she carefully peered out the window. Fortunately, the figure in the courtyard was familiar. Even in the early morning darkness, she recognized Vlad. He waved, and her heart's rhythm shifted from something terrified to something warm and exhilarating.

Vlad gestured toward the stables. She hesitated before nodding and moving away from the breath-fogged glass.

Her father would be furious.

All the more reason to meet Vlad outside.

Down the hall in her own bedroom, gray moonlight spilled through the shattered window. A glassmaker from Târgoviște would arrive in the afternoon, but until then the broken pane's jagged edges remained to remind Ilona about her close brush with death.

She dressed quickly, donning her hideous mourning gown. As she navigated the manor's shadowed staircase and dark hallways, the gown's black train swished along behind her, collecting dust off the floor.

Outside the air was frigid. Yet again she had lacked the common sense to put on a coat. But had she really forgotten, or was she simply giving Vlad another chance to be gallant? Shivery warmth tingled through her heart again.

The stables were thick with the musty tang of horsehide and dung. She wrinkled her nose.

"Jó reggelt!"

Ilona jumped and spun, but smiled when she saw Vlad.

"Bună dimineața," she said, responding to his Hungarian greeting in Romanian.

Vlad closed the stable doors and uncovered a lit lantern. "Honestly, Ilona," he teased. "You're going to die of consumption. Wear something warm next time you come outside." Grinning, Vlad removed his velvet coat and swung it around her shoulders.

"I wasn't planning on being outside," she replied lightly. "My father would be quite angry if he found us here together. Thankfully he leaves early to fulfill his duties at the border."

"He would be angry even though I'm the voivode's son?"

"Especially because of that. I'm betrothed to your brother. I shouldn't be alone with you."

Vlad laughed. "It's not like Mircea isn't spending time alone with any pretty girl he can get his hands on."

Ilona frowned, and Vlad stopped laughing.

"I'm sorry," he said quietly. "Mircea's a pig. Someone should have told you."

Ilona diverted her gaze. "All men are pigs."

"Not all of us. I'm not like Mircea. If you were my betrothed, I would never look at another girl again."

Her face warmed, and he smiled.

"Why did you come here?" she asked, still struggling to compose herself. "You must have left Târgoviște at the crack of dawn."

"I had to make sure you were all right. After what nearly happened to you, I . . . I . . ."

Her blush drove the frosty bite off her nose and chased the cold from her cheeks.

"Are you all right?" Vlad asked. He took both her hands into his. "Andrei told me the whole terrible story."

Andrei . . . Andrei had saved her. A faint smile touched her lips. Vlad moved closer, and she blinked and focused on him again.

"He said the arrow grazed you. Where?"

Ilona pulled one hand free and lightly touched the top of her head. Vlad gently brushed her hair aside and grimaced.

"It's nothing serious," Ilona said. "It bled for a little while, but it was only a bad scratch. It didn't even need stitches."

Vlad clenched his teeth. "It should have never happened. The voivode should have known something like this might happen and taken precautions."

"Why do you call your father 'the voivode'?" Ilona asked. "Why that and not 'Father'?"

Vlad stared at the floor. "I don't know. Radu and Mircea call him 'Father.' I do sometimes, but . . ." He shook his head. "Maybe because sometimes I don't feel like a real son."

He looked at her helplessly, as if he would like to explain but didn't know how.

He didn't have to. Ilona understood the feeling.

She took his hand again. "Where's Andrei, by the way? I don't think I've ever seen you without him."

"Him?" Vlad shook his head. "He's exhausted. I didn't want to wake him. He's had a rough few days and could use some sleep."

Ilona nodded. She was exhausted, too. Run-ins with assassins could do that to a person.

She looked into Vlad's green eyes again. "Thank you," she said. "Thank you for coming to check on me."

Vlad grinned sheepishly. "I had to. You're family. Mircea should be checking on you, too, but he probably hasn't."

"No," Ilona confirmed. "He hasn't."

Vlad's face darkened. "If Mircea doesn't wake up and get

his priorities straight . . . ," he growled. "If he doesn't figure out how important you are . . ."

Ilona surprised Vlad by leaning forward to kiss him on the cheek. As quickly as she did it, she lowered her eyes and pulled away.

"I . . . I'm sorry," she said. "I—"

Vlad pressed a finger against her lips. "You don't have to apologize. Remember? We're family?"

She nodded.

"Andrei and I figured out who sent the assassin."

All the warmth she'd felt a moment before drained away.

"It was one of Golescu's men," Vlad continued. "A hired soldier. His nose is broken and his face is bruised from Andrei punching him."

Ice snaked up Ilona's spine. "You're certain?"

"There's no question about it, and I'm going to make Golescu pay."

"My mother always said it's best to leave vengeance to God," Ilona whispered. "We're supposed to love our enemies. We're supposed to turn the other cheek."

"You think a murderer deserves forgiveness?"

"He didn't kill me."

"But he tried!" The muscles in Vlad's jaw tightened. "In cases like this," he said, "I think Burchard—the Bishop of Worms—has a much better idea. '*Propter vindicta noxiorum gladium fuisse permissum.*'"

"To bring vengeance upon the wicked," Ilona translated, "the sword has been permitted."

Vlad looked impressed. "You've studied your Latin. Have you read Burchard's *Decretum Burchardi*?"

"I haven't."

"Burchard says princes and kings are authorized by God to carry out His vengeance. So according to God, it's my *responsibility* to avenge you."

Ilona shifted uncomfortably. "It's enough that you and Andrei have been looking out for me," she said. "I'll be all right. My father says he's going to post extra guards at the doors."

"Like the guards who stopped me from throwing rocks at your window? The ones who stopped you from slipping outside?"

She didn't have an answer for that.

"Golescu should have never sent someone to hurt you! He—" Vlad stopped speaking and stared over one of the stall gates. "Didn't you say your father leaves early to be at the border?"

"Yes . . . ?"

"Not today. His horse is still here."

Ilona walked to the stall and looked in. Her father's big black charger snorted at her and stomped its hooves.

"How did you know this was my father's horse?"

"The voivode says it's my business to remember and recognize everything. Horses, weapons, faces . . . Allies become enemies, enemies become allies. You never know when small details might become useful."

"Like which bedroom someone's sleeping in?" Ilona raised her eyebrows, and Vlad laughed. He laughed easily—a trait Ilona found attractive.

Attractive?

Yes. She was attracted to Vlad Dracula. Why not admit it? Mircea wasn't faithful to her. He didn't care that she'd nearly been murdered. Why should she be faithful to him?

Because Mother would have expected it. Because Mother would have wanted me to be a proper lady.

But her mother was dead. Ilona rolled her shame into an iron ball and pushed it down into the pit of her stomach.

"Before Codru Conac was yours," Vlad said, "it belonged to the voivode. I know its rooms almost as well as the rooms at the Princely Court. Once I spotted the broken window, it wasn't hard to guess which other room you would be in."

"You're lucky you didn't guess wrong and throw pebbles at my father's window."

Vlad chuckled, and Ilona allowed herself a small grin.

"You're beautiful," Vlad said. "You know that, don't you?"

Her face warmed and his grin illuminated his entire face. Somehow his hand found hers again atop the stall gate. She tried to pull back, but his fingers tightened around hers. She stopped resisting and his touch sent warm prickles up her arm.

"You've probably noticed," Vlad said, "what a dangerous place Wallachia can be."

"I figured it out when that man tried to kill me."

"Every girl needs a protector," he said, moving closer. "Someone to watch over her."

His green eyes were mesmerizing. Ilona gazed into them and found herself unable to look away.

"You never know what the future holds," Vlad murmured. "Mircea might be assassinated. I'm next in line for the throne. Without him around, you could be with . . . someone else."

One of his arms went around her waist and his warm lips unexpectedly touched hers. She had never been kissed before.

Not this way. It was wrong. She was betrothed, yet she didn't pull away.

Vlad ended the kiss first.

"I'm sorry," he whispered. "That was wrong of me. It won't happen again."

Ilona avoided his lingering gaze. Her head spun. She searched for words but found none.

Vlad stood straight. "Someone's coming."

Footsteps and voices. Ilona heard them too.

"My father!" she whispered. There was no time to exit the stables. Anton Csáki and his personal guards were almost at the doors.

"In here!" Vlad whispered.

He opened a creaky gate, and they both stepped in. A huge warhorse—a brown destrier—whinnied and shied to one side as they pushed past it. It wasn't one of Ilona's father's horses; it had to be Vlad's. The stable doors swung open, freezing air rushed in, and Ilona's father entered.

Ilona moved her foot and placed it in something squishy. She pressed her lips together, silencing the exclamation that nearly betrayed her.

"Saddle Arnyék," her father said, "and be quick about it."

"Yes, Your Excellency. You heard him, Sorin. The big black one."

The marshal and the groomsmen. He'd brought them, too. The situation was getting worse and worse.

"And two rouncys for my guards."

"Of course, Your Excellency. Iancu! Iuliu! Get to it!"

Ilona heard activity throughout the stables. If she was found in this stall with Vlad, the humiliation would be unbearable. She glanced at Vlad, but he didn't look worried. He seemed to enjoy the thrill of possible discovery. His smile faded, however, when his horse chose this inopportune moment to urinate all over his boot.

An eternity passed before her father's party exited the stables. Vlad took her hand and helped her out of the stall.

"Things will get busy soon," Vlad said. "The servants will be back to feed the horses. Sneak out the back while there's still time."

"What about you?"

"I'll wait until I hear your father's horses leaving. Then I'll hurry back to the Curtea Domnească before anyone notices I'm missing."

"The marshal will see you. He'll ask questions."

Vlad waved her concern away. "Haven't you heard?"

"Heard what?"

"I'm the voivode's son. No one questions me. At least no one outside the Curtea Domnească. Commoners just bow and wish me a good day."

He unbarred the back doors and ushered her out.

"Hurry," he said. "Now's your chance."

"Wait!"

"What?"

"Your coat."

She pulled it from her shoulders and handed it back to him. "*La revedere*, Vlad."

"*Viszontlátásra*," he answered.

He started to swing the doors shut again but changed his mind and whispered three parting words.

"*Gladium fuisse permissum.*"

The sword has been permitted.

Ilona shivered, and Vlad closed the doors.

CHAPTER TEN

"I DON'T UNDERSTAND WHY WE NEED TO INTERROGATE THE housemaids," Andrei said. "We already know Golescu was behind the attacks."

"But we don't know *how* the voivode's attacker got the wooden key," Vlad said. "I've been thinking and thinking about this. I don't want to tip Golescu off that we're onto him, but I think one of the maids has to be behind the wooden key. Maybe the voivode forgot to wear it around his neck one day. Maybe a maid traced a picture of it or pressed it into something to save its shape. I don't know, but it's important to know how it was passed on to him. We need to question the maids."

Andrei placed a hand against his forehead. "Do you at least have some kind of plan for what kinds of questions we're going to ask? And how we're going to start the conversation without making it sound unnatural?"

"You're going to flirt with them," Vlad said. "Make them laugh. Make them think you're attracted to them."

"Oh no!" Andrei took a step backward, shaking his head. "Count me out! I'm not having any part in this."

"Just leave it up to me," Vlad said. "I already have an idea about how to get the information we need. And I know exactly which maid to start with."

"Just questions," Andrei said. "And *you're* asking them. No flirting."

"Trust me. This is going to be well worth our time."

They followed the sound of sweeping to Radu's bedroom. A maid stood in a corner, removing cobwebs from the plaster ceiling with a birch-twig broom. She didn't notice them until Vlad was standing right behind her.

"Oh!" The housemaid dropped the broom, gathered her long skirts, and bowed, nearly falling over in her haste. "Your Serene Highnesses . . . How may I serve you?"

"You can serve us by answering a few questions."

Vlad's manner was overtly threatening. Andrei raised a hand to protest, but Vlad waved him off.

"You were cleaning the voivode's personal chambers the other day," he growled.

"Y-yes, Your Highness."

"Have you been in his room before?"

"Only the one time. Only yesterday. I—"

"I don't believe you," Vlad interrupted.

"Vlad . . . ," Andrei said.

"Which means you've had access to everything in his room," Vlad continued. "A misplaced key. A piece of gold or two."

At the mention of gold, the young woman's face turned white.

"I . . . I don't know anything about gold, and the . . . the voivode carries the only key on a chain around his neck. He . . . he never takes it off except . . . except to unlock the door . . ."

"You seem to know a great deal about the voivode's personal habits."

The housemaid glanced toward the open door. Vlad drew his sword, and the young woman's eyes widened.

This wasn't the plan. This wasn't a few harmless questions like Vlad had made it seem it would be.

"*Vlad!*" Andrei snapped.

"Close the door, Andrei. Hold it shut and don't let anyone in."

But Andrei didn't move. What sort of person intimidated frightened young housemaids at swordpoint? His cousin was taking this too far.

"The voivode must remove the chain sometimes," Vlad pressed. "At night before he sleeps. In the morning when he dresses. I think he forgot to put it on at all one morning. I think you were cleaning his room, and you found it."

"N-no, Your Grace! I-I would never—"

"And you've taken gold from his room and accepted payment from his enemies. You would betray the House of Drăculeşti for a little money."

The maid looked like she wanted to scream, but she glanced at Vlad's sword and the impulse was silenced.

"It . . . it was someone else! I-I've heard rumors! Something whispered among the scullery maids!" With that, she burst into tears.

Vlad took a step back from her. "Tell me," he commanded.

"It's . . . it's only rumors."

"*Tell me.*"

She gulped air and gasped out the words: "A mistress! A boyar's daughter!"

Vlad scowled. "Give me her name."

"I . . . I don't know it . . ."

"Who would know the name?"

"Maybe one of the cooks or one of the scullery maids. Raluca! She would know. She knows everything that happens inside the palace. Please, I . . . I don't know anything else!"

Vlad glanced at Andrei, then back at the weeping maid. "You will tell no one what was said or done here today. Is that clear?"

"Yes . . . Thank you, Your Serene Highness!"

"Because if I learn you've spoken about it, I will find you, and I'll put your body somewhere where your family will never find it."

He said it so coldly—with a voice so like the voivode's—even Andrei almost believed the threat. The maid's mouth opened and closed in a way that made her look like a suffocating fish. Vlad turned his back on her and strode toward the door.

Andrei cast a nervous glance at the young woman before following Vlad back into the corridor.

"Was that really necessary?" Andrei demanded once they were out of earshot.

"It's what the voivode would do. Sometimes a prince has to rule by fear."

Andrei wasn't sure he agreed with that assumption, but now wasn't the moment to argue that point.

"That was useless," Vlad muttered.

"You don't believe her?"

"I believe her, but the voivode probably has a hundred mistresses. Any one of them could have gotten her hands on that key. We're no closer to the truth than we were before."

"Maybe no one took his key. Maybe his enemies found a smith who had saved a copy."

"Maybe."

Clearly Vlad wasn't convinced, but perhaps he now saw how impossible this was for them to investigate on their own and would stop terrorizing servants.

"The voivode will be away from the palace tonight, and we will, too," Vlad said.

Andrei didn't like the sound of that.

"Ask Raluca about the boyar's daughter the next time you get a chance. She loves you like a son. I think she'll give the woman's name to you."

Andrei nodded hesitantly.

"We're going to solve this mystery if it kills us to do it," Vlad said. "We're going to keep our family safe."

He should have refused to come. The first trip to Golescu's manor was risky. This one was like taunting a hungry lion by placing your hand in its mouth. At least Vlad had enough sense to make the visit under cover of darkness. Andrei lurked beside him in an outbuilding's concealing shadows and hoped Vlad had some kind of exit plan if things went wrong.

"This one looks right. Try the door."

"What?"

"We're going inside."

"What if someone's in there?"

"At this time of night?" Vlad pushed past Andrei and tried the door's latch himself.

The door creaked as it opened. Alarmed, Andrei scanned the manor grounds, but Vlad plunged, unworried, into the building's dark interior. Andrei waited only a moment before following.

Inside it was pitch-black and warm. A few paces ahead Vlad bumped into something solid, and a variety of unseen metal objects clanged loudly against the floor.

"Oh, great," Vlad muttered.

They froze.

When no hint that anyone had heard them reached their ears, Vlad crept forward again.

"Ah! Here it is."

Andrei heard a sound like shifting grain. Something crackled. A dull orange glow lit the room.

"Shut the door."

Andrei did as commanded, turned back, and saw Vlad standing over a blacksmith's forge. Vlad was still holding the poker he had used to stir the forge's slumbering coals to life.

"Why are we in Golescu's blacksmith's shop?"

"We're looking for clues."

"Like a key?"

"That, or lock parts. Anything that could tie Golescu to the palace assassin."

"He probably needs locks and keys for his own house. If we find any of those, the only thing it will prove—"

"It will prove that he *could* have been involved with that key."

Andrei shook his head.

"I *will* find evidence," Vlad said. "And when I prove that Golescu sent the assassins, the voivode will reward me. Mircea will become second best in his eyes."

Andrei doubted that, but it was better to keep his mouth shut until Vlad discovered the flaws in his argument on his own.

"You search that side," Vlad said. "I'll search this side. If you find anything suspicious, let me know."

Andrei nodded. The quicker they got this over with, the happier he would be. He glanced at the closed door and shuttered windows and a shiver ran up his spine. He hoped that no light was escaping because, if it did, someone would surely come to investigate.

Vlad tucked his crossbow under one arm and searched a table's contents. He wasn't worried about being discovered, but Andrei carried enough worry for both of them.

Keys. Lock parts. Find one or the other and Vlad would be satisfied. Then they could get out of here.

Andrei touched a tarnished anvil and searched around it. Tongs. Horseshoes. Hammers. No keys or lock parts. Vlad was having no better luck. He was shoving objects aside, muttering under his breath, making far too much noise.

"Nothing!" Vlad snarled. "What have you found?"

Andrei shook his head.

"Come on. I should have known he would be too smart to leave evidence lying out in the open."

They went to the door, slipped quickly into the night, and shut the door behind them. Yellow slivers of light escaped around the door's frame.

"What now?" Andrei asked. "Back to Târgoviște?"

"No, I've got one more thing I want to see."

Vlad turned toward the manor, his feet crunching noisily over the frozen earth. Other than that, all was eerily silent. Lanterns still burned in a few of the manor's windows. Smoke from the chimneys cast a thick haze across the star-studded sky. The smoke gave the moon a reddish tint. Like blood. A bad omen.

"You're not planning on breaking into the manor, are you?" Andrei whispered.

"Shhh!"

Vlad sprinted across an open space and crouched beside a squat, dark building. Andrei paused to take a shaky breath before following. From their new vantage point, they could see into almost every window on the manor's southwest side. There wasn't much to see.

Andrei's mind drifted to Ilona's window. He remembered her long dark hair framed in the rippled glass. He remembered the twanging bow and the screams that followed. He shuddered, blinked, and hastily returned his thoughts to the present.

Something was moving behind one of the manor's lower windows, and when Andrei recognized the silhouette, he went rigid. It was none other than the Grand Boyar Golescu. He stood at the sill, hands planted against it, staring into the darkness as if he sensed Vlad and Andrei's presence. The boyar moved his lips, speaking to some unseen occupant behind him.

"Look at him," Vlad growled. "So pleased with himself. So sure no one lurks outside *his* manor waiting to put an arrow through *his* head."

Shattering glass. Girls' screams. Andrei shivered and blinked again.

They watched for several minutes until Golescu turned and moved away.

"Help me," Vlad whispered.

"Help you what?"

"Help me climb onto the roof."

Vlad leaned his bow against the squat building they'd been using for cover.

"Hurry," he said. "I want to see who he's talking to before they leave the room."

Vlad grasped the roof's low overhang and lifted a boot, waiting for Andrei to boost him up. Andrei made a stirrup with both hands, and Vlad clambered higher. As he did, his foot struck the wall. Something stirred inside the building.

Startled clucks and squawks echoed across the manor grounds. From the manor house itself, the bell-deep voices of Golescu's hunting hounds split the night.

"Pass me the bows," Vlad said. "Quickly!"

Andrei hesitated.

"If we leave them, someone will see them!" Vlad pressed.

Andrei handed up the crossbows. As they left his grasp, a tired, mildly annoyed voice cut through the darkness.

". . . probably a marten or another fox after the hens again . . ."

Andrei looked at Vlad.

"Hide!" Vlad whispered.

A lantern's flickering light bobbed through the shadows. Trudging footsteps echoed closer. No time to climb. No barrels or crates to hide behind. Andrei hurried to the far side of the coop and flattened himself against a wall.

"See if it got inside. I'll check out here."

The lantern's light expanded, stretching past Andrei's inadequate hiding place. To his left something rattled and a door squeaked open. The chickens' worried clucks grew louder.

The light faded, but fingers of illumination escaped through cracks in the walls. Outside, stealthy footsteps came Andrei's way. He tensed his legs and prepared to run.

Thud! Something hit the ground at the other end of the coop.

"Sandu!" a voice called. "Quick, bring the lantern!"

The lantern's yellow illumination softened the darkness, its light bobbing wildly. Andrei held his breath as he peeked around the corner.

Two serfs, both carrying wooden cudgels, were creeping toward an empty field.

"Was it a fox?"

"I don't know, couldn't see it. Whatever it was, it's gone now . . . Anything inside?"

"Nothing. The chickens are safe."

"Then I'm going back to my bed and my warm fire."

The thin man with the lantern lowered his cudgel and mumbled agreement, and they walked back the way they had come. Andrei remained where he was—motionless, pulse pounding in his ears—until their footsteps finally faded.

"They've gone back into their hut. Get over here and help me down."

Slavă cerului! Someone was watching over the two of them tonight. Trembling, heart still pounding, Andrei tiptoed back to Vlad.

"I'm here."

"Thanks to my quick thinking. I had to toss my dagger into the field."

"Mulțumesc."

"You're welcome."

"Hand me the bows," Andrei said, "and I'll help you down."

"Wait a second."

Vlad lifted himself off his stomach and balanced on his knees. He stared at the manor.

"What is it?"

"He has a woman with him."

"His wife?"

"No."

Andrei contemplated the other possibilities and played with his collar.

"Get your mind out of the cesspit," Vlad said. "It's not what you think. But I swear I've seen her before . . ."

Vlad scratched his head a moment, scowling, but froze when another movement at a higher window caught his attention. Andrei saw it, too. Golescu's daughter, Daciana.

She wore a nightdress. Her hair was down, and she was slowly combing it out. She was attractive—physically at least— but her haughty nature detracted from her looks. Until Ilona came along, Vlad had been infatuated with Daciana Golescu. Now he didn't talk about her anymore. Andrei almost wished Vlad would regain a little of that lost interest. Vlad could have whatever fantasies he wanted about Daciana, but Ilona was betrothed. She was off-limits.

"If you're done peeping at Golescu's daughter, I'll be happy to help you down now," Andrei said dryly.

Vlad didn't answer. He balanced his crossbow on his shoulder, lips twisted into a frown of concentration.

"Vlad? What are you—"

The string twanged. The bolt hissed. Daciana's window shattered and her shrill scream pierced the night.

"*Gladium fuisse permissum*," Vlad muttered.

His boots hit the earth, and Vlad tore through the darkness like the devil was on his tail.

Andrei followed. He ran until he thought his lungs would burst, stumbling often.

They vaulted onto their horses, spurred them forward. There were no sounds of pursuit, but Golescu's men would come.

"What have you done?" Andrei demanded.

Vlad didn't answer.

Andrei would never again take part in Vlad's dangerous adventures. Never again!

CHAPTER ELEVEN

Cântecul Lebedei was as different from Codru Conac as spring was from winter. The Csáki family's manor was darkly forbidding, a gathering of sharp angles and angry, scowling lines. Magda's home, on the other hand, was almost as swanlike as its graceful name. If the two manors were artwork, Magda's would be an oil painting brought to life with loving strokes. Codru Conac was a cold gray statue pounded into existence with a rusted war hammer.

But Ilona's family wasn't here to admire the Racoviţă family's architecture. They were here because Anton Csáki called a secret meeting of Prince Dracul's supporters. Ilona counted four. There had been at least five times that number on her father's scribbled list.

"Lead my horse to the stables," Ilona's father said, swinging down from his saddle and handing Ilona the reins. He lifted Gizela out of her saddle, gently steered her away from the restless horses, shaded his eyes, and scanned the horizon.

"Ah, good!" he muttered. "I was worried Mihai wouldn't come. I'm glad to see he still has his priorities straight."

Ilona followed his gaze toward a group of distant, galloping horses. A final boyar with his retinue. Five Dracul supporters. Six, if she counted her father. Still too few.

"Take these horses, too."

"What?"

"My men's horses. Take them."

Her father motioned his hired guards forward, took their reins, and slapped the leather straps into Ilona's hand. Still seated atop her chestnut palfrey, she struggled to control the three big chargers. They jostled irritably and would have knocked her into the dirt if not for Magda, who was already hurrying across the courtyard to assist; she took the reins so Ilona could steady herself.

"My father has servants waiting at the stables," Magda whispered, watching Anton Csáki stride away. "Your father should have taken these horses to them."

"He didn't want to waste precious moments riding the extra distance." Ilona's voice was tight.

"Maybe he's irritable like my father," Magda said, "because of the threats."

"What threats?"

A pair of pages had now come to Magda's aid. She handed the bundled reins to them before answering Ilona's question.

"Dragoş Golescu and his friends," she whispered. "They want my father to join with them against the voivode. They know if they get him on their side, only your father will stand against them."

Ilona bit her lower lip. Both girls fell silent for several moments. Gizela cheerfully skipped over to join them.

"This is your first time at Cântecul Lebedei," Magda said to Ilona and Gizela, clearly forcing herself to speak in a lighter, more cheerful voice. "Would you like me to show you around the manor?"

"That would be wonderful," Ilona replied.

"And I definitely must show you my father's new toy."

"Your father plays with toys?" Gizela wrinkled her nose in amusement.

"BIG toys," Magda answered. "Just wait. You'll see what I mean."

The last boyar had just entered the courtyard, and Ilona's father, along with the other Drăculeşti supporters, moved stiffly to meet them. Ilona wondered why the newly arrived boyar didn't dismount and why her father seemed so unwelcoming. She figured it out when she recognized the man atop the nearest horse.

"Golescu," her father said. His voice was colder than ice.

"Csáki," Golescu answered in an equally frosty tone.

"I had no idea you were such an avid supporter of our voivode," Ilona's father said. "It's so kind of you to ride all the way from Târgovişte to attend our meeting."

His comment brought tense chuckles from the voivode's real supporters. But Golescu surprised and unsettled them by laughing too.

"Always so funny, Csáki. I see you've managed to rally a *vast* crowd of Dracul admirers. But before you start your 'secret' meeting, you might want to hear what I've come to say."

Ilona's father narrowed his eyes. "Whatever it is you have to say, Golescu, be quick about it. Those of us who aren't traitors to Wallachia have important business to attend to."

Golescu's teeth shone like white daggers through his thick black beard. He scratched his wrist and made himself comfortable in his saddle.

"Traitors? We'll see which boyars are considered traitors once that nasty business in Transylvania has been settled." He paused a moment and swept his cold dark eyes over the gathered Dracul supporters. "I trust you've informed these men about the situation in Transylvania? Frostbite. Sickness. It's all Mezid Bey can do to keep his cowardly troops from deserting him."

"These men don't need to hear your twisted lies," Ilona's father said.

"You would know about twisted lies, Csáki. Except your style is more about withholding important information when it doesn't look good for your precious voivode."

This comment spurred uncomfortable murmurs from Dracul's supporters and questioning glances in Ilona's father's direction. For a moment she thought he would lose his composure, but he squared his shoulders and brushed Golescu's accusation aside.

"My information comes directly from Transylvania. You rely on rumors. Your faith in Hunyadi will be your downfall. Now if you don't mind, my colleagues and I have important things to do."

He turned his back on his adversary and headed toward the manor, but Golescu wasn't ready to let it drop.

"Csáki!"

Ilona's father kept walking.

"*Csáki!* I'm not finished talking to you!"

The rage in Golescu's voice stopped Ilona's father. He turned slowly.

"Last night someone paid my family a visit," Golescu snarled. "I believe you know what I'm referring to."

"I have no idea what you're referring to."

Golescu removed a broken crossbow bolt from his belt and held it aloft. "This was left by an assassin. He nearly killed my daughter."

Ilona's father looked surprised but not sympathetic. "How unfortunate. It seems no family is left untouched in these troubled times."

Golescu ground his teeth. "The surgeon removed this from Daciana's shoulder. A hand's width lower and it would have struck her heart."

Ilona's father stayed quiet a moment before responding to the angry boyar's words. "Your daughter is fortunate. A different assassin might have tried for her head. I hear the chances of recovering from that are minimal."

Ilona shivered in the wintry chill of the two men's mutual hatred.

"There's something else," Golescu said. He retrieved a dagger from his belt and tossed it into the dirt. "Do you recognize that?"

Ilona's father picked it up and turned it in his hands. "Fine craftsmanship. Saxon-made. Like the bow I found in the woods after someone attempted to kill *my* daughter."

"Look more closely."

Irritated, Ilona's father stared at the dagger again.

"I'm sure you recognize the symbol on its hilt?"

"A dragon and a shield."

"Not any dragon. The symbol of the Order of the Dragon."

"No doubt planted near your manor," Ilona's father calmly

replied, "to incriminate the voivode. Not very convincing unless a man is foolish enough to believe a prince would personally carry out a task he could hire another man to do."

Golescu's self-assurance faltered. He wheeled his horse around but kept his gaze on Ilona's father.

"Think about what I've told you." He now spoke to everyone but Anton Csáki. "It's not too late to change your allegiance. Don't be caught on the wrong side when Hunyadi repels the Ottoman army and rides on Wallachia to take his vengeance on the voivode."

He tossed the broken bolt into the dirt, spat at it, and galloped away in a cloud of dust.

Gladium fuisse permissum . . .

The sword has been permitted.

Magda touched Ilona's arm. "Are you all right?"

"What? Oh . . . Yes. Of course. Are . . . are you ready to show us the manor?"

"Yes!" Gizela exclaimed. "The manor! Show us the toy first!"

Magda nodded. "Follow me. We'll begin with Papa's pride and joy."

She led them behind the stables to a new building. Its stone walls bore fresh chisel marks and the wood planks in its double doors glistened with piney sap. Magda grasped an iron ring and slowly pulled one of the doors open. Ilona and Gizela followed her inside.

Gizela sucked in her breath. "Oh!"

Ilona stared, speechless as well.

"It's a *chariot branlant*," Magda said. "It arrived two days ago from Hungary. Papa commissioned it over a year ago and paid a small fortune for it."

To refer to it as a wagon, or even a carriage, would have been like calling a priceless diadem a chunk of metal decorated with pretty rocks. This was nothing like the occasional carriage Ilona had seen in Sighişoara's narrow streets. It was a lordly vehicle like she imagined she would see in the great cities of Italy and France.

"It's wonderful!" Gizela exclaimed.

Magda smiled and opened the carriage door. "Climb inside."

Gizela scrambled up immediately, but Ilona held back. The carriage seemed too beautiful to touch. It was decorated top to bottom with scrolling brasswork that gleamed like gold. Its iron-rimmed wheels were decorated with brass-covered spokes, and its polished axle caps shone like stars. A magnificent pearly-white body was suspended on thick chains over a sleek, long undercarriage. Ilona felt that if she touched it, a higher power would strike her dead.

"Go on," Magda urged. "Papa won't mind as long as we don't scratch or tear anything."

Reluctantly, Ilona slid in and the carriage swayed gently beneath her.

"The chains give a smoother ride," Magda explained. She placed herself on the opposite-facing seat. "I was hoping to convince Papa to take us for a ride today, but . . . I don't think he'll be in any mood after what just happened."

Ilona nodded. She was certain her own father's mood would be a foul one for the rest of the day. She wasn't looking forward to the trip home.

Ilona absently stroked one of the cold seat covers and tilted her head back to stare at the ceiling. The moment she looked up, a surprised noise escaped her throat.

"Oh, look!" Gizela exclaimed, following her gaze. "It's like the pictures Mama used to hang on our walls!"

"Papa spared no expense," Magda said proudly. "He wanted everything to be beautiful. He wanted his carriage to be a masterpiece."

He had succeeded. Everything about this vehicle—from its brassy wheels to its vibrantly painted ceiling to the upholstered panels on its walls—turned it into a stunning work of art.

The mural was especially enchanting. It depicted four girls dancing in a forest while delicate winged fairies bobbed around their heads. The *Sânziene*. The Midsummer's Night festival. It was supposed to be a magical, supernatural event.

"He commissioned a wheelwright from Kocs to build the carriage," Magda said, "but the painting and scrollwork were done by Italian artisans."

"Why go to so much expense for a wagon?"

Ilona's blunt question caught Magda off guard and wiped the smile from her face.

"I mean . . . It's wonderful," Ilona quickly added, "but why bring such a beautiful and expensive thing to a place like Wallachia?"

She sounded so superior. She sounded so much like her father. Anton Csáki had no patience for impractical things. It bothered Ilona to realize she harbored the same bias.

"Papa thinks people should surround themselves with beauty," Magda quietly answered. "He wishes to encourage art in Wallachia, and he thinks this is a way to do it."

"I like beautiful things," Gizela said. "I like your papa's carriage."

"I like it, too," Ilona said, hoping she sounded sincere. "You're lucky to have a father who appreciates beautiful things."

Magda's face brightened.

"Have you had many chances to ride in it yet?" Ilona asked.

"I've ridden once. It was wonderful. It's far more comfortable than traveling on horseback." Magda giggled. "And when it sways, it almost lulls you to sleep."

"Someday I'm going to have a carriage like this," Gizela said. "It will be pulled by four white horses, and I'll be married to a prince."

Ilona ruffled her sister's hair. "When you're of age, madárka, princes all over Europe will want your hand in marriage."

Gizela beamed, then shivered and rubbed her arms.

"I'm cold," she complained. "Can we go inside?"

"We'll sneak in through the kitchen," Magda said, "and warm up next to the cooking fire."

"Your cook won't mind?" Gizela asked.

"She's much friendlier than yours. As long as we stay out of the food and keep away from the great hall, we should be all right."

Ilona carefully exited the carriage, and Gizela and Magda bounced out behind her. She gave the expensive carriage one last look before Magda hid it behind the outbuilding's plank doors.

Maybe Magda's father was right. Maybe it was a good thing to introduce a little beauty to Wallachia. But Ilona couldn't help but wonder how long anything beautiful could survive in this place.

"Your face is looking better," Raluca said. "The swelling has gone down."

She touched Andrei's face and he flinched. Not because it hurt—it was an instinctive reaction.

"Still red," Raluca said, "but that will fade with time. You'll still be the handsome young man your mother hoped you would grow up to be."

The kitchen servants paused their conversations long enough to turn and grin at Andrei. He ducked his head, face warming.

"So what have you and Vlad been up to lately?" Raluca asked as the kitchen noise resumed. "I haven't seen either of you around the palace the last few days. You haven't been breaking your promise, have you? You haven't been doing anything that would dishonor your mother's memory?"

Andrei avoided her gaze. "No," he mumbled. "Just practicing our archery. Training for war with the Transylvanians if it comes to that. The usual routine."

Raluca frowned. "Those events in Transylvania worry me. Practically on Wallachia's doorstep. And if the Ottoman Empire gets what it wants in Transylvania, what's to stop it from turning on us next?"

"The voivode thinks his treaty will protect us."

"He once had a treaty with the White Knight. Then he broke it. That's the problem with kings and princes. Their promises are easily made, easily broken." Raluca scowled and shook her head. "But what do I know about such things? I'm simply the lowly servant who gets to stitch wounded boys back together if the latest treaty goes wrong."

Andrei heard bitterness in her voice, and he didn't think it was all related to the voivode's treaties, but Raluca saw the way he was looking at her and forced a smile.

"So, what brings you to my kitchen tonight? Supper is almost ready. You're not here to beg for an early meal, are you?"

"No, I . . . I just haven't seen you in a while." He lowered his eyes again. "I wanted you to know I'm still alive."

Raluca ruffled his hair. "You're a good boy, Andrei. If I had a son, I would want him to be just like you. But you're really here for food, aren't you?"

"I am a little hungry," he admitted.

"Of course you are. Boys are always hungry."

She took a warm bread roll from a serving tray and tossed it at him. He snatched it out of the air and grinned.

"That should keep you alive until dinner is served," she said.

If only this were his actual reason for visiting her . . . Andrei watched one of the servants turn a slab of meat on a spit. He perspired as if he himself were being roasted over open flames. How to begin? He took a bite out of the roll and chewed it slowly to buy himself more time.

"Vlad and I overheard something we weren't meant to hear," he said, lowering his voice.

Raluca stepped closer.

"One of the maids said something about the voivode." He stared down at his warm roll. "About a former mistress . . . A boyar's daughter . . ."

When he looked at her again, Raluca was acting very interested in the kitchen's flour-powdered preparation table.

"I wouldn't put much stock in anything the housemaids say," she said, dusting a small pile of flour and dried dough flakes into one hand. "There's always gossip around the palace. Half of it isn't true."

Andrei shifted uncomfortably. She still wasn't looking at him. She was watching the kitchen staff, making sure they were engrossed in their own conversations.

"But just out of curiosity," she said, "what exactly were they saying about this supposed mistress?"

"Just that he had one. Maybe still has one." He hesitated before saying what he was thinking, but the assassination was common knowledge even if this detail wasn't. "Vlad thinks she might have provided the assassin with a key."

Raluca straightened, smiled, and shook her head. "Impossible. The voivode is far too cautious. If someone took his key, he would know about it. If the assassin had one—however it came into his possession—it had nothing to do with the rumor you've heard."

"Oh . . ."

Andrei had no idea what to say now. He felt embarrassed that Vlad had even convinced him to bring it up.

"All right . . . So . . . Where do you think the wooden key came from, then?" he asked.

"Maybe the smith who originally made the lock carved it in case he later needed a pattern for replacing a lost key. Perhaps he saw an opportunity to make a profit by selling it to the voivode's enemies. With all that's happening between the Ottomans and the Transylvanians, the voivode has no shortage of those. It would be the perfect time for an unscrupulous locksmith to fill his pockets with extra ducats."

As far as Andrei was concerned, that settled it. The key

didn't come from a mistress or a maid. There was no reason to pursue it further.

"Thank you for the roll," Andrei said, stepping backward toward the exit. "I'll get out of your way now. You probably have lots to do."

He turned, but Raluca stopped him.

"Andrei."

"Yes?"

"Whatever Vlad is up to, stay out of it."

She knew Vlad too well. And Andrei, for that matter.

"La revedere," Raluca said.

"Goodbye."

Next time Vlad wanted the sordid details of the voivode's secret relationships, he could ask for them himself.

"What did you find out from Raluca?"

"Nothing."

The eager smile faded from Vlad's face. "Sometimes you're next to useless, Andrei."

"She didn't want to talk about it. She told me not to pay any attention to the things the maids say."

"Probably because of the new things I found out."

Andrei didn't want to show interest, but he couldn't help himself. "What did you find?"

"I got another maid to talk."

Andrei flinched. "You didn't threaten this one with a drawn sword, did you?"

"No, but she told me a few interesting things about Raluca. Did you know that Raluca is a boyar's daughter? Or that, once upon a time, she was younger and prettier and the voivode was very interested in her?"

"Raluca isn't like that!"

Vlad stepped back, surprised by Andrei's anger. When he recovered, a slow smile spread across his face. "Then explain why she was Vasilisa's lady-in-waiting one day and a scullery maid the next."

"Maybe because she rejected him! Maybe because she has dignity and self-respect!"

Vlad thought for a moment. "That's a possibility," he said. "She rejects him, so he humiliates her in return. And then she wants revenge and gives his key to his enemies."

"She didn't give the voivode's key to his enemies. How could she possibly do that? She works with the servants, remember? A scullery maid would never get close enough to the voivode to get her hands on his key."

"Unless she didn't really reject him. Unless he demoted her for some other reason . . ."

Andrei balled his hands into fists. "It wasn't Raluca."

Vlad smiled, and decided to leave off egging on his cousin, despite how much it amused him. "You're probably right. Which brings me to the story of *another* boyar's daughter."

"I'm listening."

"Apparently she was very young. And she gave birth to a son. He's about Mircea's age now. She named him Vlad, after his father. Just like I was."

Vlad paused a moment, an angry expression darkening his face. He took a moment to compose himself before continuing. "The boyar's daughter followed the voivode from Sighișoara to Târgoviște. He sent for her after he took Wallachia's throne.

133

At that time, she'd already given birth to his illegitimate son. Apparently their relationship lasted for several years after she came here until, for some reason, she decided to join a monastery. She eventually became its abbess. It's been a decade or more since she had anything to do with him."

Andrei stared at Vlad and shook his head. "You're telling me a *nun* is behind the plot to kill the voivode?"

"Or her father," Vlad said. "Think about it. If any man wanted the voivode dead, it would be that girl's father."

"Maybe." Andrei pondered the information. "Probably. But that still doesn't explain how the girl's father got the key."

"It could have happened years ago."

"And her father didn't do anything about it until now?"

Vlad gave Andrei a disgusted look. "Learn to think like a boyar, Andrei. Timing is everything. The voivode is unpopular now. And the nun's son . . ."

". . . would be a contender for the throne," Andrei finished for him.

"Exactly."

A chill crept up Andrei's spine. "And where is her son?"

"The maid said he followed in his mother's footsteps and became a monk."

"So, what now?" Andrei asked. "Are we going to start searching monasteries?"

"I didn't think of that, but since you mentioned it—"

"It was a joke, Vlad! A joke!"

Vlad smiled. "Don't worry. There are too many monasteries in Wallachia, and we have other things to do."

"Like what?"

"Dinner's waiting. I'll tell you later."

Maybe they weren't going to search monasteries, but Vlad wasn't going to let this drop.

The voivode led a twisted life and now it was twisting Vlad's and Andrei's fates.

"I'm feeling ill, darling," Vasilisa said. "Will you help me to my bed?"

Radu hopped off his chair to rush to his mother's side. Vlad looked at Radu as if his younger brother were something he wanted to scrape off the bottom of his boot.

"You'll excuse me, won't you, boys?" Vasilisa fanned herself with a pale hand. "This business between the Ottomans and the Transylvanians has left me completely out of sorts. I don't know how a prince can expect his princess to manage when he's off making treaties and wars all the time."

She closed her eyes, pressed the back of one hand against her forehead, and Vlad stifled another disgusted expression.

"It must be a great burden for you," he said tightly, "running the palace all by yourself when you're not feeling well. You should definitely go to bed. Andrei and I will set the servants about their evening tasks. You don't have to worry about a thing."

He was far too eager to get Vasilisa out of the room, but the cneajna was too distracted by her "throbbing" head to figure it out.

"Mulțumesc," she said. "You're such a good boy, Vladislav. I'll be sure to let the voivode know how kind you were to me while he was away."

Vlad nodded and smiled, but Andrei could tell if Vlad had to speak with Vasilisa another minute, he was going to gag.

135

"And you . . ." Vasilisa turned to Radu to kiss him on the forehead as he helped her out of her chair. "You are my constant sunshine. Thank you, darling. I haven't the strength to tuck you into your own bed tonight, but you can sleep next to me and protect me while your father is away."

This time Vlad did gag. When Vasilisa looked in his direction, he pretended to be choking on a chunk of meat.

"I'm all right," he said, pounding a fist against his chest. "Need to chew before I swallow."

Vasilisa smiled sweetly, and Vlad nodded at her as she, Radu, and her ladies-in-waiting exited the room. He remained silent until they were well beyond hearing.

"I don't know how the voivode puts up with her," he growled through clenched teeth.

Andrei speared a chunk of roasted pork and chewed it slowly.

"She's turned Radu into a simpering weakling," Vlad said. "I'm ashamed to call him my brother."

Andrei stopped chewing. "Radu isn't that bad. He's just a little boy."

"By the time we were his age, we both knew how to ride horses, fight with swords, and shoot bows. What does *he* know how to do?"

"It isn't his fault."

"You're right. It's the cneajna's fault."

"No family is perfect."

Vlad scowled. "Are you almost finished eating?"

"Almost."

"Good, because we're going back to Golescu's manor."

Now it was Andrei's turn to choke.

"We *have* to go back," Vlad explained. "I threw my dagger to save you from those peasants. We need to find it before Golescu does."

"If he was looking for evidence, he probably already found it."

Vlad frowned. "For both our sakes, let's pray he didn't."

"Why? It's just a dagger. It could belong to anybody."

Vlad shook his head. "Not this dagger."

Ice crackled up Andrei's spine. "Your ceremonial dagger?"

Vlad bit his lip and nodded.

"I'll get the horses," Andrei said.

"I'll gather our weapons," Vlad replied.

"No crossbows."

Vlad rolled his eyes. "Fine. Just the swords."

I risked my life to bring you to Wallachia. Your mother sacrificed *hers.*

He could hear Raluca's disapproval as clearly as if she were standing here beside him. He remembered the promise he'd given her after she finished stitching his face up. But what choice did he have? If Golescu found that dagger . . . If it came to the voivode's attention that Vlad and Andrei were responsible . . . He shuddered at the possible consequences.

The stables were dark and quiet. No one here to catch Andrei and Vlad with the horses. Umbră whickered a soft greeting when she spotted her master, and Andrei affectionately patted her neck.

"More adventure," he whispered. "Are you up to it?"

The black mare scraped a hoof against the floor and tossed her head.

"Good. Let's get a saddle on you. The sooner we finish tonight's business, the better."

Both horses were saddled and ready by the time Vlad arrived.

"Clouds are blowing in," Vlad said. "We need to get moving while we still have moonlight to ride by."

Vlad grabbed Invictus's reins and the charger's hooves clopped hollowly over the stable's wooden floor. Andrei led Umbră along behind.

"Any problems with the stable master or the grooms?" Vlad asked.

"Everyone's gone to bed early tonight."

"Of course they did. The voivode's away. When he's gone, we all shirk our duties. It won't be that way when I'm voivode, though. I'll make everyone fear me. Fear keeps people in line."

"There are other ways to motivate people."

Vlad laughed. "Name one."

"I'll name three. Love. Loyalty. Respect."

"You should move to a monastery, devote yourself to a life of prayer and study. The voivode says peasants and boyars only respect the people and things they fear."

"It's good to know I managed to teach you at least one useful thing."

They stopped so suddenly their horses nearly bowled them over. Andrei's throat closed off. Vlad whispered a curse. Two horse-mounted shadows came out of the darkness toward them.

The voivode dismounted slowly. Mircea remained in his saddle. It was hard to see Mircea's face, but Andrei thought he was grinning. The voivode peeled off his riding gloves and tucked them under his belt.

"Going for an evening ride?"

Neither Vlad nor Andrei answered. Neither could loosen his tongue enough to speak.

The voivode lifted one hand and both boys flinched, but Dracul was merely holding up an object for both of them to see. It was Vlad's dagger.

"Do you recognize this?"

Vlad gulped.

"What puzzles me," the voivode said, "is how it could have possibly ended up at Dragoș Golescu's manor."

Andrei shuffled backward. He should have remained still; his movement drew the voivode's attention.

"Take your shirt off."

Hands shaking, Andrei gave Umbră's reins to Vlad and quickly obeyed the voivode's command.

"Turn and kneel."

The voivode took his time unbuckling his belt. He tested it against an open palm before snapping it across Andrei's back. The second lash curled over Andrei's shoulder. He clenched his teeth to bite back a cry.

Crying was an unacceptable sign of weakness. The smallest whimper would increase the severity of the beating. The belt came down again and again. He received twelve welt-raising lashes before the voivode decided he had suffered enough.

"Get up."

Andrei got shakily to his feet.

"Return the horses to their stalls. Now."

Vlad handed Andrei his shirt and the reins.

"Kneel."

Andrei didn't dare look back as he led the horses back to their stalls.

Crack! Snap! Crack! Snap!

Fear. The voivode held it over Wallachia like a sharpened sword.

But the rest of Wallachia was lucky. They didn't feel its bite nearly as often as Vlad and Andrei did.

CHAPTER TWELVE

Anton Csáki departed for the border fifteen minutes after the sisters' new tutor arrived. Unable to lure the girls' former teacher out of Transylvania, he had hired a stern-faced, gray-haired scholar from Moldavia instead.

After only half a day under the new teacher's tutelage, Ilona already missed her former tutor. Old Master Kedves was happy to indulge Ilona's interests in mathematics and science. Master Sîrbu was of a different mindset.

"Why," he demanded, "would a woman need to know such things?" Like Ilona's father, he believed a woman's education should consist primarily of calligraphy, languages, and grammar. It made her furious.

She had become an expert at birds and learned a great deal about anatomy and art almost entirely on her own. If Sîrbu wouldn't teach her, she would teach herself, and she dared anyone to stop her!

Her anger quickly simmered back down into unhappiness as

she and Gizela descended the stairs to take their midday meal. When she thought about teaching herself, she also thought about her priceless sketchbook and the years of work she had lost when it disappeared. She was certain she'd left her sketches on the log where she was seated when Vlad shot the bolt that frightened the nuthatch away, but when she went back to search for it, it wasn't there. Losing that book was almost as great a blow as losing her mother.

"Do you think the cook has poisoned our food?" Gizela asked when they entered the great hall and sat down to a lunch of cold chicken and day-old bread. "Papa isn't here to stop her."

"If the cook wanted us dead, it would have happened weeks ago. Father couldn't have stopped it."

Gizela didn't look convinced. "I'm not hungry," she announced. "I'm going to my bedroom to play with my dolls."

"At least take a piece of bread with you. And make sure you're back at the library before our afternoon lessons begin."

Gizela didn't listen; she skipped cheerfully out of the hall. In less than an hour, she would be complaining about her empty stomach. She would say she had a headache and was too sick to study. That got her out of lessons with Master Kedves, but Ilona had a feeling it wouldn't work with this new tutor. She shook her head and selected a chicken leg.

The meat was greasy. She cleaned her fingers on a hunk of bread before pouring a cup of lukewarm water. As she lifted the cup, she reconsidered Gizela's ridiculous suggestion. Was it possible? Could the cook actually be thinking of killing them?

It wasn't beyond the realm of possibility. Someone had tried to shoot Ilona in the head. What was to stop them from poisoning her instead?

"Is there a fly in that cup?"

Ilona spilled water down her dress and stood up so fast she nearly knocked her chair over. The unexpected visitor was half-concealed behind a tall brazier in one of the shadowy corners.

"Vlad?"

He grinned.

"How did you get in here?"

"The door was unlocked. I apologize for frightening you, but I couldn't stand to go another hour without seeing your radiant face."

She blushed. Then she remembered his last visit and blushed again.

"You eat like a princess," Vlad said. "So dainty. So careful."

"It's not polite to watch a lady eat when she doesn't know you're in the room."

"Forgive me, my lady."

He gave her an exaggerated bow, and she stifled a giggle. She was acting like Daciana. The reminder of Daciana was enough to make her sober. Vlad moved closer.

"What brings you to—" She stopped speaking, suddenly noticing the bruise on Vlad's cheek. She touched the dark mark, and he winced and pulled back.

"What happened?" she asked.

"I fell off my horse."

She didn't believe him. The bruise was as big and as round as a man's clenched fist.

"It doesn't hurt," Vlad said. "At least not as much as not seeing you for days and days."

Ilona's cheeks flushed, and Vlad touched her face, his grin reappearing. His hand was warm. His eyes were hypnotizing.

He'd shot and almost killed Daciana Golescu.

Ilona blinked and stepped away from him.

"Did I say something wrong?" he asked.

"Was it you?" she asked. "Did *you* shoot her?"

"Shoot who?"

"Daciana."

He hesitated a moment. "Yes."

Dark horror curdled in the pit of Ilona's stomach.

"How did you—" Vlad began.

"Golescu found your dagger. Accused my father of having something to do with it."

"I only did it to protect you," he insisted. "It wasn't even supposed to hit her. Just shatter the window and send a message."

This didn't make her feel any better about what had happened, but at least he was penitent.

"It was stupid," he said. "I know. Can you ever forgive me?"

He seemed so earnest it was hard for Ilona to stay angry. She looked again at the bruise on his face. "Your father . . . Did he do that to you?"

Vlad nodded, and Ilona reached out and grasped both of his hands.

"You can't put yourself at risk for me that way," she said. "You have to promise me you'll never do anything like it again."

Vlad shook his head. "I can't make that promise. To give you a long and happy life, I'd take a thousand beatings from the voivode."

Ilona's head swam. Vlad laced his fingers through hers.

I shouldn't be doing this. Whether she liked it or not, she was still betrothed. She tried to regain her balance and step away

144

from him, but Vlad's lips were already against hers. His kiss was fevered. His arms were strong.

Guilt and pleasure. She didn't know which to feel . . .

Something crashed to the floor behind her.

Ilona broke out of Vlad's embrace and spun wildly. The cook stood in the doorway, gawking.

Ilona glanced at the dropped platter, and the cook followed her gaze. The discomfited woman crouched to collect the spilled contents before backing out of the room.

"That was inconvenient."

Ilona gaped at Vlad. *Inconvenient?*

What would her mother think of an eldest daughter who disgraced her family's name?

"I . . . I think you should leave now," she said.

"Why? Because that peasant woman saw us kissing?"

"I'm betrothed to your *brother*. If my father finds out . . . If . . . if *your* father finds out—"

"Who's going to tell them? The cook? The only person she gives information to is Dragoş Golescu."

"What?"

"She's Golescu's spy. She's been collecting his gold ever since your family moved into this manor. Bring that up and she won't dare say a word about our kiss."

"How do you know this?"

Vlad looked away.

"Tell me! How do you know?"

"I saw her the night I shot the bolt through Daciana's window," Vlad explained. "She was in a different room with Golescu. He was questioning her, counting out ducats to pay her for her information."

145

Ilona blinked.

"But you don't need to fear her or Dragoş Golescu or anyone else," Vlad assured her. "As long as I'm around, I'll make sure no harm comes to you. As long as I live, I will be your protector."

"Vlad . . ."

"I won't go anywhere near Golescu or his property again, but if he or any of his people come near you, they'll do so at their own risk."

Ilona wilted. "Thank you."

She allowed him to hold her hand a few more moments before reluctantly pulling away.

"I need to get back to my lessons," she murmured. "If I don't, Master Sîrbu will come looking for me."

And find her here. With Vlad.

"I understand. I'll come back when your lessons are over."

"No . . . I mean . . . that wouldn't be a good idea. Not today."

"All right. Not today, but I still have to come back to deliver your present. I'll bring Andrei with me. It will all be very proper."

"Present?"

"For your birthday. You haven't forgotten your own birthday, have you?"

She had forgotten, but Vlad had remembered. She smiled and lowered her lashes.

"Who told you?"

Vlad gave her a roguish grin. "I make it my business to know about important events. The sixteenth of March. Your sixteenth birthday. I'm going to make it special for you."

She self-consciously met his gaze. Then her focus shifted yet again to the purplish-blue shadow marking his jaw.

"You shouldn't come. What if your father finds out and punishes you?"

"I won't get caught. I almost never do."

He wanted to celebrate her birthday, and he was probably the only one who remembered it. Her father certainly wouldn't. But . . .

"You're not afraid of me, are you, Ilona?"

"What?"

Vlad grinned. "I won't kiss you again. I promise to be on my best behavior. I give you my oath as a knight of the sacred Order of the Dragon. I vow to protect your reputation and your honor."

She blushed so fiercely she was certain he must feel the heat radiating off her face.

"I'll bring Andrei," he said, "to chaperone us."

He leaned forward as if to kiss her, but stopped himself and stepped back.

"You see? My best behavior. I'm a man of my word."

He strode to the great hall's doors, bowed, and blew her a kiss. Ilona smiled at him as he exited the room.

A golden ring in a swine's snout . . . Rottenness in the bones . . .

She was a terrible person. She would never be as good as her mother.

But she wasn't sure she wanted to be.

CHAPTER THIRTEEN

VLAD WAS SUPPOSED TO TAKE PART IN THIS PUNISHMENT. Andrei had already shoveled half the stalls, and Vlad wasn't here. One part of Andrei was annoyed. Another part felt small and mean for harboring such thoughts.

Andrei's face wasn't bruised like Vlad's. He didn't have blue finger marks around his arms. The voivode had saved the worst of his temper for Vlad. Maybe Vlad hurt too much to get out of bed.

This was at least the thirtieth return trip from the steaming mountain of manure Andrei had now heaped up outside. The handles would fall off this wheelbarrow before the job was done! Andrei wiped perspiration from his forehead and rubbed his neck. His muscles burned. He was permeated with manure stench. The voivode wanted this to be a punishment he would never forget.

Skritch. Scratch. Skritch. He moved the shovel across the stall floor until the worn planks were spotless. Another stall down.

Twelve more to go. Andrei led a skittish chestnut rouncy back into its newly tidied home.

Plop!

He frowned and wrinkled his nose before scooping the fresh dung into the barrow.

"All right, Invictus. Your stall is next . . ."

He swung the adjacent gate open and froze.

Empty. Nothing but shadows.

Brisk footsteps echoed through the stables. Andrei had just enough time to latch the gate shut before a thin man with hunched shoulders appeared.

"Hard at work, are we?"

Pavel. The voivode's marshal and stable master.

"Isn't the high and mighty princeling supposed to be here helping you?" he sneered.

"Vlad . . . um . . . he had to run to the garderobe."

The marshal shook his head. "The gutter isn't good enough for his likes, is it? Well, today neither of you is so high or mighty, are you?"

Pavel moved to a gate and looked over it, scrutinizing the floor inside.

"Missed a spot. Clean this one again."

He moved to the rouncy's stall.

"Oops! Looks like Briză's left a new mess for you. Clean it, too."

Andrei pressed himself against Invictus's stall, but the marshal had already lost interest.

"The voivode says the both of you are mine for the entire day. When the princeling returns, tell him I want all the saddles oiled and the cobwebs swept out of the rafters. When that's done, clean the stalls top to bottom again. I don't want one dropping on the floor when I return to inspect."

Andrei's heart sank. It must have shown on his face because Pavel chortled. The marshal was about to say something more when a new set of footsteps distracted him.

"Ah! Here he finally is, back from his business."

Vlad sauntered forward, leading Invictus by the reins.

Pavel examined the fully saddled horse. Its flanks were lathered from what had obviously been a long ride. Pavel raised one eyebrow.

"What's this? Disobeying the voivode again?"

Vlad's sword hissed out of its scabbard and pressed into the flesh under the marshal's bobbing Adam's apple.

"The voivode is *never* going to hear about this." Vlad's voice was cold. Andrei took a halting step forward, but Vlad waved him back.

"If you say a word," Vlad snarled, "I'll kill you in your sleep. Do you understand?"

The marshal stared down his nose at the flat blade. A thin rivulet of blood trickled down his neck, but he still attempted a sallow smile.

"You can threaten me, princeling, but it won't change anything. The voivode will still hear of it, and when he does—"

Vlad's pommel strike sent the marshal to the floor. His booted foot flew into the man's rib cage before Andrei managed to insert himself between the two.

"Vlad! What are you doing?"

Vlad looked at him, wild-eyed, panting. It was like the ax incident all over again.

"I . . . I don't know," Vlad mumbled. "I . . ."

They were distracted by scuffling noises and rapid movement toward the exit. They turned to see Pavel fleeing the stables.

"He's going to report this to the voivode."

Vlad shook his head. "The voivode's gone. Something's happening at the northern border, I'm not sure what. He and Mircea left this morning. There's no telling when he'll be back."

He paused a moment, still catching his breath.

"I visited Codru Conac today," he said, staring at the floor.

"You . . . visited Ilona?"

"Yes, and I promised to go back for her birthday."

"Why are you telling me this?" Andrei tried to make his voice hard to read, but it was difficult.

"Because you're coming with me. Because I need your help to choose her gift."

Andrei leaned his shovel against a gatepost.

"I have something to confess," Vlad said. "I think I love her. I *know* I love her."

He looked at Andrei. This time it was Andrei who stared at the floor.

"She's betrothed to your brother," Andrei said.

"And he doesn't deserve her!"

Andrei held a hand palm outward. "I'm not disagreeing with that, but how do you know you love her?"

"I . . . just do. I think about her all the time. I'm miserable when I'm away from her."

"You barely even know her."

"Some things you just know," Vlad said. "I think I knew it the moment I set eyes on her."

Andrei said nothing.

"Somehow I'm going to make her mine," Vlad said, staring

off into space, "and take the throne as well. Mircea isn't fit for either of them."

He blinked, shook his head, and looked at Andrei again.

"So what do you think she'd like most—jewelry? Furs or silks?"

Andrei didn't think she would like any of those things, but he didn't say this to Vlad. Instead he said, "You'd have to get those things from a merchant. If you buy it in Târgovişte, half the city will know about it before nightfall. There's no way the voivode—and Mircea—won't find out that you bought her a gift."

"Mircea and the voivode will never hear about it," Vlad said, "because they'll think we were shopping for Vasilisa."

Andrei frowned. "I don't understand. How will shopping for Ilona seem like we were shopping for Vasilisa?"

"Because Vasilisa is still complaining about having headaches. I'm going to tell her I've heard of a merchant who imports pain remedies from Venice. I'll find some so-called remedy and convince her it's the one I was telling her about."

"And how will that explain buying whatever it is you decide to get for Ilona?"

"I won't be buying Ilona's gift. While I'm finding the 'remedy,' you'll purchase Ilona's present for me. No one cares what *you* buy. No one will say a thing about it."

"I don't like this plan."

"Of course you don't. You're afraid to take chances. You need to stop being afraid if you plan on ruling Moldavia someday."

Andrei laughed. "I'll never rule Moldavia."

"It's your birthright. The voivode intends to put you on Moldavia's throne."

"What?"

"I thought you knew that," Vlad said. "Why do you think he took you in when your mother sent you with Raluca to save you from your uncles? His treaty with the sultan is a temporary one. He wants you on Moldavia's throne and Anton Csáki on Transylvania's."

"To form a triumvirate," Andrei mused.

Vlad nodded.

A political alliance the voivode would control.

Vlad put an arm around Andrei's shoulder. "Come on. Let's go sympathize with the cneajna about her headache."

So that Vlad could do some politics of his own. But rather than attempting to win a kingdom, Vlad was after Ilona's heart.

CHAPTER FOURTEEN

VLAD WASN'T HAPPY. RADU HADN'T BEEN PART OF HIS PLAN. Vasilisa insisted, however, that he join them. This required five additional escorts handpicked from the cneajna's own guards; the princess refused to take any chances with Radu's safety.

"I have an idea," Andrei said as they walked down the cobbled street together. "Radu can come with me to pick out the gift you said you wanted to get for the cneajna. While we're doing that, you can go and find her the medicine you were telling her about."

"Gift? I didn't—"

"Of course, I'll need a few extra ducats," Andrei interrupted, nodding his head ever so slightly toward Radu. "Since it's for the cneajna, it ought to be something extra nice."

"Oh . . . *That* gift," Vlad said, catching on. "*Bine. Cum vrei tu.* Do whatever you want."

Vlad fished a handful of ducats out of the pouch on his belt and put them in Andrei's hand. "Don't spend them all."

Andrei nodded. "Don't worry. I'm not a neispravit. I'll spend wisely."

Vlad grunted something that sounded like, "You'd better," and stalked away with two of the royal guards.

"Don't mind Vlad," Andrei said, glancing down at Radu. "He's still in a bad mood because he and I had to clean the stables this morning."

Radu shook his head. "He isn't mad about that. He hates me. He's always angry when I'm around."

"If it makes you feel better, he's angry even when you're not around. He carries a lot of anger inside."

"Like Father," Radu said.

Andrei thought a moment and nodded.

"My father hates me, too," Radu whispered. "He thinks I'm weak."

There was pain in Radu's voice. The same kind of raw pain and isolation Andrei so often felt as an adopted member of the House of Drăculeşti. The same pain he guessed Vlad also felt.

"Let's go spend Vlad's ducats," Andrei said. "Tell me what kinds of things the cneajna likes."

"She likes pretty necklaces. And silver bracelets," Radu said. He stared at the coins in Andrei's hand. "Where does Vlad get ducats? Father doesn't even give Mama money."

A good question. One Andrei couldn't answer.

He shrugged his shoulders. "Maybe he robbed a boyar."

Radu laughed and Andrei grinned.

"How about that shop over there?" Andrei suggested.

Radu nodded and they cut through a small crowd of fur-clad shoppers.

With spring on the horizon, the weather was gradually

warming, and many of Târgoviște's wealthier residents were out and about. A few of them recognized the voivode's youngest son and gawked at Radu, but they moved hastily aside when his guards glared at them.

Andrei was grateful to escape the street and duck into the shop. It was a cheerful place; lanterns cast bright illumination over glittering display counters. Colorful tapestries clung to its walls. An armed man sat on a stool near a soot-blackened fireplace. He gave Radu's guards a nervous look.

The shop's exuberant keeper had no misgivings about his new customers. The door hadn't even finished closing behind them before he was shaking their hands.

"*Bună ziua!* Welcome, welcome! How may I serve you, young masters? What may I do for the sons of an esteemed boyar?"

He didn't yet recognize them. All the better.

Andrei straightened his collar and cleared his throat. "We've . . . come to buy a gift."

"For my mother," Radu chimed in.

"Of course! Of course!" The merchant hurried to the other side of his counter, eager to show his wares. "And what do you seek today? Something gold? Something with gemstones? You won't find finer merchandise in all Târgoviște."

"Mama likes rubies," Radu said. "Do you have a necklace with rubies?"

The merchant beamed. "I am positive I can show you something your mother will adore. Right this way!"

Radu followed the merchant along the counter and the guards followed him. Andrei was left alone to move in the opposite direction.

He scanned the display counter, searching for something that called out Ilona's name.

Silver bangles. Golden earrings. No. No again. Nothing.

Then he saw it.

A small brooch. A silver swan with a sky-blue gemstone set as the elegant bird's eye.

"How much for this one?" Andrei heard Radu asking.

"This? This is one of my finest pieces. I won't part with it for anything less than one hundred ducats."

"I'll buy it!"

"How about this one over here, Radu?" Andrei called across the room. "The cneajna would love it."

He realized his mistake the instant the word "cneajna" left his mouth. The shopkeeper's eyes widened and a hungry look crept across his face.

"The Princess Vasilisa? If only you had told me sooner!" He bowed. "These trinkets are far beneath the wife of our esteemed voivode. Allow me to retrieve my finest pieces from my workroom."

"No!" Andrei cried.

The merchant blinked.

"I-I mean . . . That won't be necessary," Andrei stuttered. "The cneajna prefers simple jewelry. And . . . and the voivode doesn't believe in unnecessary luxuries."

That last part was true.

Andrei waited for Radu to contradict him, but his cousin merely watched with a curious expression on his face.

"This necklace . . ." Andrei pointed at the one Radu had been examining. "Prince Radu likes it and the cneajna will like it, too. I can pay fifty ducats for it."

"I'm a poor man . . . I have a wife and children . . ."

"How much, then?"

"This is the purest gold and the ruby is flawless. I cannot part with this piece for anything less than ninety ducats."

Andrei wasn't going to walk away from this with a fair deal. Vlad would be upset, but Andrei couldn't see any way out of it.

"I will give you ninety-five if you include the swan brooch over there."

"A fair price," the merchant said. He said it far too quickly. A better bargainer would have walked away from this with more ducats remaining in his purse. Andrei, however, had no experience with business transactions.

The merchant wrapped Andrei's purchases in two squares of white linen, took Andrei's ducats, and accompanied him to the door.

"Thank you! Please come again anytime!"

"You're smart," Radu whispered as they headed down the street. "I wouldn't have thought to get two things for one price."

Andrei smiled weakly. "I saw the swan and thought of someone who might like it."

"What's that?"

Andrei followed Radu's pointing finger to a small crowd gathered around a wagon. No, not a wagon. A carriage. A finer carriage than any Andrei had ever seen.

"Let's go look!" Radu grabbed Andrei's hand and dragged him forward.

Virghiliu Racoviţă beamed as he displayed his carriage to the admiring crowd. Two or three of the more daring spectators attempted to run their hands over the vehicle's gleaming body, but the boyar's hired guards put their arms out to block the would-be touchers.

"A friend in Kocs—a skilled wheelwright—built it for me," Racoviță was saying. "The chain-supported undercarriage is a new development. One day all carriages will be built this way . . ."

"Impressive, isn't it."

The voice—a whisper in Andrei's left ear—made him jump.

"You shouldn't sneak up on people like that," he growled at Vlad. "I might have drawn my sword."

His cousin quirked an eyebrow. "Anyone who is unobservant enough to let me get that close would be dead before I gave him a chance to use his sword."

"Did you get the 'medicine'?" Andrei asked.

"Of course. Did you get the gift?"

"Yes."

"Well, let me see it, then."

Andrei handed Vlad the linen-wrapped swan. Vlad unwrapped a corner and scowled.

"That's all? It's rather . . . plain."

"Ilona will like it. Trust me."

"You'd better be right." Vlad glared. "What did you get the cneajna?"

Andrei reluctantly handed him the other package.

"You got *this* for Vasilisa and that tiny brooch for Ilona? I'm giving Ilona the necklace. Vasilisa can have the stupid swan."

"Ilona will like the swan better, and you'll have to give the necklace to Vasilisa because Radu already knows it was purchased for her."

Vlad cursed under his breath. "At least tell me you got a good deal for them."

"I . . . I have six coins left."

"What!"

Andrei was saved by a happier voice.

"Prince Vlad! Prince Andrei! Bună ziua! Come see my new carriage!"

Vlad tucked the wrapped gifts beneath his coat and painted a false smile on his face. The crowd parted to let him and his guards through.

Virghiliu Racoviță embraced Vlad and patted Andrei's shoulder.

"This is amazing," Vlad said, looking the carriage over and nodding.

Racoviță beamed. "It's a new type of carriage. Join me for a ride. You too, Prince Andrei."

Radu was already seated beside Racoviță's wife and daughter. While Vlad and Andrei were discussing Ilona's gift, he had made himself at home.

"It's beautiful," Vlad said, brushing his fingers over one of the carriage's large wheels. "Fit for an emperor."

"Perhaps not an emperor," the boyar said, his voice modest, "but it suits my humble needs."

There was nothing "humble" about that carriage, Andrei thought. It was luxurious and ornate. He examined its pastel panels, burnished ornamentation, and the horses' polished harnesses. The carriage must have cost Racoviță a small fortune—enough to buy a hundred shiny, bejeweled gifts for Ilona and the cneajna.

Vlad seated himself beside Radu. One of the boy's guards

was already in the carriage with him, and this left only enough room for the jovial boyar. Racoviță frowned as he examined the situation.

"It's all right," Andrei said. "I can walk to the palace. It's not far."

"No, no! It wouldn't be right to leave you standing here! How about up there?" Racoviță pointed. "Would you be opposed to climbing into the boot with Matyas?"

"I don't mind."

Racoviță clapped Andrei on the back, and the driver reached down to help him up. Vlad and Andrei's guards watched unhappily as the carriage rolled away.

"Have you ever driven a carriage?"

"Huh?"

The driver, a young man—probably in his early twenties—with dark-blond hair and a Hungarian accent, smiled and waited for Andrei's answer.

"Um . . . No. I've never had that privilege."

"Are you good with horses?"

"Yes."

"Then this will be easy for you. It is not much different from guiding a horse from a saddle. The important thing is to not turn too sharply. This would tip the carriage over."

"You wouldn't want to tip *this* carriage over," Andrei muttered.

The driver laughed. "Most definitely not. The good boyar would be in tears. He loves his carriage like he loves his wife and his child."

Andrei smiled and watched the driver navigate around a horse cart, two street urchins, and a boyar in a tall fur hat.

"You aren't Wallachian," Andrei said.

The driver shook his head. "I am from Kocs. I came here to deliver the carriage. I will drive it and care for it until I have taught one of the boyar's own servants the necessary skills."

"Did he pay you well to travel so far?"

"The boyar is very generous. When I return, I will have enough money to marry my sweetheart, Piroska, and start a new life as a master wheelwright."

A bright future. Something Andrei could only hope for. He nodded and forced a smile.

"My name is Matyas." The driver extended his free hand.

"Andrei."

They shook.

"Would you like to drive the rest of the way to the palace?"

"What?"

Matyas put the reins in Andrei's hands.

"I don't know if—"

"Do not worry. I will take the horses back if you have trouble. These are good, well-trained Hungarian horses. They will do most of the work for you."

Andrei nodded and allowed himself a small grin. For the first few moments, he worried he might roll the wheels over one or more of Târgoviște's unsuspecting citizens, but anyone who saw the carriage coming moved quickly aside to stand and gape.

"You know horses and riding," Matyas said. "I can see this by the way you hold the reins."

"I'm better with animals than people," Andrei admitted.

"People are no different from horses. They respond to love and respect. They find ways to rebel against a tyrannical hand."

Andrei nodded.

"You serve the voivode's sons?" Matyas asked.

"Well . . . Not really. They're my cousins. Almost like brothers."

"You are a prince, then?" Matyas bobbed his head. "My apologies for my mistake. You are then visiting from another land?"

"My parents are dead. The voivode took me in and made me part of his family."

"That is a shame. I only say this because if you were a servant, I could make a wonderful carriage driver out of you."

Andrei grinned, warmed by Matyas's joking compliment. "This carriage rides so smoothly," Andrei observed. "I barely feel the bumps in the street."

"This is because of the special undercarriage," Matyas said. "Because of the chains." He took a few moments to explain how the carriage was constructed, how the horses were hitched to equally pull the load.

He loved his work. He loved being a driver and a wheelwright. Without meaning to, Andrei found himself envying Matyas.

"You said you have a girl waiting for you at Kocs?" Andrei said.

Matyas nodded and smiled.

"Is she pretty?"

"More beautiful than blossoms in springtime or stars at night."

"You must miss her."

A longing expression crossed the young wheelwright's face. He didn't have to answer with words. "And you?" Matyas teased. "Is there someone your heart beats for?"

A blush crept out of Andrei's collar.

"I thought so," Matyas said. "And I am guessing she is pretty. Pretty like my Piroska."

Andrei shifted uncomfortably. It was fortunate Vlad was inside the carriage where he couldn't hear or see any of this.

"The Princely Court," Matyas said. "We have arrived."

It had been a short ride. Andrei reined in the horses and the carriage rolled to a stop. "Thank you," he said. "That was fun."

"Visit me at the good boyar's manor if you decide to give up life in the palace to become a carriage driver."

CHAPTER FIFTEEN

Early Spring 1443

"I'm sorry it's been so long since I've stopped by," Magda said. "We had visitors at Cântecul Lebedei this week, my sister Călțuna and my nephew. Papa fetched them in his carriage because he has to show it to *everyone*! Mama says it will soon belong to thieves if he doesn't stop putting it on public display."

Magda laughed and Ilona smiled. Gizela sat on her bed, braiding and unbraiding her hair.

"I didn't know you had a sister," Ilona said.

"Yes. She's much older than I am. We usually only see her on holidays, but Papa is creating his own holiday to celebrate the carriage's arrival. Even though he didn't warn her in advance, Călțuna humored him with a weeklong visit."

"Does she live far from here?"

"No, not far."

"I suppose she's married to a boyar. One of the voivode's supporters?"

"Not a boyar."

Magda looked uncomfortable now, and she seemed relieved when Gizela changed the subject.

"It's Ilona's birthday today."

"Your birthday?" Magda grinned. "Why didn't you tell me? I would have brought a gift!"

"Ilona is too old for presents."

Magda looked at Gizela and frowned. Gizela shrank under her gaze.

"That's what our papa says. Not me. *I* don't think she's too old."

"Father is probably right," Ilona said, shrugging. "I'm sixteen, too old for silly celebrations."

"Nonsense! My father says you're never too old to celebrate a birthday. We always have a big party for my birthday. We—"

Magda saw Ilona staring at her own toes and cut herself short.

"My birthday will be next month," Magda said. "I'll tell Papa I want to celebrate your birthday and mine at the same time. We'll make it the grandest birthday celebration either one of us has ever had!"

It did little to lighten Ilona's glum mood, but she appreciated Magda's kind sentiment. It reminded her that Vlad told her he had something special planned for today. Warm anticipation suddenly flowed over her.

"Your father and my father are so different," Magda said. "Sometimes I find it funny how they're such good friends. Maybe it's because they knew each other in Transylvania."

Ilona looked up. "Your family's from Transylvania?"

"My family's ancestral home has always been Wallachia, but we lived temporarily in Transylvania. Since your father and mine were acquainted, I assumed your father would have said something about it to you."

"Our father doesn't tell us anything," Ilona replied. "Not even if it's something that will drastically change our life."

Like an unexpected move to Wallachia or betrothal to a voivode's self-absorbed son.

Magda must have guessed what Ilona was thinking, because she nodded sympathetically. "It must be difficult for you."

"Very."

They sat in awkward silence a moment.

"I thought you'd always lived in Wallachia," Ilona said, returning to the original topic. "I'm guessing there's a fascinating story behind how your family ended up in Transylvania."

"Not fascinating. Interesting, perhaps. My father was in exile when he met your father. Vlad Dracul was military governor of Transylvania at the time, and my father was taking refuge at his court in Sighișoara. Our fathers met there. Both supported the voivode in his efforts to raise an army to throw his half brother off Wallachia's throne."

"Alexandru Aldea," Ilona said.

Magda nodded. "My father rode in battle with the voivode. He received Cântecul Lebedei for his service."

"That means we both lived in Sighișoara. We could have grown up together as friends if your father had stayed."

"Better late than never," Magda said, grinning. "But it's still funny your father said absolutely nothing about it. Especially since their friendship has grown so strong over the past few months. Mama is constantly complaining about all the time Papa spends at Codru Conac. Almost every evening since your father arrived."

Every evening? Ilona glanced at Gizela, but her sister looked as confused by this as she was. Wherever Magda's father was spending his evenings, it wasn't here at the manor. But Ilona's father wasn't, either.

Strange.

If the two men were going off somewhere together, what were they up to?

"Hurry up!" Vlad said. "She's going to think I've forgotten her! Do you think you could saddle those horses any slower?"

"I could do it faster if you would help me," Andrei retorted.

Invictus, as jittery as his master, danced around the stall. Andrei was forced to dance with him to keep from being pinned against a wall.

"If you want to speed things along," he said, "try getting your horse to stand still so I can cinch up these girth straps."

Vlad stepped into the stall and held Invictus's head, patting the horse's muzzle. But he was paying more attention to the silver object pinched between his thumb and forefinger.

"Are you sure she's going to like this? It's so small. How can this possibly show her how much I care about her?"

Andrei winced. "Because she loves birds."

Why was he helping? If Vlad knew Ilona well enough to "love" her, he should already know this on his own.

"And you know she loves birds because . . ."

"Because she told me. And because of the book." Andrei froze. "The book . . . I have to return the sketchbook!"

"What the devil are you talking about?"

"She has a sketchbook that she's filled with bird drawings. It's the book she was holding when you shot at that nuthatch."

"And how is it that *you* now have her sketchbook?" Vlad demanded, his eyes narrowing.

"It was on the log where we left our crossbows. I took it to keep it safe. I've been meaning to return it to her for days now but haven't had a chance to ride to Codru Conac."

"Go and get it, then. It might make up for this insignificant gift if I hand her her lost sketchbook. She's probably been worried about it. You should have told me, I could have taken it to her the other day."

"Yes," Andrei mumbled. "You would have been her hero."

"What did you say?"

"Nothing. The horses are ready. I'll get the sketchbook and then we can leave."

He stepped toward the gate, but Vlad slapped an arm across his chest to stop him.

"Wait," Vlad whispered. "Listen."

Andrei frowned, but then he heard it, too.

Horses. Voices. Commotion.

Fear.

"Something's wrong," Vlad said.

Andrei nodded. Together they exited the stables and ran to the castle.

The Curtea Domnească was in chaos. Soldiers on horses jostled one another. Frightened servants flung hastily loaded panniers over rouncys' backs. A servant bumped into Vlad, and Vlad seized him.

"What's going on here? What's happening?"

"The White Knight!" the pale-faced servant said. "He's coming!"

Vlad looked at Andrei, and the servant pulled away.

"You told me the voivode rode to the border because something was happening," Andrei said. "This must be it."

"Then where's the voivode?" Vlad asked. "Who's in charge of . . . of *this*?"

He swept a hand around, gesturing at the chaos. As if to answer his query, a fully armored warhorse—a white destrier— pushed through the crowd toward them.

"There you are! Two more minutes and I was going to leave both of you behind!"

"Mircea," Vlad said. "Where's Father?"

"Fleeing with the sultan's army to Adrianople."

"What do you mean?"

"I mean exactly what I said. He and Csáki are riding south to the sultan's capital. Mezid Bey is dead and without their general, the Ottoman army is in full retreat. The White Knight and his armies will reach Târgoviște by nightfall. We have to leave. *Now*."

Vlad stared at his brother, dumbfounded.

"Get your horses," Mircea said. "Father sent me here to collect our family and take us all into hiding."

"What about Csáki's family?" Vlad said. "They'll be in danger, too. What about Ilona?"

"She'll have to fend for herself. There isn't time."

"She's your future wife!" Vlad exclaimed. "You can't leave her behind!"

Mircea gave Vlad a weary look. "She's just a girl. Women are only useful for producing offspring. I can find another wife."

If Andrei hadn't held him back, Vlad would have probably drawn his sword and attacked. If Andrei wasn't busy holding Vlad back, Andrei would have likely done the same.

"Get your horses. Now."

Vlad bared his teeth. "I'll get my horse. I'll get my horse so I can ride to rescue Ilona."

"If you defy me, you're also defying the voivode," Mircea said. "We have our orders, and they don't include bringing Csáki's daughters with us."

Vlad turned toward the stables, but Mircea snapped his fingers and three mounted soldiers blocked Vlad's way.

"Go with him," Mircea said. "Don't let him out of your sight. If he gives you trouble, you have my permission to bind him."

"Curse you, Mircea!" Vlad exclaimed. "You're a complete and utter *zevzec*! Let me ride to Codru Conac!"

"There's no time," Mircea said.

He nodded again at the soldiers, and they moved threateningly toward Vlad.

"I'll go back for them."

Both brothers shifted their gazes toward Andrei.

"I'll get Ilona and Gizela," Andrei said. "I'm the least important member of this family. I'm dispensable."

Mircea shook his head. "By the time you reach Codru Conac, Hunyadi's armies will already be there. I can't wait for you, and I can't risk revealing our destination. You and Vlad are both riding with me." Mircea turned toward a passing soldier. "Have the treasure vaults been emptied?"

"Yes, Your Excellency. The carts are packed. We're ready to leave."

Mircea nodded. "Give the command. I'm leading the way."

"Someone will need to let the voivode's allies know you and he are still alive," Andrei said, thinking quickly.

Mircea looked at him again.

"If you intend to recapture the throne from Hunyadi," Andrei continued, "you'll need the boyars' help,"

"If the White Knight catches you, he'll kill you," Mircea said. "Or he'll hand you over to your relatives in Moldavia. Either way you'll be dead."

Andrei took a deep breath and squared his shoulders. "I won't let that happen. Boyar Racoviță supports the voivode. I'll go to him for help."

He'd only had a few seconds to come up with this plan, so it surprised him how logical it sounded.

Mircea pondered the suggestion, and Andrei pushed his advantage.

"Virghiliu Racoviță is respected by all the boyars. If you come back with a large enough army, he can convince the majority of them not to stand against you."

"You think you can accomplish that?"

"We won't know unless I try."

Mircea stroked his chin and thought some more.

"If you're captured, you might be tortured. They'll want to know where the royal family is hiding. Like I already said, I can't tell you where that is. You won't be able to find us. You'll be on your own until our forces regroup and we come back."

"I understand the risk."

"If you manage to get a message to Racoviță . . . If you

convince him to stand with the voivode and me, I won't forget your service to the House of the Dragon."

"I won't let you down."

Mircea removed his ring and handed it to Andrei. It was a replica of the voivode's medallion—a circling dragon carrying St. George's cross across its scaly back.

"Show my signet to anyone you think you can trust," Mircea said. "They'll know by the ring that you represent me."

Andrei nodded, slipped the ring over his middle finger, and bowed.

Vlad pushed forward to stand shoulder to shoulder with Andrei. "If he's staying, I'm staying with him."

Mircea shook his head. "We can't take that risk. If the voivode and I get killed, you're next in line for the throne."

"You'll still have Radu."

Mircea guffawed. "We both know he'll never be fit to rule Wallachia. No. You're going into hiding like the rest of the family. I have my orders and you have yours."

Vlad fumed, but Andrei saw in his eyes that he knew Mircea was right.

"You have one minute to change your mind," Mircea said to Andrei.

"I won't change it."

"Good luck, then."

Mircea wheeled his horse around. "You," he said to one of the soldiers. "Get Prince Vlad's horse. And you two. Keep him here until I say."

Vlad cast Mircea a hateful glare as his brother trotted away. Andrei turned toward the castle, but Vlad's hand grasped his arm.

"What you're doing is suicide."

"It's the same thing you were going to do."

"No, I was going to get Ilona and bring her with us," Vlad argued. "You're staying behind. Here. Where the White Knight will have a better chance of finding you."

"I'm going to take Ilona and Gizela to Racoviţă's manor. Even if he won't take me in, he'll at least hide them. If it means I fall into Hunyadi's hands . . ." He shrugged. "Whatever happens to me, at least they'll be safe."

Vlad surprised Andrei by embracing him. "Don't get yourself killed."

Andrei gave him a halfhearted smile. "Try not to kill Mircea."

They laughed, but their laughter sounded tense.

"*Pe curând*," Vlad said.

"See you soon," Andrei agreed.

He strode back toward the palace. Every minute mattered, but he couldn't leave Ilona's sketchbook behind. And there was something else he needed: his mother's carved swan. One quick detour and then he'd be on his way. He picked up his pace and ran.

For some reason he wasn't frightened, but he wondered what his dead mother would think about the risk he was taking today. If she could meet Ilona, he was certain she would understand.

CHAPTER SIXTEEN

ILONA WAITED ALL MORNING, BUT VLAD AND ANDREI DIDN'T come. If they had, it might have saved her from Master Sîrbu's tedious lessons. Now afternoon lessons had begun, and she was losing hope in Vlad's promise. Maybe, like her, he had obligations that made it impossible to slip away. Or maybe he had simply forgotten.

"Please smooth out your wax tablet," Master Sîrbu said to Gizela. "You will practice Latin noun declensions while I complete a special lesson with your sister."

"*I* want a special lesson!" Gizela folded her arms and gave the tutor her most petulant glare.

"Fine. You can practice nouns *and* adjectives."

"Never mind. I don't need a special lesson."

Ilona twisted her fingers into her skirt.

"Your father has requested," Sîrbu said, gazing down his long nose at Ilona, "that I make you well versed in the history of Wallachia's royal family. As you will soon be marrying into the

House of Drăculeşti and providing young Prince Mircea with an heir, the grand boyar deems it prudent that you familiarize yourself with the family's genealogy and accomplishments."

Ilona nodded and attempted to shake away the unpleasant thought of "providing young Prince Mircea with an heir." She was already formulating alternate plans to deal with that situation. They were still vague, but they involved dressing herself as a boy and making her way to Florence or Genoa. Thanks to her former tutor, she spoke passably good Italian. Perhaps one of the great Italian masters would take pity on the runaway "boyar's son" from Wallachia and make him their apprentice.

Master Sîrbu rubbed his thin hands together and paced slowly around Ilona.

"Let us begin with a test of your current knowledge. In which year did Basarab the Great found the Principality of Wallachia?"

"I don't know."

"Something easier, then. Which battle, fought in November of 1330, secured Wallachia's independence from the kingdom of Hungary?"

"I don't know that either."

Master Sîrbu scowled.

"One more question. Perhaps the most important, as it will most assuredly affect you and your children. Other than the House of Drăculeşti, which family—also descended from Basarab cel Mare—claims the rightful heirship to Wallachia's throne?"

"The House of Dăneşti."

"Yes! I was beginning to lose hope!"

Perhaps God was punishing Ilona for kissing Vlad. Twice.

"To fill in the prodigious gaps in your knowledge," Master

Sîrbu said, "I think we should quickly run through the genealogy of Prince Vlad Dracul and his Dăneşti cousins." He thrust a stylus and a writing tablet into her hands. "Please record each name beginning at Basarab and paying special attention to the division of his lineage with Dan the First and Mircea the Elder. You must commit the name of each voivode to memory along with the approximate dates each ruled Wallachia."

This lesson was going to be even more tedious than Gizela's grammar exercises.

Despite the tedium, Ilona learned one thing quickly: Membership in Wallachia's royal family was a bloody affair. Brother betraying brother. Cousin murdering cousin. Treachery. Violence. Bloodshed. Death. This was the legacy Ilona's children could look forward to.

She shuddered and wrote names on her tablet. Radu Chelul, Dan II, Alexandru Aldea, Vlad Dracul . . . Would Mircea and her Vlad be willing to kill each other like those who had come before them?

Her Vlad?

She shook her head. She shouldn't be having such impure thoughts!

"Am I beginning to bore you?"

"What?"

Master Sîrbu made an exasperated noise. "Give me your slate so I can see what you've written."

Ilona handed it over and the tutor grilled her on names, dates, and important events. The test continued until Gizela interrupted them with a startled noise.

"Heavens!" Sîrbu exclaimed, his voice nasal with annoyance. "What on earth is the matter, child?"

Gizela pointed out the window. "Look! Soldiers! Lots of them!"

Ilona brushed past the tutor to stand beside Gizela. What she saw made her eyes grow as wide as her sister's.

Ottoman soldiers. Hundreds of them, thousands, spilling out of the forested hills. Some limped, some ran, and all wore fear on their haggard faces. These weren't the tall, proud soldiers Ilona saw from the hilltop months earlier. These soldiers' red boots were crusted with mud, and their daring blue robes hung in sorrowful tatters. Most wore filthy, bloodstained bandages, and all moved like hunted animals.

"Janissaries," Master Sîrbu whispered.

He pushed Ilona and Gizela aside so he could squint through the window's thick glass panes.

"*Vai de mine!* We must bar the doors!"

He dashed out of the library, leaving Gizela and Ilona alone.

"What's happening?" Gizela said. "Why are there soldiers at Codru Conac?"

"I don't know, but it looks like . . . they're running from something."

Gizela pressed closer to Ilona. "Will they come inside and hurt us?"

Ilona stroked Gizela's hair. "No."

But whatever army that came after these soldiers might.

"Come with me," Ilona said, grasping Gizela's quivering hand. Her own hand was already slick with perspiration. To her credit, when she spoke again she did so with a steady voice. "Let's go to my bedroom and read Mama's Bible."

"Why?"

"Just do as I tell you."

She towed Gizela into the hallway.

"Quickly."

Her pulse thudded in her ears. It was difficult to think. They entered the bedroom, and Ilona closed the door behind them and locked it.

"We're going to play a game," Ilona said. "It's called 'Fortress.' We're going to turn my room into a castle. Help me build a wall in front of the door."

She pasted a smile to her lips, grabbed her high-backed chair, and dragged it across the room.

Gizela stared at her. "I'm not stupid, Ilona. Are . . . are they going to kill us?"

"Don't be silly, madárka. The voivode has a treaty with the sultan."

"But not with the vajda. Not with Transylvania."

Gizela had grown older and wiser since coming to Wallachia.

"Help me with the cedar chest."

Their pitiful barricade might protect them from soldiers intent on pillage, but if the Transylanian victors were intent on burning, Ilona might quickly come to regret her defensive strategy.

"Hurry, madárka."

They pushed and pulled the heavy chest until it was flush against the door.

Still panting from exertion, Ilona risked a glance out her window. Her father's marshal with his stable boys were frantically closing and barring the stable's doors.

"The White Knight is coming," Gizela whispered.

Ilona turned from the window. "Yes."

"Papa hates him, and he hates Papa. Will Papa come home to protect us?"

"I don't know."

"If he doesn't, who will?"

"God will. And I will. Come. Sit on the bed beside me. Let's read."

It had grown suddenly very quiet outside. Ilona no longer heard janissaries' running feet or clanking armor.

Gizela began to cry. "I'm frightened, Ilona."

"Don't be." *What would Mother do?* "Hold my hand. I'll pray with you."

She wasn't strong like their mother, but she could pretend. She held Gizela's hands and helped her recite a familiar prayer. She was proud of herself for keeping her own voice from quivering.

Help would come, but if it didn't, she had already hidden a crossbow under her bed. She closed her eyes and remembered the assassin's attack. The shattering glass. The quivering bolt. The vow she made afterward that she would never feel helpless again.

It was a vow she was already having difficulty keeping.

The retreating Ottoman soldiers paid little attention to Andrei, but he kept his distance anyway lest one or more of the foot soldiers be tempted to steal his horse. The bigger problem would be Transylvania's pursuing soldiers. They were wolves after prey. They'd either capture him or kill him on sight.

Mircea was right. There was no time. Even if Andrei reached Codru Conac before the Transylvanians did, he would still have to spirit Ilona and Gizela to Boyar Racoviţa's manor. Andrei's pulse thudded noisily in his ears, and the muscles in his stomach tightened.

By Andrei's calculations, the blue-coated janissaries were coming almost directly from Codru Conac. That meant Hunyadi's forces would also cut a swath right through Anton Csáki's properties.

"Faster, Umbră!"

He spurred the black mare forward, and she bunched her muscles to leap over a shallow ditch.

He likely only had minutes, but even at full gallop Codru Conac was still a half hour away. He could only hope Hunyadi's men would be in too big of a hurry to stop and search the manor. For everyone's sake, he hoped that would be the case.

Huddled on the bed, Ilona and Gizela listened to the booted footsteps coming up the stairs. Ilona set the crossbow's tiller over her shoulder and aimed it at the door. The doorknob rattled, and the footsteps moved away.

She slowly let out a breath, but more feet now approached. This time when the doorknob rattled, the footsteps didn't move onward.

A deep, frightening voice spoke in Saxon just outside the room. Gizela whimpered as a sharp blow shook the door.

"Shhh," Ilona soothed. "I won't let them hurt you."

Gizela made the sign of the cross, but her prayer was interrupted by an echoing voice from the hallway.

"Have you found them yet?"

"No, but this door is locked."

Gizela squeaked excitedly, extricated herself from Ilona's

arms, and scrambled off the bed. Ilona was slower, but in a moment she was at her sister's side, helping her pull the chair and the cedar chest away from the door. When they finally got it open, Magda's father stood in front of them, looking almost as relieved as Ilona was feeling. Master Sîrbu stood with him, and two burly Saxons stood behind them.

"We hid ourselves in here," Gizela chirped. "In case the White Knight came to hurt us."

"Good girl," Magda's father said, ruffling her hair the way Father often did. "That was smart of you, Gizela, but you can rest reassured that the White Knight would never harm a child. He's an honorable man. You'll have nothing to fear from him."

He mopped perspiration from his forehead and grew suddenly sober.

"If the Ottoman army makes it past Wallachia's southern border, Hunyadi will be back to tie up loose ends. Your father was the voivode's staunchest supporter. He's also a candidate for Transylvania's throne. That will naturally draw János's attention to you. I think it's best that you lodge with my family until the White Knight makes his intentions known."

"You already said he wouldn't harm us. Gizela and I can take care of ourselves."

Ilona didn't know why she said it. She didn't feel capable of taking care of either her sister or herself, but the words flew out of her mouth before she had time to carefully think them through.

"I said he wouldn't harm a 'child,'" Magda's father quietly replied. "You, Ilona, are Mircea Dracul's betrothed. He won't consider you a child."

He gave her a moment to let the words sink in. Ilona felt her extremities grow cold.

"In any case, I'm afraid I must insist. If I don't bring you home with me, Magda and my dear Sofia will make my life unbearable."

He chuckled, clearly meaning for his joke to relieve Ilona's anxiety, but the smile she gave him was forced.

"Can we at least have a few minutes to gather some clothing?" she said.

"Certainly. Pack whatever clothing you need. And bring anything else you feel might be important for a long stay. In the meantime, I'll be at the stables getting your horses ready."

Ilona nodded. "Thank you, Boyar Racoviță."

"Please," he said. "Feel free to call me Virghiliu. I consider you girls to be practically family. If you can't call me Virghiliu, consider calling me *Uncle* Virghiliu!"

Ilona wasn't sure she could refer to him by either of those names, but Gizela beamed.

"And can we call Magda's mama 'Aunt Sofia'?"

Magda's father tousled Gizela's hair. "Aunt Sofia would be delighted!"

He was very kind. Too kind. Ilona didn't want to impose on the good boyar and his family, but for Gizela she couldn't decline.

"Come with me, madárka," she said. "Tell me which dresses you want. We should also find the wooden doll Father brought you from Nuremburg. I know you wouldn't want to leave it behind."

CHAPTER SEVENTEEN

ANDREI IGNORED THE BRAMBLE SCRATCHES THAT BURNED HIS face and stared through the grass at Ilona's manor. Was she still here, or did Hunyadi's men take her? If she was the White Knight's captive, he wouln't hesitate to rescue her. The only problem was . . . he wasn't sure how.

Two serfs carrying sloshing buckets walked past his hiding place. Andrei turned an ear toward them, hoping to learn something about Ilona's fate.

"Who do we water these nags for now?" the younger of the two peasants asked. "For Hunyadi, or for whichever member of the House of Dănești he puts on the throne?"

"What does it matter," the older peasant answered, "as long as we're receiving food and a home? Csáki . . . Hunyadi . . . They come and go. We suffer. We remain. It's all the same."

"I could get myself better food and a better home if I took one of Csáki's pretty palfries and sold it."

"Do that and you'll find yourself sleeping in a cold grave."

They moved beyond earshot and Andrei slumped against the earth. He was accomplishing little out here in the grass. What he really needed was to get inside the house.

He had seen two Saxons—possibly from Transylvania—patrolling the grounds. Maybe Hunyadi had Ilona locked in a room inside. If Andrei could find out which one, he might be able to get her out.

The bucket-carrying serfs entered the stables, and Andrei scanned the grounds. No sign of the Saxons at the moment, and no trace of any other servants. He rose to his feet and dashed toward the outbuildings.

"Dashed," at least, was his original intention, but his legs were so cramped he barely managed a hobble. He made it to the boyar's atelier right before the two serfs came back out of the stables. Luckily the small workshop's door wasn't locked.

Panting, Andrei held the door open a sliver and watched the slouching men to make sure they hadn't seen him.

"One horse. That's all I'm suggesting. The White Knight will never miss it . . ."

They walked past the shop, oblivious to Andrei's presence. He slumped against the doorframe, closed his eyes, and waited for his heart to stop racing. Maybe he should wait until dark to break into the manor. But maybe Hunyadi would move Ilona to a more secure place before then.

Andrei took a moment to scan his new surroundings. The shop was dark, its only illumination the thin shaft of light falling through its almost-closed door. It only took a few moments, however, for his eyes to adjust. The floor was covered with wood shavings. Two benches were crowded with gimlets, adzes, hammers, and braces. A third bench displayed an unstrung longbow and the rough beginnings of a crossbow.

Andrei moved to the bench and ran his hand over the crossbow. It would be beautiful when it was finished, but there were no finished weapons here. Only blocks of wood and metal bands. Andrei searched the benches for any tool that might be useful for breaking into a locked manor. He weighed a chisel in one hand, reached for a gouge, and paused when a splash of vermilion caught his eye.

The orange-red object was half covered in sawdust. Andrei brushed the debris aside and found a lump of wax. There was also something under it—a carefully folded sheet of parchment.

A block of wax was nothing out of the ordinary in a bowmaker's shop—Andrei waxed his own bowstrings to increase their life expectancy—but this wax was different: It was sealing wax for official documents, perfumed with a sweet, earthy odor. The expensive scent of aged ambergris.

He was about to set it aside and reach for the parchment, but as he turned the block, a deep impression in the wax turned his body to stone. It was a hollow outline of a key. An oval bow . . . a front-notched bit . . . four comb-shaped teeth to engage a bolt . . .

The voivode's key.

A mold of it, at least. Andrei didn't need the pieces from the broken wooden copy to know they would fit this mold perfectly.

He slipped the wax block under his coat and reached for the parchment, his fingers trembling. He unfolded the paper, expecting to read a damning letter, but what he found instead were names in three columns. Some of them he recognized. Some of them he didn't. Ice prickled up his arms, leaving goose bumps across his flesh.

"We'll move the horses in the morning."

Andrei jerked around to face the door.

"He wants them transported to his own stables. Some of us will stay here to guard everything else until Hunyadi announces what he intends to do with Csáki's manor."

Andrei stuffed the parchment under his coat next to the wax, and searched for a hiding place. It was the Saxon soldiers he had seen patrolling the grounds.

"Maybe we should throw in our lot with the White Knight," one of them said. "He probably pays his soldiers better."

"And loses more of them to Ottoman scimitars! I'll take the boyar's gold and live a longer life."

Andrei drew his sword, clenched it tightly, and wiped beading moisture from his forehead. He should have pushed the door all the way shut. If they noticed it was partly open . . .

"What's this? I thought you and that seneschal locked everything up."

"We must have missed this one."

He could easily kill the first man before either of them realized he was there. If he was fast enough, he might even take down the second and escape.

The door swung inward. Andrei lifted his sword, then startled both soldiers when his fingers loosened to toss it at their feet.

This was why he would be dead while Vlad one day ruled a kingdom.

He couldn't kill another man to save his own life.

The royal caravan had moved forward at a slow trot since leaving the Curtea Domnească behind. They likely would have moved faster if not for the wagons that were loaded down with food supplies and gold from the treasury. Finally, Mircea raised one hand and slowed the column to a walk. Vlad took advantage of this to spur Invictus forward, push between Mircea's guards, and match pace with his brother's white destrier.

"Where are you taking us? I have a right to know. I'm also the voivode's son."

Mircea laughed. "You're nothing, Vlad. A useless princeling. A joke."

If he was trying to make Vlad furious, it was working, but Vlad held his temper in check. A show of anger would get him nowhere at the moment.

"If something happens to you, it will be up to me to take charge and keep our family safe," Vlad growled through clenched teeth. "You already said as much before we left the Curtea Domnească. Wherever it is our father told you to take us, I need to know his plans, too."

Mircea turned in his saddle to stare at Vlad with one of his characteristically arrogant smirks. "I told you that because I knew it was the quickest way to get you to shut up and do as you were told. Nothing is going to happen to me, and you haven't got the slightest chance of sitting on Wallachia's throne. You're *nothing*, Vlad. A mere speck. A name that history will forget. The sooner you learn that lesson and accept your insignificant place in Wallachia's royal hierarchy, the happier you'll be."

Heat rushed through Vlad's body. He lunged for Mircea's

throat, but his brother was expecting it, and he grabbed both of Vlad's wrists and twisted him out of his saddle.

Vlad hit the earth hard. Their mounts snorted, shied back, and barely avoided crushing him under their hooves. Mircea's guards circled around Vlad, looking down at him and laughing along with Mircea.

"You're pathetic," Mircea said. "Not worthy of *anyone's* throne, let alone *mine*. Weak. Reckless. Foolish. An embarrassment to the family name."

Vlad stood and dusted himself off.

"What's going on up there? Why have we stopped?" Vasilisa's voice called out.

"Vlad wants to walk," Mircea called back. "I've given him my permission to walk for the next half an hour."

Mircea would pay for this. It wouldn't happen today, but vengeance would come. One day soon, Mircea would kneel before Vlad while a crowd far bigger than this one laughed at *him*.

"Why so angry?" Mircea called down. "You want to know where I'm taking us, don't you? Well, this will give you the opportunity to memorize the path up close."

Still laughing, Mircea turned to one of his guards. "Don't let him fall too far behind. Give him an occasional kick between the shoulder blades if you feel like he's lagging."

Mircea spurred his horse forward, and Vlad staggered out of the way. A second guard led away Vlad's horse, and the long line of soldiers, family, and courtiers rode past, their eyes observing Vlad's shame.

"You heard him," the mounted guard said, pressing his booted foot against Vlad's back and pushing him so hard he stumbled forward. "No lagging."

Vlad turned, the palm of his right hand pressed against his sword's pommel. "Do that again, and I'll pull you off that horse and gut you like a fish."

The guard laughed again, but this time his laughter wasn't so hearty. Maybe he saw the vicious intent in Vlad's threat.

Fear. It was a useful tool Vlad could use to accomplish his ends. It had worked against Lupescu's peasants. It had procured information from a close-lipped housemaid. And he shouldn't forget Daciana Golescu: there had been a dearth of assassination attempts since he put that crossbow bolt through her shoulder.

Vlad looked up at the guard, and this time he was the one wearing a smirk.

"*Gladium fuisse permissum*," he said. "The sword has been permitted."

"We'll make the two of you cozy in the room next to Magda's," Magda's father said. "She'll be thrilled to have your company until we learn what's become of your father."

Father . . .

Ilona should have been worried about him, but until Magda's father brought it up, she hadn't paused to wonder if her own father was even still alive. She should probably feel guilty about it, but she only felt hollow. She doubted he was spending even a moment of his time worrying about her.

She pressed her mother's Bible tight against her chest. Other than clothing, it was the only personal item she'd brought with her. She would have also brought her sketchbook if it hadn't been lost to the woods.

Although Gizela had at first been excited to come to the

Racoviță family's manor, the seriousness of their situation now seemed to be settling over her. As they stood in Cântecul Lebedei's entryway, she clung to Ilona's skirt.

"While you're with us," Magda's father said, "please view this home as your own. Supper will soon be ready. Let me find Magda so she can entertain you until it's time to eat."

He gave Ilona and Gizela an encouraging smile—one so big it lifted his entire bushy mustache—then ambled down the hallway bellowing Magda's name.

Ilona heard a sniffle near her waist and fought back her own tears so she could comfort her younger sister.

"I'm scared, Ilona."

"I know, madárka, but there's no reason to be afraid. Boyar Racoviță will keep us safe."

"He said we can call him Uncle Virghiliu."

"So he did, and you can call him that if you want."

"When is Papa coming back?"

"I don't know."

Gizela stared at the floor a moment. When she spoke again, she spoke in a whisper. "What if he never comes back? What if he's dead?"

"He's not dead, but even if he was, you still have me and I won't let anything bad happen to you."

Gizela allowed herself a small smile and unclenched one hand from Ilona's skirt. Quick footsteps echoed down the hallway and Magda appeared. She saw Ilona and Gizela, grinned, and swept them both into a warm embrace.

"Papa told me what happened! Soldiers crossed our property, too. Transylvanian peasants armed with pitchforks and spears. They damaged Papa's carriage, broke into our barns, and stole a few horses. They might have burned the manor, too, except their officers intervened and stopped them."

She paused a moment.

"We were terrified about what might be happening at your manor. Papa knew your father was away with the voivode's cavalry at the border. I'm so glad you're safe! Come into the *sală mare* and tell me everything."

She led them a few dozen steps into the manor's great hall, and they seated themselves near the hearth. Cântecul Lebedei's hall was larger and brighter than the one at Codru Conac. These walls were draped with red and yellow tapestries, and the mounted heads of bears, stags, and boars stared down from high places. A huge painting—the room's focal point—graced the space directly above the fireplace mantel.

"Papa's portrait," Magda said, following Ilona's gaze. "Mama says it looks nothing like him. She says the painter should return our ducats, but Papa says it's wonderful."

Ilona agreed with Magda's mother. The portrait bore a vague resemblance to Magda's father, but the painted face was too stern to belong to Virghiliu Racoviţă.

"Mama doesn't like having dead animals on her walls either. She says they smell bad and ruin her appetite. But Papa threatens to hang them in the bedroom if she won't let him have them here." She laughed. "My parents are always bickering over the silliest things."

There was so much warmth to be found in this home. It was a kind of warmth Ilona hadn't felt since her mother died.

"What do you think will happen now?" Magda asked. "What will happen to Wallachia with the White Knight in charge?"

"He'll probably put a new voivode on the throne," Ilona answered. "A Dănescu."

Another prince to add to Master Sîrbu's list.

"But if a Dănescu takes the throne," Magda wondered aloud, "what will become of Prince Dracul's family? They must have been at the Curtea Domnească when the Transylvanian army arrived. Do you think Hunyadi will . . . execute them?"

Fear knifed through Ilona. Vlad . . . He was a potential heir—a threat to the Dăneşti clan.

"If the boyar council gets a say in it," Magda said, "my father will vote for merciful treatment. I hope Hunyadi is the good man everyone says he is."

A bevy of servants entered the hall, arms filled with steaming trays.

"Suppertime!" Magda said. "I hope you've come with an appetite. Our cook makes the best roe salad and venison stew you'll ever taste!"

She closed her eyes, inhaled, and smiled in anticipation. When she opened her eyes again, she noticed the Bible in Ilona's arms.

"I'm so sorry. I'm such a bad hostess. Let me have someone take that heavy book upstairs to your room."

Before Ilona could protest, Magda waved one of the servants over.

"Rahela, please deliver this book to Lady Ilona's room."

The servant, a pretty girl, bowed and smiled. Ilona locked her fingers around the Bible. Since her departure from Codru Conac, she had clung to it the way Gizela had clung to her skirt. She wasn't ready to give that source of comfort away.

Rahela shot Magda a questioning glance, and Magda stared quizzically at Ilona. It was too awkward. Exhaling slowly, Ilona relinquished the heavy book.

"So many terrible things have happened lately," Magda said as the servant departed. "First the arrow through your window, then poor Daciana, and now this thing with Transylvania. And I already mentioned what happened to my papa's beautiful carriage."

Ilona's fingers fluttered in her lap. She felt guilty. Nothing that bad had happened at Codru Conac. Perhaps a few barrels tipped over and some trampled shrubbery, but nothing worthy of discussion.

"Why would they do something like that?" she asked. "What was the point of such destruction?"

"Revenge for allowing the sultan to attack them," Magda replied. "Anger because the boyars have so much and they have so little."

"Poor Uncle Virghiliu!" Gizela said.

Magda smiled at Gizela and clasped her hand.

"How badly was the carriage damaged?" Ilona asked.

"Terribly damaged! Matyas says it could take months to repair. That's if it even can be repaired. Fortunately, Matyas has agreed to continue in Papa's service for another month to see what he can do." She fell silent a moment. "I've never seen Papa so angry. Or depressed."

More servants arrived with more steaming trays, distracting the girls from their conversation. The dining table filled quickly, and, as if on a signal, Magda's parents entered the hall.

Lady Racoviță was a short, stout woman with graying hair. When she saw Ilona and Gizela, she descended upon them like a mother hen fussing over newly hatched chicks.

"Poor dears!" she clucked. "When I think about what you've been through, it simply pains my heart!"

She placed a hand over her bosom to emphasize her words, then embraced both girls and kissed their foreheads. "Come to the table. You're both so thin! Don't they feed you at Codru Conac?"

"They have a terrible cook," Magda said, winking at Ilona. "She burns everything and never cooks pastries."

Lady Racoviță scowled. "Is that so? Well, we'll make sure you aren't mistreated that way here. I'll have Doina cook up a sweet batch of scovergi first thing tomorrow morning."

Magda's lips curled in a triumphant smile—which she quickly hid when her mother glanced her way. Gizela didn't hide her enthusiasm at all; she bounced in excitement, bringing a glow to Lady Racoviță's face.

"Speaking of food," Magda's father said, "I don't like my soup cold like the Russian boyars do. Gather around the table. I'm about to starve to death."

Magda's mother patted her husband's ample stomach. "You? Starve to death? You're a fat old bear! You could sleep all winter, wake up in the spring, and still have enough meat on those bones to last you through the summer."

Magda's father pretended to be offended, but his wife pinched his cheek and kissed his nose, drawing a laugh from him.

Ilona watched their playful exchange with an aching heart. Even when her mother was alive, Ilona had never seen such affection between a husband and wife. Ilona's mother was an ornament, something beautiful for her father to show off to other men.

Ilona didn't want that for herself. She wanted a relationship like this.

She wanted *love*.

The family gathered around the table, and Magda's mother slapped her husband's hand as he moved his fork to spear a slice of meat.

"Not without giving thanks to God. You know the rules, Virghiliu."

"My apologies. I forgot."

"You always forget," Magda said with a giggle.

"Because the food always looks so tempting. Perhaps my beautiful wife will consent to pray over it before the soup turns to ice."

"The poor shall eat and be satisfied," Lady Racoviță said, head bowed and hands clasped, "and those who seek the Lord shall praise Him . . ."

It was an Orthodox prayer, not a Catholic one, but Ilona could almost hear her mother's voice in the words. Mother always prayed over meals; Ilona's father had tolerated it while she was alive, but quickly ended the tradition after she died.

The prayer ended, and Magda's mother proceeded to heap horse-size servings onto Ilona's and Gizela's plates—potatoes, stuffed cabbage, bread rolls, and boiled eggs. The venison stew was as delicious as Magda promised it would be.

"Your Excellency . . ."

They stopped chewing when the soldier appeared at the great hall's doors.

"Enter."

The soldier came in and bowed.

"My lord . . . We've apprehended someone. We found him at Codru Conac."

Magda's father stood. "A thief?"

"He claims to be a messenger. He says he was on his way to speak with you but lost his way."

"A messenger? What's his name? Who sent him?"

"He refuses to say."

Magda's father scowled. "Where is he now?"

"At the front door. Shall we escort him in?"

"Yes."

The soldier bowed and disappeared. Magda's father tugged at his drooping mustache until the soldier returned with a nervous-looking boy at his side.

Ilona stood in a rush. "Andrei!"

His body jerked as he turned toward her voice. He looked at her first in disbelief and then relief. Awkwardly, they smiled at each other . . . until they noticed everyone else watching.

Ilona sank back into her chair.

"Andrei Muşat," Magda's father said. "Indeed, welcome! Welcome to Cântecul Lebedei!"

Muşat . . . Why did that name sound so familiar? Then she realized: Master Sîrbu's House of Drăculeşti lessons. Andrei was a member of the cneajna's family—the House of Muşat—and Vasilisa's nephew. Ilona recalled her courtyard conversation with Andrei about his parents, and now it all made sense. Andrei's uncles—Iliaş and Stephen—murdered their own brother, Roman, so that they could become Moldavia's co-rulers.

"You've arrived safely from Târgovişte," Magda's father said. "Does that mean the royal family is also safe?"

"They've gone into hiding. I'm here to deliver a message."

"A message from the voivode?"

Andrei shook his head. "From Mircea. The voivode fled with the sultan's army to Adrianople." Andrei's eyes flickered toward Ilona. "And the Grand Boyar Csáki went into exile with him."

"Then they are out of the White Knight's reach. Welcome news for the grand boyar's daughters, I am sure."

Was it? Ilona didn't know. She entertained the unrighteous thought that her life might be better if her father and the voivode never came back.

"Mircea and the rest of the royal family . . . Where are they?"

"Mircea took them into hiding. He's going to raise an army."

Magda's father rubbed his chin. "Which is why you are here. To gain my support for Mircea's return."

Andrei looked uncertain. "Yes."

"The voivode is short on allies . . ." Magda's father met Andrei's nervous gaze. "The House of Drăculeşti, of course, can count on the support of my house as always."

Andrei visibly relaxed.

"The boy looks exhausted and half-starved," Magda's mother said. "Invite him to sit and eat, Virghiliu."

Magda's father nodded. "Join us for supper," he said, "and tell us what has happened at Târgovişte."

Magda's father gestured toward an empty seat—the one next to Ilona. Andrei's eyes flickered like a shy butterfly, close enough to touch Ilona but too uncertain to linger or land. He sat stiffly, careful not to brush against her. She pretended to be interested in the food on her plate.

The meal resumed, but Ilona was now too distracted to eat. Magda's father grilled Andrei, and Ilona listened for details about Vlad.

Why was she so concerned? Why did she care what happened to Vlad Dracula? She twisted her fingers in her skirt, crossed and uncrossed her ankles. She knew why. It was because, despite all common sense, she had feelings for him.

When Magda's father ran out of questions about the royal family, he asked a question about Andrei. "And what of you? What will you do now? Where are you going to stay?"

Andrei stared at his hands. "I don't know. Perhaps I'll hide in the woods until Mircea comes back. I know how to hunt and forage."

"Nonsense!" Magda's father exclaimed. "You'll stay here!"

An expression only Ilona could decipher flashed across Andrei's face: guilt. He felt as uncomfortable about accepting the kind boyar's hospitality as she did.

Andrei's eyes stayed fixed on the table. "I can't stay."

"Why on earth not?"

"It will put your family in danger. It wouldn't be right. I'll find another place to hide."

"You'll stay here under my protection," Magda's father said curtly. "End of discussion. Now fill that plate again."

Despite his earlier protests, Andrei looked visibly relieved. With some surprise, Ilona realized that she was relieved, too.

It would be good to have another friend here—someone who could probably understand what she was feeling. Even with Mircea out of the picture for now, she had a feeling she could still use an ally.

CHAPTER EIGHTEEN

HE FELT LIKE A CAGED RAT SCRATCHING AND GNAWING ON unbreakable bars. While Mircea went to scout the path ahead, Vlad had been left like a child with the women. If things didn't change soon, he and Mircea would come to blows again, and this time Mircea wouldn't escape unscathed. Vlad didn't care that the voivode left Mircea in charge or that Mircea was family. It didn't matter that Mircea commanded a small army. Vlad would hurt him. He would best Mircea with all Mircea's soldiers watching.

"Don't go too near the stream. I don't want your boots getting wet."

Vlad turned toward Vasilisa, realized she was speaking to Radu, and fought to hold down his rising rage.

Humiliation. That was why Mircea left him here; he wanted to humiliate Vlad not only in front of his army but also in front of the curious villagers.

He'd had enough.

Vlad strode toward the forest, but it took less than three seconds for two guards to sidle in the same direction and block his path. He thought about drawing his sword and fighting his way through, but more soldiers would converge on him and his inevitable defeat would be even more humiliating.

Vlad glared at the soldiers. He hated Saxons; their loyalty only ran as deep as the gold in their master's pocket. If Mircea weren't as dumb as he was ugly, he would have left Wallachian soldiers in charge of the treasure wagons. It was only a matter of time before his hired Saxon army turned on him and departed with the funds from the royal treasury.

Vlad stalked toward the village, fuming again. He should have stayed at Târgovişte. If he weren't so well known—if his face weren't so recognizable—he could be home doing something useful rather than wasting precious hours listening to Vasilisa complain about all her hardships to her ladies-in-waiting.

The only positive decision Mircea had made since ordering the family's evacuation was to leave Andrei behind to unite the boyars. For once in his life, Andrei had shown a tactical shrewdness worthy of a prince. Vlad knew why Andrei really stayed behind, and he hoped for Ilona's sake that Andrei's gamble had paid off.

Not just for Ilona's sake, but for Vlad's as well. He couldn't stand to be away from her. If something happened to her . . . If she wasn't there when he got back . . .

He shook his head. If any harm came to Ilona, he would see to it that Mircea suffered as well.

Vlad's jaw tightened, and he ground his teeth. He should be there with Andrei. He should be protecting Ilona. He was a warrior—a highly trained soldier. Definitely not the exhibit in a traveling show that Mircea was turning him into. Even now the local villagers gawked at him from the safety of their straw-roofed cottages. Vlad pushed his hair out of his eyes and turned to glare at them.

His latest audience consisted of two teenage peasant girls, and they were tolerably attractive. They had the same pale skin, and the same light brown hair tucked beneath matching head scarves.

Twins. Neither was comparable to Ilona in beauty, but Ilona wasn't here, and Vlad needed a distraction from the torture of thinking about her.

He walked to an age-blackened tree stump—near enough to draw the two girls' attention but far enough so it wouldn't seem like that was his intention. He removed his sword from its scabbard, rested it across his knees, and proceeded to polish its blade with a corner of his coat.

One of the twins pushed her sister toward him. The pushed sister turned, grabbed her twin's arm, and pulled her with her. They laughed. Vlad pretended not to notice.

A few more steps in his direction. Conspiratorial whispers. Vlad finally looked up.

"Bună dimineața," he greeted them.

They giggled and covered their mouths.

Too easy. When he was voivode, he would have any woman he wanted. But the only woman he would want was Ilona, so it was a skill he would never need to put into practice.

"I'm Vlad."

"I'm Brândușa," the first twin said.

She was slightly taller than her sister. Other than that, they were virtually indistinguishable from each other. They stood barefoot despite the cold. They were much prettier up close than they had appeared from a distance. Vlad smiled. Maybe his circumstances weren't so intolerable after all.

"And what's your name?"

"Viorica," the shorter, shyer sister answered.

"And what's the name of your village?"

"Gruiu," they answered in unison.

"Can you tell me which boyar you serve?"

"Boyar Ghica," Brânduşa answered.

Vlad nodded. Ghica was loyal to the House of the Dragon. Most of these southern boyars were.

"Are you a prince?" Brânduşa asked. "Viorica thinks you're a prince."

"Vlad Dracula," he said, standing and bowing. "Second in line to Wallachia's throne."

The girls beamed.

Mircea had given orders for the family to keep their identities secret, but Vlad didn't see the point. If Hunyadi came looking, he wouldn't need to use much imagination to figure out it was Mircea's tiny army that had passed through here.

"Is it true?" Brânduşa asked. "The White Knight chased the Ottomans back to Adrianople? Did he really take Târgovişte?"

"He has Târgovişte," Vlad admitted, "but he won't have it long. As soon as my family raises a proper army, we'll take it back."

"Will you be leading that army?"

"Of course. This sword isn't for decoration."

He brandished the weapon, and Viorica stepped back. Brânduşa touched his hand and examined the blade.

"It looks sharp."

"I've split my fair share of skulls with it. Soon it will make Transylvanian heads roll."

Brânduşa looked impressed. Viorica seemed frightened. Encouraged, Vlad grew bolder.

"A few years ago—not far from here—I single-handedly lured a hundred Ottoman *sipahis* to their deaths. It happened while I was patrolling near the Danube. They ambushed my party and killed everyone but me. They thought they could take me prisoner, but I evaded them in the swamps and led them straight into the spears of the voivode's army."

Brânduşa gasped and clapped.

"Making up tall tales for the local girls, Vladislav?"

Vlad spun.

"Put that away before you hurt yourself," Mircea said, pointing at Vlad's sword.

Vlad's face reddened. He considered putting the sword somewhere where it would do irreparable damage to Mircea, but the two guards flanking the crown prince dissuaded him from that idea.

"Ladies," Mircea said, bowing.

Brânduşa and Viorica giggled, quickly returning his bow. Mircea returned his attention to Vlad. "I told you not to leave the family. Get back there. The White Knight's men are headed this direction and we're leaving for a new location."

Vlad glanced at the twins. They were admiring Mircea now. He clenched his teeth, turned, and stalked away.

Someday . . . Someday very soon he would humiliate Mircea the way Mircea humiliated him. He would take Mircea's crown. He would take Mircea's bride. He would slash that stupid smirk off Mircea's ugly face.

But not today. Today he would plot his escape so he could raise a rival army to retake Târgoviște before Mircea did.

Andrei stood at the window, watching his breath paint fog across the glass. He wiped a circular peephole, stared into the darkness, and pressed his knuckles against the sill. He felt guilty about being warm and secure while Vlad was hiding from Hunyadi's army in some forsaken place, but someone had to make sure Ilona and her sister were safe.

Safe . . . Anton Csáki's daughters were anything but. If the wax mold meant what Andrei thought it meant, they would be in even more danger if Mircea and the voivode ever came back.

He stepped away from the window. Under his shirt, the lump of wax from Anton Csáki's workshop pressed against his ribs. Andrei reached for it but touched the parchment first. He smoothed it out and held it in the circle of light cast by one of the room's flickering candles.

Three rows of names carefully penned in flowing script. Three sets of underlined letters above these names. VD. BD. VC. The names under the letters belonged to boyar families. Under the first column, Andrei recognized several boyars who frequented the palace and the voivode's official functions. These were supporters—or at least had been supporters—of the House of Drăculești.

VD. Vlad Dracul. Easy enough, and the second set was no harder. BD. Basarab Dănești. Andrei figured it out the moment he found the name "Golescu" penned beneath it. Enemies. Supporters of the House of Dănești.

But who did the third set belong to?

Andrei shifted his gaze from the initials VC to the names underneath.

Florescu . . .

Weresmarth . . .

Longo Campo . . .

The only one he recognized was the one at the top: Vintilă Florescu. Florescu was one of the voivode's most outspoken opponents—so outspoken he had been forced years ago to flee into exile.

Noticeably absent from the lists were the names Csáki and Racoviță. Boyar Racoviță was a Dracul supporter, so why was his name missing from the Vlad Dracul list?

The room's door shook under the weight of a knock, so loud that it made Andrei jump. He quickly shoved the parchment under a pillow, then crossed the room to open the door.

"I hope I didn't wake you," Racoviță said.

Andrei shook his head.

"Can I speak with you a few moments before you retire for the night?"

Andrei nodded.

The boyar glanced down the hallway, scanned the room, then shut the door behind him.

"I need to tell you something, and I need you to listen carefully: Wallachia is crawling with spies," Racoviță said. "The voivode's enemies have infiltrated every important household in the land. This household is no exception."

As if to emphasize his point, he scanned the room again as if enemies lurked in every shadow.

"I don't know how many of my servants are currently in my enemies' pockets, but I do know no conversation—even this one—is completely safe. By morning, Dragoş Golescu and others like him will know you're a guest at my manor. You will be safe as long as you remain on my property, but the moment you set out on your own, they will find you, and they will torture you until they've extracted every piece of information they think they can get."

A drop of perspiration trickled down the back of Andrei's neck. "I don't know where the royal family is," he mumbled. "Mircea wouldn't tell me where they were going. I can't tell anyone anything."

"Very wise of Mircea, but unfortunate for you," the boyar said. "It won't stop the torture, only prolong it. And when they've finished with it, they will kill you. Do you understand the danger you're in?"

Andrei nodded and fidgeted with his collar. "If Golescu and his friends know everything so quickly, what's to stop the White Knight from knowing it as well? What's to stop him from coming here to take me?"

"Nothing," Racoviţă admitted. "But Hunyadi has something Golescu and his friends don't have: a sense of honor. You'll be safe with him as long as you can convince him you're a person of integrity, too."

Andrei nodded.

"When the White Knight questions you," Racoviţă continued, "answer his questions truthfully. If Mircea didn't tell you anything that could compromise him or the royal family, this shouldn't be a problem."

"I have no reason to lie."

"Good!" The boyar clapped a hand on Andrei's shoulder. "All will be well. And whether or not Mircea and your kin return from exile, I'll make sure you have a home and a future in Wallachia. Noapte bună."

"Good night," Andrei answered.

The boyar stepped into the hallway and closed the door behind him. Andrei stared at the scrolling patterns in the doorframe, his nervous suspicions roiling in his mind. The names of two men were missing from that parchment list.

Was he in a friend's home . . . or an enemy's?

CHAPTER NINETEEN

ILONA FOUND ANDREI IN THE GREAT HALL. THE REST OF THE house was still asleep, but like her he'd probably had a restless night. He heard her echoing footsteps and looked up, but only gave her a weak smile before returning his gaze to the fireplace's glow.

Ilona was glad he was here.

"It must have been frightening," she said tentatively. "Staying behind to complete your mission, I mean."

"A little," he replied. "But . . . I had lives I was worried about other than my own."

"Vlad's? His family's?"

"What? Oh . . ." Andrei smiled and nodded vigorously. "Yes."

"I'm glad you made it here safely."

"Me too."

"Magda's father kept Gizela and me safe. Without him, I don't know what we would have done."

"He's a good man," Andrei said, but his eyes seemed troubled. "I like him."

"Yes, me too."

They both fell silent and listened to the pops of the dying embers.

"How is Vlad?" Ilona asked. "What I mean is . . . How was he when you last saw him? Was he safe? Was he well?"

She must have sounded too eager, because Andrei stared at her a moment before answering. "The entire House of Drăculeşti is safe. As far as I know."

"That's good. I would feel terrible if anything happened to them."

She approached the hearth and hesitantly sat—just far enough away from Andrei to leave a comfortable, appropriate space. But she didn't sit long.

"Oh! What's that?" Ilona jumped to her feet and stared at the ceiling.

Andrei stood beside her, following her gaze. A squeaking, erratic shape swooped through the shadows above their heads.

"A bat," he said. "It must have found its way in last night."

Ilona didn't like bats. She didn't like any furry, rodent-like creature. She pressed up against Andrei, nervously following the bat's movement with her eyes.

"Bună dimineaţa!"

Ilona and Andrei jumped apart, hiding their hands behind their backs. An amused grin parted Magda's father's lips.

"I'm not interrupting anything important, am I?" the boyar said innocently.

"No," they answered in unison, so quickly it sounded incriminating.

The bat fluttered between the chandeliers, and Magda's father looked up.

"An unexpected visitor," he said. "There's been a lot of that here lately. I'll have to get some servants to show this one out."

He returned his attention to Andrei and Ilona. "You're up early this morning. That's good. Another visitor showed up late last night asking about both of you."

Ilona and Andrei stiffened.

"I've received a summons from Târgoviște. The three of us must travel there immediately."

Fear cramped Ilona's stomach. "Târgoviște?"

"The White Knight," Andrei mumbled.

Magda's father nodded. "His soldiers are waiting outside."

Ilona and Andrei looked at each other. When Magda's father motioned for them to follow him, Ilona moved like one of Gizela's dolls—as if her legs were being controlled by someone else.

Mircea's guards were watchful about preventing Vlad from leaving the camp, but they were far less observant about his doings in and around the tents. Mircea should have left someone to watch his own. Fortunately, he was so arrogant he saw no need for it.

Vlad peered through the tent flap, making sure no one saw him enter. When he decided no one was after him, he turned to examine Mircea's possessions.

A large map hung like a tablecloth over a log Mircea had commandeered for a table. His bedroll was twice as thick as any other bed in the camp and topped with more pillows than a pasha's mattress. He had a chair. He had a cedar chest. He had an Ottoman rug on his floor. All this Mircea had brought with him while Vlad was barely given time to get out of the Curtea Domnească with the shirt on his back. It made him seethe inside to see Mircea living in luxury while the rest of the family suffered.

Helpfully, Mircea had used sticks and a pebble to mark locations on his map. Vlad guessed the white pebble signified the family's current position while the sticks marked places where Mircea's scouts had come across the White Knight's troops. According to the map, Mircea had set up camp near an obscure village named Bucharest. It was a good place to hide from Hunyadi's search parties.

If you were a coward.

Vlad couldn't take the big map, but several smaller maps were curled around one another in a round leather case. He would need one when it came time to go back for Ilona, so he slipped one free. Folded into a square, it fit nicely in the drawstring pouch tied to his belt, and there was still room for other useful items. He cast his eyes around the tent, deciding what else he should take.

Two bottles of wine. A plate of half-eaten smoked ham. Mircea was living large while the rest of the camp lived off stale bread and old cheese. Vlad couldn't fit these in the pouch, but he seriously considered pouring the wine into the dirt. That, however, would only make Mircea surlier than he already was.

Vlad was poking through a pile of clothing when he heard voices.

He rushed to the flap, but it was already too late. Mircea strode slowly toward his tent. Vlad frantically searched for a hiding place. There! Between the bedroll and the wall. It wasn't ideal, but it would have to do.

He had just enough time to pull Mircea's pillows over himself before his brother and the captain entered.

"We need to head south," Mircea said. "As close to the Ottoman border as possible."

Vlad peeked through the pillows. Mircea was pointing at his large map.

"The voivode will meet us here. His plan is to return with the sultan's janissaries, join forces with us, and drive Hunyadi back into Transylvania. I've already received pledges from the southern boyars that they'll supply us with soldiers when I call for them."

"What about the White Knight's search parties?" the captain asked. "We don't have enough men to hold them off if they discover our location."

"We just need to stay out of sight for another week or two," Mircea said. "We need to give my father time."

A breathless soldier skidded to a halt at the tent entrance. "Your Highness!"

"Yes? What is it?"

"Your brother . . . He's nowhere to be found."

Mircea cursed and stepped back outside.

Vlad's jailers weren't as oblivious as he'd hoped they would be.

Luckily, the tent's walls were loose enough for Vlad to stretch a bottom edge up and slip under it. Vlad scooted out, stood, and dusted himself off. Then he casually sauntered around the tent. Mircea now stood under a tree, speaking heatedly to the soldiers who had been assigned to watch his brother.

Vlad walked toward his own tent, pretending not to notice Mircea but making sure his path crossed Mircea's line of sight.

"You!"

Vlad turned, hoping his face looked suitably surprised. "Yes?"

"Where have you been?"

"Where I always am. Wasting away in this prison you call a camp."

Mircea stomped toward him.

"Don't play your games with me! I know you left the camp-site. How did you get past the guards? How did you get back in?"

"I never left the camp."

Mircea shoved Vlad so hard he nearly fell over.

"Do that again," Vlad snarled, "and I'll kill you."

Mircea punched him in the stomach, and he doubled over.

"I'd like to see you try," Mircea said. He turned to Vlad's guards. "Escort the princeling to his tent. He can stay there for the rest of the day."

Saliva dribbled off Vlad's lower lip as he held his stomach and gasped for air.

He *would* kill Mircea.

There was no longer room enough in Wallachia for two princes.

CHAPTER TWENTY

COLD SWEAT DAMPENED ILONA'S NECK, AND SHE SURREPTI-
tiously wiped it away. She was still being punished for kissing
Vlad, she was sure of it. If she were as pure as her mother, God
wouldn't allow this to happen to her.

The horses' hooves clopped loudly as Captain Török led
their party through Târgoviște's narrow, cobbled streets. Magda's
father took advantage of the noise to bring his horse close and
whisper near Ilona's ear.

"The fact that we've been summoned and not dragged
here," he said, "is a very good sign. I think I can bargain with
Hunyadi to keep you and Andrei out of trouble. Mircea left
both of you here with little thought for your safety. Use that to
your advantage if you have to."

Any comfort Magda's father hoped to give Ilona with this
thought vanished when they approached the Curtea Domnească's
gates. The plaza was crowded with ragged, dirt-streaked soldiers.

Transylvanian peasants—lean, hungry men armed with pitch-forks, axes, and scythes.

Ilona shivered. As a Transylvanian, a part of her was grateful for these men. As a Wallachian, she feared them.

Her anxiety only grew when the peasants spotted Virghiliu Racoviţă's *kalpak*. They pointed at his tall boyar hat, murderous expressions flickering across their faces.

Magda's father paid them no attention. Ilona wished she could be so unconcerned, but her heart nearly stopped when Török led them directly through the angry mob. She didn't breathe until they were safely within the palace's chilly shadows. Here they dismounted and the captain motioned them inside.

Andrei walked close beside her. Vlad would have taken advantage of this frightening moment to hold Ilona's hand. She wouldn't mind if Andrei made the attempt, but his arms were folded tightly across his chest. He was taller than Vlad, she noticed . . .

Ilona diverted her gaze.

"In here, please."

Török ushered them into a familiar room—the voivode's great hall. Ilona still remembered very vividly the last event that brought her here, but things had changed at the palace since the night of her unexpected betrothal. The hall's once-bare walls were now decorated with tapestries, banners, and brightly painted shields; the White Knight was wasting no time making himself feel at home.

Two men waited for them in the room. One was thin, of medium height, and had a narrow nose and close-cropped beard. Ilona didn't have a clear view of the other man. He sat near the fireplace in the voivode's comfortable chair. The chair's back was to Ilona, but she saw the seated man's calloused fingers tapping a slow rhythm on the armrest.

"Your Excellencies, the guests from Cântecul Lebedei have arrived," Török said.

Guests. Such a benign word, but this "visit" seemed anything but friendly.

The man in the chair rose from his seat and turned to face them. He wasn't particularly tall, but there was something about him that made him as imposing as a giant. Maybe it was the reddish-brown hair that fell like a lion's mane over his broad, muscular shoulders, or his thick, drooping mustache and his penetrating brown eyes.

"*Jó napot! Isten hozta!*"

His voice surprised Ilona. It was as pleasant as Magda's father's and radiated warmth. "*Bun venit!*" he added, switching from Hungarian to Romanian. "I hope Ladislaus made your journey here swift and safe."

He crossed the hall with smooth, even strides. His companion followed a few steps behind him. His arms were open and smile lines lifted his mustache at the corners. Magda's father bowed, and Ilona and Andrei quickly followed his example.

"As we've never met," the man said, "allow me to introduce myself. I am János Hunyadi." He turned and gestured at the man behind him. "And this is Wallachia's new and rightful ruler, my good friend and ally, Basarab of the House of Dănești."

Ilona and her group bowed, and Basarab nodded back at them. Hunyadi clapped a hand onto Boyar Racoviță's shoulder. Magda's father flinched. "Join us at the fire," Hunyadi said. It was both an invitation and a command. "You may leave us, Ladislaus."

Captain Török nodded, stepped out, and quietly shut the hall's doors behind him. Hunyadi took a few moments to examine his "guests" before addressing them.

"You know why I've summoned you here."

"To ask us what we know about the whereabouts of Dracul's family, I presume," Racoviță answered.

"And do you know where they are?"

"I have no idea, and neither do these children."

"We'll be the judge of that," Basarab said, threateningly lowering his eyebrows.

The White Knight turned his piercing gaze on Andrei.

"You were the last one to have any contact with Prince Dracul's family. Where were they off to when you left them?"

Andrei fidgeted with his hands and didn't answer for several moments. When he did, his voice was strained.

"I saw them here, at the south gate. But I left before they did. I didn't see where they were going, and Mircea didn't tell me."

"Why did you stay behind?" Basarab chimed in.

Andrei looked even more uncomfortable now. Before answering the question, he glanced at Magda's father. The boyar nodded.

"Mircea left me to gather support to take Wallachia back."

Hunyadi smiled. "An unlikely proposition, but very brave of you to take such a risk for the Drăculești clan." He pointed at Andrei's hand. "You have Mircea's ring."

Andrei stopped spinning it around his middle finger and nodded.

"May I see it?"

Andrei handed it over. Hunyadi examined it a moment and

returned it. "My own sources confirm everything you have just told me."

Hunyadi shifted his attention to Ilona now, and she shivered.

"You are betrothed to Mircea of the House of Drăculeşti?"

"Yes."

"But before his departure, you were spending time alone with his younger brother."

Ilona folded her hands in her lap and stared back and forth between his brown eyes and her twitching fingers. "I . . . I don't know what you mean."

"Let me help your memory. An early morning visit in your father's stables. An intimate moment in Codru Conac's great hall."

Ilona twisted her fingers into her skirt. "I don't know what you mean by 'intimate.' Vlad and I are just friends."

"And yet he made solitary trips to spend time alone with you. What type of 'friendship' should I infer?"

Ilona cast a fleeting glance at Andrei, but he looked away. Magda's father coughed into his hand and studied Hunyadi's shiny boots.

"Vlad kissed me," Ilona admitted, "but I didn't invite it. And that's the *only* inappropriate thing either of us ever did."

"So you would also have me believe that nothing inappropriate happened between you and Vlad Dracula on the night of your betrothal? You didn't see him that night? You weren't with him when you left your bedroom and were unaccounted for for several hours?"

Her mouth dropped open in confusion, then she tightened her fingers around the edges of her seat, her face burning hotter than the coals in the fireplace. "No!"

The White Knight and Basarab watched her for several moments. They watched long enough that it should have made the silence uncomfortable, but Ilona glared back at them, refusing to look away.

"Did Vlad Dracula tell you anything about where his family was going?" Basarab asked. "About where they might be at this moment?"

"No." Her tone was level and icy. "Mircea left me here. Does that sound like someone who would think to tell me where he was going?"

Hunyadi studied Ilona, frowning.

"She's telling the truth," Andrei said. "She's here. Mircea isn't. She has no reason to lie to you."

Hunyadi stared at Andrei again. Andrei straightened his shoulders, and Hunyadi chuckled. "I think I've heard everything I need to know," he said. "Thank you . . ." He glanced at Ilona. ". . . for your honesty."

The White Knight turned to the fireplace, took an iron poker from its hearth, and stirred the crackling logs until sparks darted like angry fairies up the flue. The fire rose from its glowing bed to shake out its red-gold mane. When it blazed, Hunyadi faced them again.

"Racoviță, may I have a few words with you in private?"

"Certainly, Your Excellency."

The White Knight motioned for Andrei and Ilona to go, and they wasted no time reaching the exit. Ilona trembled as Andrei pushed the heavy doors open. She was no longer frightened, but the sudden release of tension left her dangerously close to tears.

Andrei put one hand on her arm and led her into the

hallway. Captain Török and three other soldiers stood just outside the doors. They nodded at Andrei and Ilona as they exited. Ilona kept walking. Andrei glanced over his shoulder before following her. She didn't stop moving until they reached a side corridor where no one but Andrei could see her. Andrei stared uncomfortably at his boots—the walls, the ceiling—while Ilona dabbed at her tears.

"Thank you," she whispered, "for helping me."

Andrei nodded.

Ilona clenched her teeth and blinked angrily. It bothered her that Hunyadi could break her so easily. "You probably have a terrible opinion of me."

"No. Why would you say that?"

"Because of the things the White Knight said—the insinuations he made about Vlad and me."

"I didn't believe any of it."

She stopped wiping at her tears and met Andrei's gaze. He hunched his shoulders and looked away. Despite what he said, she wasn't sure he believed her.

"What do you think they're talking about in there?" she asked.

Andrei shrugged. "I don't know. Probably us."

They stood in silence, looking at anything but each other.

"The night of the betrothal . . . ," Ilona said. "When I left my room . . . I wasn't with Vlad, I was in the courtyard. The only person I was with that night was you."

Andrei nodded. "I remember."

"You left before I did. I stayed so long that my hands got so cold I could no longer feel my fingers. I wanted to freeze to death in that courtyard. Freeze or run away, sneak back to

Transylvania. I might have done it. I might have taken that risk . . . but I met you. And I hoped I'd made a friend."

"You did make a friend."

They looked into each other's eyes.

"You told me about wanting to spend your life studying birds," Andrei said.

"Yes."

"I found your sketchbook. I've brought it back for you."

Ilona placed a hand over her mouth, a smile creeping back to her lips.

"It's at Boyar Racoviță's manor," Andrei explained. "I was going to give it back to you immediately, but chaos broke out at the Curtea Domnească and one thing after another happened after that. I'm sorry about taking so long. Life gets complicated when you're a part of the House of the Dragon."

"Yes . . . Yes, it does."

Ilona smiled at him a moment . . . then threw her arms around him.

"Thank you," she whispered. "Your friendship . . . It means a lot to me. And I don't even know what to say about the sketchbook . . . It . . . It's my life's work. Thank you. Thank you so much for rescuing it for me."

Andrei's face warmed as she pulled away. "I also brought you a present," he mumbled. "For your birthday. It's nothing like what Vlad has for you, but . . . I hope you'll like it."

He fumbled with a bag he had tied to his belt, retrieving something small enough to conceal in his closed hand. "Here."

"Oh!" Ilona smiled. "It's wonderful!"

She carefully took the carved swan and examined it.

"Did you make this?"

"My father did. He liked to carve. He made it for my mother. I . . . I know you love birds, so I thought . . . Well . . . I thought you might like it."

Ilona pressed the small carving against her heart.

"It's beautiful! I love it! But . . . but how can I possibly accept it? It must be precious to you. It's too much."

Andrei shook his head. "I want you to have it so you can remember that we're friends."

She hugged him again, and a blush burned fiery red across his cheeks. An embrace with another young man might not be the best decision after what the White Knight tried to accuse her of, but Ilona didn't regret it.

"I'm here for you, too," she said. "You and I . . . We're allies." She glanced in the direction of the throne room. "We'll stand by each other."

Andrei nodded.

Voices echoed down the corridor, accompanied by footsteps moving in their direction.

Magda's father appeared with Captain Török. The boyar seemed relaxed and was smiling. It eased some of Ilona's tension.

"Ah! There you are!" Racoviță said as he and the captain drew near. "I have good news for the both of you." He came close and put a hand on each of their shoulders. "Basarab and the White Knight have granted me official status as your guardian," he announced. "You are both absolved of any crimes against the kingdoms of Transylvania and Hungary and will remain under my protection for as long as Basarab, Hunyadi, and I deem it necessary."

Ilona allowed a hopeful smile to warm her face.

"Captain Török will escort us back to the manor," the boyar

continued. "We can share the news with the family and have a small feast to celebrate our good fortune."

Ilona glanced at Andrei. He was smiling and looked just as relieved as she was.

The captain led them to their waiting horses, and Andrei helped Ilona into her saddle. But they had barely made it beyond the Curtea Domnească's protective walls before their progress was halted by a raucous crowd.

Hundreds of people—Wallachians and Transylvanians—formed an arena-like circle around five soldiers and three bedraggled prisoners. The prisoners were bound in rusty chains and knelt stoically on the cobblestones while the crowd jeered, cursed, and spat at them.

Ottoman soldiers. One was a fair-haired janissary, clad in the remnants of a once-flowing blue robe. His companions wore tan robes and drooping black mustaches.

"This way," Captain Török said, leading them around the crowd. "You don't need to see this."

A public execution. Ilona's blood turned cold, realizing this could easily have been her fate.

This was what it meant to live in Wallachia.

Death.

Blood.

Hatred.

But it could also mean other things. She glanced at Andrei.

Trust.

Friendship.

Perhaps even . . . love.

CHAPTER TWENTY-ONE

A SMALL WOODEN CHAPEL STOOD AT THE EDGE OF VIRGHILIU Racoviţă's manor grounds. When Andrei investigated it, he found the door unlocked; apparently God encouraged visitors. Andrei ventured cautiously inside.

The chapel had three rows of unpainted wooden pews set before a small white altar. A single stained-glass window cast amber illumination across the room. Beneath the window, a gilded crucifix clung tiredly to the wall. Andrei stared at Christ's twisted, agonized image, reflecting the agony in his own heart.

He wasn't sure what it felt like to be in love, but he thought it might be happening to him. It was agony laced with happiness. It was the warmth he felt when Ilona embraced him.

But he couldn't allow himself to fall in love with Ilona Csáki. To do so would be to betray Vlad's trust. He could be Ilona's friend and nothing more. He had to fight these feelings off before they permanently took hold of him.

He knelt on the padded hassock on the back row of the pews.

"Oh!"

The voice startled him. He turned.

Ilona.

"I-I'm sorry," she babbled. "I didn't know anyone was here. If I'm interrupting something—"

"No, I . . ."

He couldn't explain why he was here. *She* was why he was here.

"Are you praying?"

Andrei blinked. Praying? He supposed that would be the logical thing for someone to do in a chapel, so he nodded.

"Would you mind if . . . if I pray, too?"

"Yes. I-I mean, no. I mean . . . if you'd like to."

Seemingly unperturbed by his awkward answer, Ilona smiled, crossed the room, and knelt beside him.

Andrei forgot the guilt-fueled agony he had experienced moments before as a warmer feeling prickled through his body.

"I apologize for disturbing you," Ilona said. "I can leave if you want to be alone."

"It's all right. I just came in to . . . think."

Ilona looked around. "It's been a long time since I knelt in a church," she said, her voice growing soft. "When my mother was alive, she took me to a church in Sighişoara almost every day. She was very pious. I wish I was more like her."

Andrei examined the curve of Ilona's half-lowered lashes, studied her face's glow in the stained-glass window's light. She looked very pious from this angle, but his gaze felt like a violation, so he quickly looked away.

"I don't think I've ever been in a church," he admitted.

"What?" She looked surprised.

"There's one at the Curtea Domnească, but it never gets

used. Not by the voivode's family, at least. Not unless he needs it for official business."

"You've never been in a *church*?"

"Well . . . I suppose when I was christened, but that was a very long time ago."

She clearly didn't know how to react to this revelation.

"This is a beautiful little chapel," she finally said. "Don't you think?"

"Boyar Racoviță likes beautiful things."

Ilona nodded. "Like his carriage," she whispered. "It was severely damaged by some of the White Knight's soldiers."

"That's a shame," Andrei said. "That carriage was more than a carriage. It was art."

Ilona smiled. "You're so different from Vlad."

"Is that a good thing, or bad?"

"Neither. Just . . . different. I can't imagine Vlad recognizing the carriage as art. You do because you're thoughtful and reflective. He's reckless and bold . . . adventurous."

"Try living with him and his adventures," Andrei said, wincing. "It's a miracle I'm still alive."

Ilona laughed. It was a soft, crystalline laugh that stirred warm feelings in Andrei's chest, but then she glanced at the door and her smile and laughter faded.

"What do you think the chances are," she asked, "that Golescu's spies noticed both of us entering this little church?"

"They seem to see everything."

"My reputation is already questionable enough," Ilona whispered, frowning. "I don't want to tarnish yours, too."

She stood and took a step toward the door. "Maybe we can talk again. In a more . . . appropriate place."

She took several more steps away from Andrei, waved, and vanished.

Andrei stared at the empty doorway.

If this was love, love was agony.

Vlad pitched a rock into the lake, watched it plunk and send a rippling wave across the water. He threw another rock, then a third. With each throw his anger grew.

Tonight.

He would make his escape tonight. He would go back to the village and start building an army. Hunyadi used peasant soldiers; Vlad's tactics could be similar. While Mircea hid in the backcountry, Vlad would ride to Târgoviște and claim the throne.

He was done with Mircea's cowardly hide-and-seek games. If his brother didn't have the spine to act, Vlad would. He would go and—

"You look angry."

Vlad searched for the source of the voice, and finally found it standing behind him.

Radu.

What does this little dăunător want?

"Maybe I am," Vlad growled. "And what business is it of yours?"

Radu didn't answer. He just stared.

"If you were older and smarter," Vlad said, "you would know to stay away from angry people who carry swords."

He placed a hand on his weapon. Radu took a step backward but didn't leave.

"Are you mad because of Mircea or because of Andrei?"

"Why would I be angry because of Andrei?"

"Because he's probably with Ilona. Because she'll probably fall in love with him."

Vlad glared a moment before kicking dirt at Radu. "Get out of here, you little pestilence!" He ran at Radu with a raised fist, and the boy bolted for the women's tents.

Vlad turned to face the lake again. Probably with Ilona? Yes, Andrei probably was. But he wouldn't make any moves where Ilona was concerned. Andrei knew Vlad loved Ilona Csáki, and he was too honorable to break that sacred trust.

That, however, wasn't what Radu said. He said *Ilona* would probably fall in love with *Andrei*. What could have possibly given him that idea?

Vlad picked up a stick, drew his arm back, and flung the stick out over the water. It spun like a dying swan before hitting the lake's surface with a slap.

Swan . . . Andrei knew Ilona liked swans. He knew she liked birds, enjoyed studying them. That meant Andrei had been with Ilona at some time when Vlad hadn't. Maybe several times.

Maybe he was alone with her someplace right now.

Vlad's rage shifted.

If Andrei so much as *looked* at Ilona while Vlad was away—

He shook his head. No . . . That wouldn't happen. Even if Ilona was slightly interested in Andrei, Vlad's cousin didn't stand a chance while Vlad was in the picture.

Vlad stooped to grab another stick, then froze.

That was the problem, wasn't it? Vlad *wasn't* in the picture, and wouldn't be for the foreseeable future.

Fortunately, Ilona had never even *looked* at Andrei.

Except for that morning on the hill.

And that night at the Curtea Domnească when Vlad cut Andrei's face.

Curse it all! He needed to return to Târgovişte immediately. Mircea and Hunyadi were going to cost him everything!

Vlad scanned the trees on the other side of the lake. A solitary soldier stood watch there. Five more watched Vlad from behind.

If he tried it now, they would catch him before he reached his horse. His best chance was after dark. The first try must be successful, or Mircea would have Vlad in chains for the remainder of their exile.

Was it worth the risk?

Ilona was worth any risk. Vlad could possess all the kingdoms of the world, and it would mean nothing if she wasn't by his side.

"The throne will have to wait," he muttered.

Tonight.

He would go to her tonight.

CHAPTER TWENTY-TWO

THE CLANKING AND BANGING WAS COMING FROM SOMEWHERE near the stables. Andrei followed the noise to a large shed, the doors of which were open. Inside, Racoviță's carriage lay in a crumpled heap, looking somewhat like a dying animal licking its wounds.

Andrei recognized Matyas from the carriage ride. The young wheelwright was coatless despite the chilly morning air. He knelt over a bent piece of metal, attempting to pound it straight with an iron mallet. His sleeves were rolled up past his elbows, and a thin sheen of sweat glistened on his forehead.

Andrei took a step backward, not wanting to interrupt his work, but Matyas turned and smiled in recognition, lifting a hand in greeting.

"Jó reggelt!"

"Hello."

Matyas set the mallet down, stood, and closed the distance to shake Andrei's hand.

"She looks bad now," Matyas said, gesturing toward the carriage, "but I am certain I can piece her back together."

"She—I mean, the carriage . . . Will it ever be as beautiful as it was before?"

One corner of Matyas's mouth pulled down into a half frown.

"I can repair the mechanical parts," he said. "I am well trained in this. But the things that gave this carriage beauty . . . Well, that would require skills beyond my own."

Andrei looked at the carriage again. "This will keep you at Cântecul Lebedei for a long time, won't it?"

"It will take weeks to repair it properly. Maybe months. Some parts I can make on my own, but others must be sent here from Kocs. I have already sent word to Piroska about my situation. I hope she will not have her heart stolen by some other man while I am away."

"If she loves you the way it sounds like you love her, I'm sure that won't happen," Andrei said. "Any man who would try to steal her from you couldn't possibly be worthy of her."

After he said it, he almost grimaced. His own words stabbed him with guilt.

"Hopefully I am worthy of her," Matyas said. "But not to worry! Sometimes good things come out of the bad. When I am finished with the carriage, I will have enough money to marry Piroska *and* start my own carriage-building business. My father has always told me good things happen to men who work hard and stay honest."

Andrei smiled weakly.

"I must get back to work now," Matyas said. "You can watch

if you like, and hopefully your ears will not be bothered by my noise."

"Is there anything I can do to help?" Andrei asked.

"You wish to set your noble birthright aside, become a humble wheelwright like me?"

"Maybe for a day," Andrei said, managing a grin.

"*Nagyon jó!* I will be glad for the help. You can stand on one end of this bar and hold it against the earth while I pound. When it is flat, we will examine the broken axle. I may have to carve a new one. If so, your help will save me much time."

It took several minutes and much rattling of Andrei's teeth for Matyas to adequately straighten the bent carriage part. Next, Andrei helped Matyas take careful measurements of the splintered axle, and they chose a potential replacement from a pile of timbers Boyar Racoviţă had acquired from a sawmill from the forests near Bran.

"Now will be the difficult part," Matyas said. "If you wish to quit now, I will not blame you. This timber must be carved into a new axletree. It will take several days to do it right."

"I want to help," Andrei said. "Give me tools and show me how to carve."

Matyas clapped Andrei on the back jovially. "You are a man after my own heart!"

They worked for hours, taking only a few short breaks, and by the time Matyas called an end to it, Andrei's hands were riddled with splinters, and blisters nestled between his thumbs and forefingers. His arms, shoulders, and back ached in places they had never hurt before, but he felt strangely satisfied with his efforts.

"I suppose you will never wish to become a carriage builder after this," Matyas teased.

"Probably not," Andrei agreed, "but I'll still be back in the morning to help you."

"Hard work guarantees a man a beautiful wife, good fortune, and a long and healthy life. This, at least, is what my father says. If he is right, you will most definitely have all these blessings."

Andrei wasn't sure today's work was enough to earn even one of those rewards, but it was a start. And it was a way to pay the boyar for his hospitality. Andrei owed Virghiliu Racoviţa a great debt for all that he'd done for him.

Mircea's guards were pathetic. If Hunyadi decided to ambush Mircea at night, the entire camp would be dead in their sleep. Vlad was halfway around the lake before one of them finally raised the alarm.

Vlad kicked his heels into his charger's sides.

"Go, Invictus!"

The big horse laid his ears back, stretched out his neck, and hurtled through the trees.

Some of the sentries were already mounted, thundering after him, but they would never catch him. Invictus moved like lightning.

Vlad inhaled the crisp night air, reveling in the chase. Mircea was going to look like a fool when word of Vlad's escape got out.

Too bad for him. He should hire better soldiers. When Vlad was in charge, he wouldn't make the same mistake.

The nearest village was somewhere to the north. Vlad

scanned the sky until he found the *Carul Mare*—the Great Chariot—and he followed it to the bright star at the tip of the Small Chariot's pole. Those boring lessons with Lupescu were finally paying off—the one about constellations, at least. Vlad already had everything else he needed—horsemanship, cunning, determination. It was about time something from the old *tâmpit* came in handy.

The surprising ease of his escape was leaving him with more than enough time to dwell on pleasant things.

Like Ilona.

He couldn't wait to stare into her eyes again. He couldn't wait to see her excitement when he unexpectedly reappeared.

Too bad for Mircea.

Too bad for Andrei.

Neither of them could match wits with Vlad Dracula.

The tree branches closed in above him, temporarily blocking the sky. He charted his course by instinct now. His pursuers had veered off somewhere to the left.

Vlad laughed. By the time they realized their error and readjusted their course, he would be so far beyond their reach he could continue to Târgovişte at a slow canter. Hunyadi's relentless search parties were a potential obstacle, but nothing Vlad couldn't handle. They were looking for a fleeing army, not a lone prince on horseback.

The forest growth was becoming thicker and denser. Invictus snorted and slowed to a trot. Vlad didn't remember traveling through anything like this to get to the lake, but it was too dark to recognize his surroundings even if Mircea had brought them this way.

Vlad ducked to avoid low-hanging branches. He could

return the way he had just come, but that might take him straight into his pursuers' waiting arms. He steered Invictus to the right and peered blindly into the darkness.

Vlad gnashed his teeth. He was losing precious time!

What he would do for a lantern or a torch right now, but even if he had one, he couldn't light it.

Stupid Radu! This was all his fault! Putting groundless fears in Vlad's heart so he would depart before he was ready.

Some kind of path seemed to be cutting through the trees farther to the right. Vlad followed it and made quicker progress.

This was much better. If only he could catch a large enough glimpse of the sky to calculate how far he had strayed from his intended course . . . No matter. It couldn't be too far. If nothing else, it had at least served to shake off his pursuers.

Ah! A glimmer of moonlight ahead! Vlad spurred his horse forward and came out of the forest on the edge of a . . .

Lake?

Vlad swore.

"There he is!"

He was surrounded before he could collect enough of his wits to make a second dash for freedom. He reached for his sword, but they pulled him out of his saddle before he could use it.

Vlad kicked one guard in the nose, punched another in the stomach, and bit a third soldier's hand hard enough to draw blood. Eventually, they managed to wrestle him to the ground.

"Let him go."

The soldiers released him and stepped away.

Mircea.

Vlad rose to his feet, dusted himself off, and glared at his brother.

"I'm not afraid of you," Vlad snarled. "The voivode's no longer here to protect you!"

"I don't need my father to protect me from a reckless little boy."

Vlad drew his sword, and Mircea laughed.

"Laugh all you want," Vlad spat, "because when you're dead, I'll be laughing at your grave."

"Put that sword away before you hurt yourself."

It was almost the same words he had used to shame Vlad in front of the peasant girls. Vlad's vision turned red. He lunged but, miraculously, Mircea's sword was out of its scabbard, swatting his blade away.

He lunged again. Mircea blocked him easily. He slashed at Mircea's face, but his brother stepped out of range. He tried once more, and Mircea sent Vlad's sword spinning out of his hand.

The tip of Mircea's blade pricked Vlad's neck. A droplet of blood trickled down Vlad's collar.

"You'll never be a voivode," Mircea sneered. "You don't have the discipline to achieve it. Why do you think Father favors me over you?"

If the blade hadn't been at his throat . . . If there weren't six Saxons standing by to stop him . . .

"Take him to his tent," Mircea said. "Don't let him out without a direct order from me. This time I think we'll leave him in there for a week. It will give him time to dream happy dreams about ruling Wallachia. And that's as close as he'll ever come to sitting on a throne."

Mircea's mercenaries laughed.

One day Vlad would cut *them* to pieces, beginning with their tongues.

And one day Mircea would live to regret every word that had left his mouth tonight.

Mircea would fade into oblivion, but Vlad Dracula's name would live forever.

CHAPTER TWENTY-THREE

SHE WISHED SHE KNEW HOW ANDREI GOT OUT OF LESSONS with Master Sîrbu. He vanished every morning after breakfast, and she didn't see him again until after sunset. Magda's father didn't seem bothered by it; Ilona wondered if he even knew.

Ilona hadn't spoken with Andrei since their meeting at the little church house, and, for some unfathomable reason, it bothered her.

"Are you not feeling well, Lady Ilona? Or am I simply boring you?"

She jerked her head up; she'd forgotten she was in the middle of one of Master Sîrbu's lessons. She wasn't sleeping well at night. Possibly because she wondered if Andrei was purposely avoiding her.

"Lady Ilona? I asked if you weren't feeling well."

"I'm all right," Ilona mumbled. "I just have a headache. And I feel a little dizzy."

Magda's father was paying Master Sîrbu to continue

teaching Ilona, Magda, Andrei, and Gizela here at Cântecul Lebedei. Even a Transylvanian invasion wasn't enough to get any of them out of lessons.

"Maybe you should walk the halls and rest your eyes for a few minutes," Master Sîrbu said. "Ovid's poetry can wait."

"My head hurts, too," Gizela piped up. "I think I need to rest my eyes, too."

The tutor glared at Gizela. "Your head hurts," he said, "from lack of proper intellectual stimulation. You spend too much time searching for ways to get out of your studies and too little applying yourself to them."

Gizela gave him an exaggerated pout, and, fearing that Master Sîrbu would change his mind about letting her leave, Ilona slipped out of the room. It was rare for Master Sîrbu to show compassion. She wasn't about to let this opportunity slip away.

She didn't know how long she could miss lessons before her diligent tutor sent Gizela or Magda after her, but she decided to use the time to search for Andrei. She pulled her skirt above her ankles and took the stairs two at a time. She exited the house, deciding to start at the wooden chapel. If he wasn't there . . . Well . . . What, then?

Ilona frowned and shook her head.

Why did she care so much? It was none of her business where Andrei went when he disappeared. And yet—

A crisp clank of metal striking metal distracted her. She paused a moment before moving toward the sound. A young man's shadow stretched past the shed's corner. The shadow swung a hammer and the metal clanked again.

Andrei.

He didn't see her as she rounded the corner. He held a

chisel against a long wooden beam. Wood shavings blanketed the earth around his feet. He was attempting to carve a square notch into the beam. Large- and small-toothed saws, broad- and narrow-tipped chisels, oak-handled lathes, and iron hammers rested on the earth around him. Carriage parts littered the earth farther beyond him. He chewed a corner of his lower lip as he prepared to carve another curl of wood out of the beam.

He must have been at this task all morning—his coat was draped over a stack of lumber and his linen tunic was damp with perspiration. Sawdust dusted his hair and clung to his muscular forearms.

Ilona took another step toward him, and something crunched under her foot.

Andrei spun. They stared at each other.

"Bună dimineaţa," Ilona said.

"Hello," he answered.

She stared at Andrei's carved beam, felt inexplicably uncomfortable, and lowered her eyes.

"I . . . heard the noise and . . ."

Andrei stared at his boots. Why did their conversations always begin so awkwardly?

"You're rebuilding Boyar Racoviţă's carriage," Ilona said.

"Helping with it," Andrei sheepishly admitted.

Ilona looked around.

"Matyas went with the boyar to Târgovişte to search for special pieces," Andrei said.

"Oh."

More discomfort. More wondering what to say.

"I want to pay the boyar for taking me into his home." Andrei stared at the chisel and the hammer in his hands.

"This"—he shifted his gaze to his work—"is a start, but it's not enough. I'll do more."

"I don't think the boyar expects repayment," Ilona said. "He's not that kind of man."

"I know, but I *want* to do this. Even if he expects nothing in return, I can't eat his food, live in his home, and accept his protection and do nothing. I don't know how to explain this, but I don't want to be . . . powerless."

He didn't have to explain. Ilona knew that feeling. She struggled with it every day.

"What can I do to help?"

Andrei gave her a blank stare. "What?"

"What can I do to help with the carriage?"

He looked at the strewn pieces around him. "This is strenuous work," he said. "I don't think—"

"You don't think a girl could handle it?"

"No—I mean . . . I just . . . This isn't something that would be done by a lady of the court."

"I'm no longer a lady of the court," Ilona said. "I'm not even sure I'm still a grand boyar's daughter. How can I help?"

Andrei shrugged. "I suppose I can show you what Matyas needs us to do."

He handed his tools to her. They were warm from his grip.

"We're carving a new axletree," he said.

"What's an axletree?"

Andrei thought a moment, shrugged again, and laughed. "I have no idea, but Matyas knows, and he marked where the wood needs to be chiseled away. Here, here, and here."

"So how do I hold this? How do I carve?"

"You hold the chisel at an angle."

Ilona tilted the chisel, looked at him, and raised her eyebrows.

"No, a little more of an angle. No, if you tilt it that far, you'll injure your hand."

He moved his hands toward the tools. His fingers hovered over hers, trembling, not quite touching.

"Do . . . do you mind?"

She smiled. Vlad wouldn't have asked permission. There was something appealing about Andrei's hesitance.

"You can show me," she said. "I don't mind."

His fingers closed over hers, and now *her* hands trembled.

"More like this," he said. He carefully wrapped his fingers around the hand that gripped the hammer. "And now you'll strike the back of the chisel so that it curls off a slice of wood like this."

He helped her strike the chisel. It was an awkward strike, and it didn't remove much wood, but she gave him a grateful smile. Or was it a flirtatious one?

What was she *doing*?

"I think I've almost got this," she said. "Can you show me again?"

"Lady Csáki!"

Andrei released her hands, and they both whirled toward Master Sîrbu's voice. He was staring at them as if he had just witnessed something scandalous, but rather than feeling embarrassment, Ilona felt . . . annoyed?

"You told me you had a headache, that you weren't feeling well. Then I glance out the window and see you coming . . . here." He looked at Andrei, fidgeted a moment, and gave Andrei a stiff bow. "Excuse my interruption, Prince Andrei, but I was under the impression that you, too, would be receiving lessons from me."

"I usually study battle strategy and swordsmanship this time of the morning," Andrei said. "Since those lessons have been disrupted I've been doing this instead."

Sîrbu straightened his collar. "Of course, as a prince that is your prerogative. But as for you, Lady Ilona—" The tutor glared at her. "This . . . *manual labor* . . . is completely unacceptable. I must insist that you return with me at once."

She wanted to refuse. She was tired of being told what she must do, but Andrei looked uncomfortable, and the shadow of her "private" encounters with Vlad still hung over her.

"Of course, Master Sîrbu," she said. "I think the fresh air has helped my headache. I can think of nothing I'd rather be doing now than studying grammar with you."

The hint of a smile flickered at the corners of Andrei's mouth, and Sîrbu's scowl deepened. Ilona, however, kept her tone so respectful that her tutor had difficulty determining whether or not sarcasm was indeed intended.

Ilona turned to Andrei and gave a slight bow.

"Thank you, Prince Andrei, for showing me the important work you're doing."

Andrei returned her bow, and they grinned at each other before Ilona and the miffed tutor walked away.

She would have to come up with more excuses to spend time with Andrei Muşat. She could be her genuine self when she was with him. That was a precious gift in a world where a boyar's daughter was either a playing piece on a political game board or a glass ornament on someone's family tree.

From now on, she refused to be either of those things.

Vlad stepped out of his tent. The soldiers Mircea had assigned to watch him stood and marched stiffly toward him.

"Where are you going?" one of them demanded.

"I can't stay in this tent for everything," Vlad snarled. "Nature calls."

The soldier who'd spoken narrowed his eyes. "Nature called less than an hour ago."

"I don't control nature. It's calling again. You can either escort me to the trees or I can relieve myself on your campfire."

The soldiers glared at Vlad, then glanced at each other, silently debating whose turn it was to play nursemaid. After a moment one of them let his shoulders sag and glared at Vlad again, gesturing stiffly toward the forest.

"No tricks. If you try to run, I have permission to hurt you."

Vlad smirked. "I'm counting on it."

The soldier's scowl deepened, and he rolled his shoulders and cracked his knuckles. "You're a smart one, are you? Maybe both of us should come and watch you do your business."

"Maybe you should. It will take more than one of you to stop me if I decide to take a midnight stroll." Vlad smirked again and walked toward the trees. The soldier nodded at his comrade and both of them followed.

"Does Mircea pay you extra to be my babysitters?"

The soldiers stiffened but said nothing.

"Or maybe he pays you less. Maybe he makes you sit around watching me all night because he knows neither of you would be useful in an actual fight."

They were both angry now. That was good. It was integral to Vlad's plan.

"I think I'll be going now," he said when they reached the tree line.

One of the soldiers snorted in amusement. "We'd like to see you try."

"Is that a challenge?"

"Call it what you want."

"I accept."

Vlad turned and darted into the night. He didn't get far, but he didn't expect to; his intentions weren't to escape. In a matter of moments, the soldiers tackled him to the forest floor, and in the brief scuffle that followed, one hit Vlad in the face, cracking his lip.

"You're going to regret that later," Vlad snarled, spitting blood at the soldiers' feet.

They laughed at him, roughly grasped his arms, and dragged him back to his tent. Vlad didn't bother to resist.

They wouldn't be laughing when they realized that in the scuffle, Vlad had stolen the tallest one's dagger and tucked it beneath his perspiration-dampened tunic.

Boyar Racoviță motioned to his servant and the man stepped out, swinging the great hall's doors shut behind him. The boyar pulled three chairs up to the fire—the same way the White Knight had done at the Curtea Domnească—seated himself, and waited for Andrei and Ilona to do the same.

Everything about the boyar's demeanor was warm and friendly, but Andrei still fought to repress a shiver. Ilona looked as nervous as Andrei felt; she gripped her chair so tightly her fingers were white, and Andrei felt an urge to grasp one of her hands.

He restrained himself mostly because the boyar was watching, but also out of loyalty to Vlad. Despite the desire to respect Vlad's feelings for Ilona, what he and Ilona were about to ask still felt traitorous. Andrei tried to tell himself he was only being supportive of Ilona—only showing friendship—but every time he was near Ilona Csáki his heart beat with something stronger than friendship.

"The two of you wished to speak with me in private," the boyar said, "and now we're alone. What brings such worry to your faces? How can I ease your fears?"

Ilona's white fingers twitched. She looked at Andrei, and he swallowed hard. He swallowed again before speaking.

"We want to talk to you about your carriage."

"Marriage?"

"No!" Andrei blushed and shook his head. "Your *carriage*."

"Slavă cerului! You had me worried. What's wrong with the carriage? Do you and Matyas need more parts?"

Andrei gulped and shook his head. "No, Your Excellency. This . . . this is about something else."

Ilona, whose face was also bright red, jumped in to speak for herself at this point. "I want to help Matyas and Andrei repair your carriage. I want to take time away from studying with Master Sîrbu to restore it to what it once was."

The boyar stroked his bushy mustache and pondered this a moment.

"I'm of course humbled by your generous offer, Lady Ilona, but as to whether or not such a thing would be appropriate—"

"I would of course only help when Matyas is there," Ilona said.

The boyar smiled. "I have no worries about your or Andrei's

behavior around each other. Rather, I'm considering how it might appear for a grand boyar's daughter to be engaged in hard, coarse labor."

Ilona leaned forward, eager now. "My part would be to repair the mural on the carriage ceiling. If you can supply me with paint . . . If you will trust me to make the attempt . . ."

She saw the look of doubt on the boyar's face and slumped a little.

"Ilona's a skilled artist," Andrei chimed in. "If you saw what she's capable of, maybe you'd give her a chance." He gestured toward the sketchbook on Ilona's lap.

Ilona hesitantly held the book toward Boyar Racoviță.

"What's this?"

"My sketchbook," she said. "I've been practicing for years."

The boyar took the sketchbook and opened it. His eyes widened as he thumbed through its pages.

Andrei noticed that Ilona was chewing her bottom lip. He extended his hand and gave hers a squeeze, but he quickly pulled back when the boyar looked up at them again.

"These images are stunning," Racoviță said. "You drew them?"

Ilona nodded.

"Astounding! Simply astounding! But to sketch is one thing and to paint is another . . . Have you ever used a paintbrush on canvas?"

Ilona lowered her eyes and shook her head. "No, only ink on parchment. But I could practice first. I could let you see my work and decide before you let me touch the carriage."

The boyar stroked his mustache again, staring at the ceiling. "I suppose you won't actually be painting an original scene," he said, thinking aloud, "simply repairing what's already there . . . It would cost more than I can justify to recommission the original artist. If you think you're up to the task, I suppose we could start with a small corner of the painting and see what you can accomplish."

Andrei couldn't suppress a grin. Neither could Ilona.

The boyar saw this and smiled with them. "I'll procure the paints," he said, "and I'll speak with Master Sîrbu."

He returned Ilona's sketchbook, then stood, stretched, and yawned.

"It has been a long few days," he said, "and this old man is exhausted. If you don't mind, I think I'll retire for the evening. Don't stay up too late."

Andrei and Ilona watched him leave, neither of them speaking until long after the hall's huge doors swung shut behind him.

The fire crackled and popped. Somehow their hands wandered across the empty space that separated them until their fingers touched.

"Thank you," Ilona said. "Thank you for supporting me."

Andrei nodded.

"Do you think I can do it?" Ilona whispered. "Do you think Magda's father will be pleased with my work?"

"I think he'll believe you trained in Italy with the masters. I think your work will be better than the original."

Ilona's face glowed, and Andrei summoned the courage to close his fingers around hers. Prickly warmth spread up his arm. He knew she was only holding his hand out of gratitude, but he decided to enjoy this moment while it lasted. He was a traitor, but he couldn't help himself.

CHAPTER TWENTY-FOUR

Blood dripped from the dagger. Vlad stooped and wiped it once, twice in the grass. The skyline was slowly shifting hues from midnight black to sapphire blue. He needed to get back inside the tent before it grew light enough for one of the camp's sleepy guards to see him.

He reentered the tent at the spot where he'd carefully dug a trench earlier that night. Once inside, he squatted in darkness, pushing dirt back into place and listening to his heart hammer.

Now he waited, panting. He couldn't wait too long but he also couldn't initiate the next step too soon. It needed to be a little lighter outside. He hugged himself and shivered. One minute, two minutes . . . He lost track of the minutes, but finally he knew it was time.

"Help!" he shouted. "*Ajută-mă!* They're trying to kill me!"

It took a moment for his guards to enter—longer than he wanted—but when they did, he was ready for them.

He tackled the first the same way they had tackled him last night. He punched hard. He fought as if he was fighting for his life. The second soldier tried to help the first, and he kicked him in the groin.

"Help!" Vlad cried again. "Someone help me!"

His lip was cracked again; fresh blood trickled down his chin. A fist struck his cheekbone just beneath his eye. What was taking Mircea's other soldiers so long?

Finally he heard it: pounding footsteps. One of his guards tried to escape the fray, but he grabbed the man's ankle and dragged him back to the earth. His guards sensed that they'd somehow been duped, he saw it on their faces, but it was now too late for them. One of Mircea's captains and two other soldiers pushed their way into Vlad's small tent.

"What's going on here?"

"They came in and tried to kill me!" Vlad said. "Don't let them escape! Get Mircea!"

He was proud of himself. His terror sounded real. All five soldiers looked at one another. Vlad's two prison keepers looked confused, but not confused enough.

"Didn't you hear me?" Vlad cried. "Seize them and find Mircea!"

The captain was reluctant but he nodded to the two soldiers who had entered with him.

"You don't believe this devil child, do you?" one of Vlad's guards protested as another soldier seized his arm.

"He tried to stab me!" Vlad exclaimed, and he held his open palm forward. An angry slice ran across it, and it dripped fresh blood. "With that dagger!"

All eyes turned to the weapon beside his bedroll. The captain stooped and picked it up.

"It must have fallen from the sheath when he attacked us!" the taller guard exclaimed, staring with horror at his empty dagger sheath. "I didn't draw it. I—"

"We'll let Prince Mircea decide," the captain interrupted. His forehead was now creased with worry. "Bring them outside," he told the soldiers who had accompanied him.

"It's a trick!" one of Vlad's two victims muttered. "He's full of tricks!"

Vlad followed the soldiers out of the tent and pushed past them to walk beside the captain. "I want those traitors hanged!" he said. "I demand to speak to my brother now!"

A crowd was gathering. Soldiers. Servants. Vasilisa and her ladies-in-waiting.

"What's happening?" the cneajna asked.

Vlad ignored her. She would find out soon enough.

The captain stopped outside Mircea's tent. "My prince?" he called.

No answer.

"Your Highness?"

The creases lining the captain's forehead deepened. Hesitantly, he parted the tent flap, then gasped.

"Prince Mircea!" the captain cried as he dashed into the tent.

"What's wrong?" Vlad demanded, following him inside.

The captain knelt beside Mircea's body. Blood stained Mircea's shirt, his bedroll, the pillows. Vlad stared for several moments—cold, numb, hollow. Then a woman screamed.

Vasilisa stood at the entrance, staring past him.

Vlad scowled and pushed her away from the tent. "You shouldn't be here. You shouldn't see this."

Gladium fuisse permissum.

Wallachia's throne was Vlad's.

And with it, Ilona.

Mircea had never deserved either of them.

CHAPTER TWENTY-FIVE

Summer 1443

"You paint as well as you draw. Is there anything you can't do?"

Ilona lowered the brush and smiled over her shoulder at Andrei. "There are a great many things I can't do, and I'm not half as good at this as I'd like to be. I'm only repairing what the real artist already created."

Andrei shook his head. "You're better than you want to admit. The way you've mixed the colors, how you blend them with the brush . . . I can hardly tell where the original artist's work ends and yours begins. There's more to that than simply repairing what's here."

Ilona blushed. "Thank you." She looked at the painting again. "I hope I've done it right. I don't want to let Magda's father down. He didn't have to take Gizela and me in. It could have put his family in danger. It probably has."

"No more than taking me in has done, but I think if danger was coming, it would have already arrived. We're not only under the boyar's protection. We're also under the protection of the White Knight. No one is going to risk crossing him."

Ilona nodded, but she allowed a slight frown to touch the corners of her lips. She remembered the sound of shattering glass, the low thrum of a feathered bolt vibrating in her door. Someone had dared risk the voivode's ire. What was to stop them from risking the White Knight's?

She realized that Andrei was still watching her, and she forced herself to smile before turning her eyes back to the painted ceiling. Andrei tilted his own head back to examine it with her.

"Those girls in the long white dresses . . . Do you think they're Greeks or Romans?" Andrei asked.

"Neither," Ilona answered. "They're Transylvanian. They're dancing to honor the 'gentle fairies.' This is a scene from Midsummer's Eve—the Sânziene festival in its final hours."

"Sânziene," Andrei said. "They celebrate it here in the villages. Something to do with a couple of girls getting possessed by evil spirits and fighting each other with scythes while they do the 'Wicked Fairy' dance."

Ilona shuddered. "That's horrible! It's nothing like that in Transylvania."

"How do they celebrate it there?"

"I've never seen it myself," Ilona admitted. "My father thinks it's a waste of time. But at Alba Iulia where my mother grew up, the most beautiful girls from each village dress all in white and spend the day gathering flowers in the forests and fields. They're not allowed to be seen by any boys until the end of the day.

"When nightfall comes, they twist their flowers into

255

garlands and wear them in their hair." She pointed at the painting. "Just like these girls have done. Do you see the tiny yellow blossoms?"

"I see them," Andrei said. "So is that it? It's just a flower-picking festival?"

Ilona scowled and Andrei grinned teasingly. During their time working together, he had slowly grown comfortable enough around her to be himself. She liked this version of Andrei. She enjoyed spending time with him.

"It isn't *just* a flower-picking festival," she said, pushing his arm playfully. "The best part doesn't come until later—after they've returned to the village. It's then that they dance around the bonfire to receive the gentle fairies' blessings for the next year's harvest. That's when each girl finds her sweetheart and dances with him. It's a special night. A night of powerful magic. The best night to fall in love."

"The last part sounds nice," Andrei said, "but I don't see any boys in this painting."

"That's because the girls haven't come back to the village yet. The gentle fairies don't like to be seen by boys. If they catch a boy watching them, they turn him blind, drive him mad, or make him go lame."

"That doesn't sound very gentle."

Ilona elbowed Andrei in the ribs.

"Ouch!" he said. "You're not very gentle either!"

They laughed until Ilona spotted another damaged portion of the painting and turned her attention back to her work. This time it was part of a wreath in one of the painted girls' hair. Ilona switched brushes and dabbed carefully to restore the blossoms.

"Sânziene," Andrei murmured. "I've just realized what the festival's name means. Holy fairies."

"That's where the festival and the flowers got their name," Ilona confirmed. "From the fairies. The flowers are also named after them, and they're my favorite flowers. Bright yellow is my second favorite color."

"What's your most favorite?"

"Green. But not any green. Green like the needles on the pines in the deepest part of the forest."

"That's a pretty color," Andrei said.

"And what's your favorite color?"

"Black."

"That's . . . an interesting choice. Is there a reason why it's your favorite?"

"I like it because it's quiet," Andrei explained. "Like a shadow. Like the darkest night sky. Without black you couldn't see the stars or the glowing blue of dawn. The best kind of black is smooth and deep and silky like . . . like your hair."

He looked away, embarrassed.

"When you describe it like that," Ilona said, "it makes it sound beautiful."

Andrei risked a brief glance into her eyes, but his gaze quickly shifted to her nose.

"You've got something on your face," he said. "Right there . . ."

Ilona wrinkled her brow and touched the side of her nose.

"No. A little higher. Here."

He placed his finger against her nose and brought it back smeared with yellow paint.

He winced.

"I think I've made it worse. I'm sorry, I'll find a damp rag."

His face was so close to hers. They were staring into each other's eyes.

They leaned closer, and Ilona held her breath.

When Vlad kissed her, it had been jarring, but she knew this kiss would be different. Ilona *wanted* this kiss. She was surprised by how badly she wanted it.

She closed her eyes, leaned toward him . . . and Andrei blinked and pulled back, an alarmed look on his face.

"The . . . the rag," he stammered. "I-I'd better go get it before . . . before the paint dries on your face."

He exited the carriage so hastily it rocked after his departure. Ilona exhaled and slumped against the leather seat. Her flesh tingled, her insides tied in knots.

What had she done?

Made a fool of herself, that's what. Now she could never look Andrei in the eyes again. She had secretly hoped he returned some of her feelings, but his hasty retreat seemed to prove otherwise.

Ilona brushed her hair forward to hide her face. If she could slip into the painting and hide forever in its surreal landscape, she would. Over the past few weeks, she'd begun to think Wallachia was a place that might actually hold happiness for her.

Apparently she was wrong.

"Who will protect us? Who will take care of us?"

Vlad stopped pacing to glare at Vasilisa, somehow resisting the overwhelming urge to slap her.

"*I* will!" he snarled. "I'm the crown prince! The responsibility falls on *me*!"

Vasilisa dabbed at her eyes with the handkerchief Raluca had provided and hiccuped between sobs. Since the discovery of Mircea's assassination, Raluca had remained at the cneajna's side. She stared at Vlad in a way that made him uncomfortable, so he turned his back on both of them.

"Captain Lutz!" he barked.

"Yes, Your Highness?"

"Get the map from Mircea's tent and bring it to mine."

Lutz bowed and marched away. Vlad headed for his tent, trying not to glance at the corpses swinging in the trees. His former guards.

This was their own fault—and Mircea's. If they had treated him like the prince he was, there would have been no need to kill them. Their deaths were necessary. God would forgive him; when he was Wallachia's voivode, he would build the largest cathedrals Wallachia had ever seen. But he first had to defeat Hunyadi and reclaim his father's throne.

Ilona . . . He couldn't stand being separated from her. The blood on his hands, the things he had done . . . he could forget all of it once she was in his arms again.

He entered his tent and started pacing, but the tent was too small. It stifled him and only stoked his anger. He needed a bigger one—one like Mircea's—but he couldn't claim that; the mere thought of entering it again curdled his stomach.

Lutz approached Vlad's tent and coughed so Vlad would know he was there.

"Come in."

Lutz entered with the map in his hand and with lowered eyes.

Did he suspect Vlad of killing Mircea? Did others in the camp harbor that same suspicion?

"It's time to go south to the border," Vlad said, "but Mircea didn't tell me where my father will meet us. Show me on the map."

"You know about the plan?" the captain asked, surprised.

"Of course I know!" Vlad snapped. "I'm also the voivode's son! Someone had to know in case something like *this* happened to Mircea!"

There it was again, that look on Lutz's face. The quickly diverted eyes.

But then the captain nodded. He looked around for a place to put the map, and finally spread it out across the dirt floor. "Here," he said. "Near Giurgiu."

"How long will it take us to get there?"

Lutz thought a moment. "A day. Perhaps two. But only if our advance scouts don't encounter Hunyadi's patrols. He seems to have made it a priority to capture the House of Drăculeşti."

"I would expect nothing less," Vlad said, "but we'll show him how costly that can be."

Lutz shifted uncomfortably. "Our forces are small, Your Highness. Our best strategy is to remain unseen until your father regroups with the sultan's army."

"That was Mircea's strategy," Vlad said coldly. "Not mine."

The captain's discomfort now showed on his face. "If I may be so bold, Your Highness, direct confrontation can only lead to your capture and our destruction."

"Who said anything about 'direct confrontation'?" Vlad asked.

Lutz scowled. "What are you proposing, my prince?"

"An ambush. Here in the swamplands." He placed a finger on the map where one of Hunyadi's patrols had earlier been seen. "We strike while they're spread thin and move on before they have time to strike back. I want to leave a message, something that will strike terror in their hearts."

Vlad stared at the captain. "Do I have your loyalty?"

Lutz nodded, but he didn't look happy.

"Prepare your men," Vlad ordered. "We're leaving now."

After handing her a wet rag, Andrei had made an excuse about needing to search for a misplaced tool. Ilona didn't see him again until the evening meal at the great hall, and neither of them added much to the usual dinner table conversation.

She was glad he couldn't see her now, tears blurring her eyes as she climbed the stairs. Her world was black, but it wasn't the beautiful black Andrei liked. This was a thick, tar-like blackness that was cold like an icy lake.

She came to an abrupt halt as she approached her bedroom door, stepped back, and wiped her eyes. Something hung from the doorknob. Flowers . . .

"Sânziene," she whispered.

But how did they get here? It took her only a moment to figure it out.

Andrei.

So that was why she hadn't seen him all day. He'd been out gathering these for her and had placed them here where she would find them. Ilona touched the flowers, a happy sob bubbling up in her chest.

He felt it, too. He felt the same dangerous, wonderful, confusing emotions she was feeling.

Suddenly her world was filled with endless, unimaginable possibilities.

CHAPTER TWENTY-SIX

"You carved that?" Magda asked, dumbfounded.

Andrei hunched his shoulders. "With Matyas's help."

"It's wonderful! A master wheelwright couldn't have done it any better."

Andrei blushed.

"He also carved the rear axle and the replacement spokes," Ilona said. "Matyas says Andrei is more than a wagon builder. He's an artist!"

"You're the artist," Andrei mumbled, his cheeks burning hotter. "You fixed the painting."

"I helped what was already there. You re-created what was missing."

Magda laughed at them. "The two of you should get together with Papa. Between the three of you, you could create the most amazing art."

"Your father is an artist?" Ilona asked.

"He's an artist like Andrei: too modest. Won't admit how

good he is. I should show you his creations. Do you want to see?"

"We would love to!" Ilona replied. She grabbed Andrei's hand and pulled him along behind her.

He still had work to finish on the carriage, but he supposed it could wait. Ilona, Magda, and Gizela laughed and chatted on the way back into the manor. Distracted by their conversation, Ilona let go of Andrei's hand, and he became a silent shadow trailing after them.

"In here," Magda said, taking them into a room Andrei had passed a hundred times but never really noticed until today. "Don't let Papa know I showed you. He would never forgive me. Like I said, he's very modest."

The room was dark; Magda pulled back a drape and flooded the room with light. The floor's tiles were mottled with bright splashes of dried paint. Tables crowded the walls and paintings crowded the tables.

"Papa loves to dabble in artwork of all kinds," Magda said. "These are his portraits. I think he's rather good."

"Very good," Ilona said in a hushed voice, leaning forward so she could more closely examine one of the paintings. It was an image of a young noblewoman, sitting on a divan with a child on her lap.

"My sister," Magda said.

"You told me about her," Ilona said. "Her name is Călțuna, right?"

Magda nodded.

"Who is the little boy on her lap?" Gizela asked.

"Her son."

"What's his name?"

"Vlad."

Gizela giggled. "He looks like Vlad Dracula and has the same name." She turned to Ilona. "Don't you think he looks just like Prince Vlad?"

"Actually," Ilona said, squinting, "he does look rather like our Vlad."

Magda smiled nervously, turned the picture around, and pointed to the other side of the room. "Come and see Papa's wood carvings. They're much better than the paintings."

Andrei remained where he was, staring at the back of the portrait.

Vlad . . .

Was it mere coincidence, or . . .

"How old is your nephew?" he asked.

"What?"

Magda looked at him—saw him staring at the turned painting—and anxiously twisted the silver bracelet on her left wrist.

"I was just wondering how old your nephew is."

"He's . . . about nineteen now. It's an old painting."

"Nineteen?" Gizela laughed. "He's older than *you*!"

"Yes," Magda said. "It's a long story. Let's look at the wood carvings before Papa finds us in here and shoos us out."

The boyar's wood carvings sat in a corner on a triangular table. Magda and Ilona crowded close. Andrei walked slowly away from the portrait of Călțuna and her child named Vlad and stood on his toes to look over the girls' shoulders.

"This one's my favorite," Magda said. "A Russian boyar on a horse. And look at this!" She held up three links of a chain carved from a single piece of wood.

So detailed. So perfect. A cold chill crept up Andrei's spine.

"Papa can carve *anything*," Magda said. "He once carved a little centaur for me. And the wooden dolls! I must show you the wooden dolls! They're up in my room."

The girls moved away from the table, but Andrei again lingered behind, examining the boyar's handiwork. A tiny elephant, a fierce janissary, a wooden bird in a wooden cage . . . The boyar really could carve anything. Anything he could imagine or see.

"Are you coming, Andrei?" Ilona said.

Andrei blinked and turned.

"I told you it was wonderful," Magda said, "but we really need to go before he catches us here."

She closed the drapes, turned her sister's portrait outward again, and led Ilona, Andrei, and Gizela out the door.

Gizela was right. Călțuna's son did look a lot like Vlad. So much, in fact, that they could have been half brothers . . .

It couldn't be.

Not Virghiliu Racoviță. Not the voivode's firmest supporter.

But then, Andrei had also thought Ilona's father was absolutely loyal to the voivode until he found the wax impression of the voivode's key at Csáki's manor.

Andrei's thoughts went back to the conversation he'd had with Vlad several months ago. *A boyar's daughter . . . An illegitimate son named Vlad . . .*

A son who was a monk. A *călugăr*. Vlad the Monk. *Vlad Călugărul.*

VC.

A marrow-deep chill traveled the length of Andrei's spine.

He finally understood the clues from the boyar's paper. And his heart sank as he realized what they were telling him.

Vlad didn't know why he hadn't already killed him. Maybe because the soldier was young. Barely older than a boy. The other survivors—there were three of them—were also young. They knelt, hands bound behind their backs. Their eyes, like the youngest soldier's, bulged with terror as they stared at the three sharpened poles set along the path.

"I'm going to let one of you live so you can deliver a message to Hunyadi," he said, pacing before them. "I want him and any of the Dăneşti who think it's safe to claim Wallachia's throne to know it belongs to the House of Drăculeşti forever."

Vlad stopped in front of the youngest soldier, placed the tip of his sword beneath the boy's chin, and pressed upward to make him look into his eyes.

"What's your name?"

The boy swallowed before answering. "Ambrus."

"Ambrus?" Vlad smirked. "Your name means 'immortal.'"

"Yes."

"How immortal are you feeling today?"

The soldier's eyes involuntarily flickered toward the sharpened poles. He swallowed again. He was clearly feeling anything but immortal.

"It's called impalement," Vlad said. "The Ottomans use it to punish deserters and thieves." He lowered his sword and paced again. "You're thieves. You came to help Hunyadi and Basarab steal what rightfully belongs to me."

Vlad stopped and stared at his prisoners again.

"Three stakes," he said. "Three examples."

He turned back to Ambrus.

"Tell Hunyadi what lies in store for the House of the Dragon's enemies. Tell him Vlad Dracula is coming to reclaim his father's throne."

Two soldiers hoisted Ambrus to his feet.

"Run," Vlad growled.

Ambrus did as commanded. He didn't look back.

Not even when his comrades' agonized screams rang shrilly through the trees.

CHAPTER TWENTY-SEVEN

IT TOOK TIME TO REPAIR VIRGHILIU RACOVIȚĂ'S CARRIAGE, BUT not as much time as Andrei hoped it would. Too soon, both the artistic and mechanical repairs were completed. Still, he couldn't help but get caught up in the boyar's "carriage" celebration.

And a celebration it was! Although midsummer had arrived, temperatures were still mild in the evening, so Boyar Racoviță gathered the manor staff, the local peasants, and his family for outdoor festivities. Food-laden tables were placed in a circle around the painstakingly restored carriage. A peasant band added to the merriment with the music of their lute-like *cobze*, their panpipes, and their elderwood flutes.

Andrei stood by one of the tables, watching the laughing boyar dance a *Sîrba* with Lady Racoviță, several farmers, and the farmers' wives. On the other side of the circle, Ilona stood with Magda and Gizela, watching the dancers and clapping to the music's rhythm. Her eyes sparkled. Andrei had always known she was pretty, but he never realized how truly beautiful she was until tonight.

Ilona noticed him watching her, and their eyes locked. He started to smile, but his smile turned into wide-eyed bewilderment when a strong hand grasped his arm and pulled him into the dizzying circle.

"Don't just stand there wistfully looking at her!" Boyar Racoviță bellowed. "Join in! Dance with the girl!"

Flustered, Andrei found himself whirling toward Ilona. The jolly boyar waved her forward, and she quickly stepped into the empty space next to Andrei. The next thing he knew, she was holding his hand. They looked at each other, and she grinned. Andrei wasn't much of a dancer, but Ilona was. He relied on her to guide him through the steps, and they danced until they were out of breath.

Somehow they eventually found themselves away from the cheerful crowd, walking under a starlit sky. They were holding hands. Andrei didn't know how that happened, either, but he wasn't unhappy about it.

"Magda's father knows how to throw a party, doesn't he?" Ilona said.

"Yes," Andrei agreed. "I think this was the best one I've ever seen."

"I wish every night could be like this." There was a wistful note in her voice. "I wish life could go on like this forever and never change."

"Me too," Andrei whispered.

Ilona stopped walking, gripping his hand tighter. "Do you think the voivode will ever come back?"

"I don't know."

"I don't want him to," she said. "Is that wrong of me?"

Andrei hesitated before answering. It also felt wrong to him and yet he wished for the same thing. "There's been news from the south," he said, "that the voivode displeased the sultan and has been cast into an Ottoman prison. That's all I've heard. It might not even be true, but if it is . . ."

"If he doesn't come back . . . ," Ilona said, "I won't have to marry Mircea. But if he does . . ." She shook her head. "If he does, I *won't* marry Mircea. If he returns, I'll run away!"

She released Andrei's hand and twisted Mircea's betrothal ring off her finger. She examined the ring a moment, as if not quite sure what to do with it, then dropped it into the dry leaves at her feet.

"I'll go with you," Andrei said quietly.

Ilona took his hand again, her fingers tightening around his.

"It won't matter if none of them come back," she said. "I have to believe God won't let them. It's the only way I can have peace of mind. But I don't want to talk about them anymore. Let's talk about us. What are we going to do now that the carriage is finished?"

"Boyar Racoviţă will probably want you to go back to your studies. He's already talked about finding someone who's good with a sword to start tutoring me."

"Why do my studies have to be confined to a library? Why do I have to spend my time with a tutor who knows less about mathematics and sciences than me?"

"Maybe you don't," Andrei said. "The boyar isn't like other noblemen. Maybe he'll let you learn the way you learn best—by reading, observing, and sketching."

Ilona laughed bitterly and shook her head. "No man would agree to that."

"I would. Maybe he would, too. You can't know unless you ask. Maybe he would agree to mornings with Master Sîrbu and afternoons studying the birds around his manor. He's already impressed by your sketchbook. We could learn together. You, Magda, Gizela, and me."

Some of his enthusiasm spread to Ilona, and a smile once more illuminated her face.

"I've been wanting to explore the woods near the monastery," Ilona said. "Magda says there are several owls nesting in the area."

Her smile faded when she noticed the troubled look on Andrei's face. "What's wrong?"

"What?" He glanced at her and shook his head. "Oh . . . It's nothing."

"It's not nothing. What is it, Andrei? You can tell me."

What could he say? That another heir to Wallachia's throne might be hiding in that monastery? That her father had put her in more danger than she could possibly imagine?

"It's nothing. Really."

Ilona frowned. She clearly didn't believe him, but she didn't press the matter.

"I would love to explore the woods near the monastery," Andrei said. "We can find out what kinds of owls live there. We can learn all about them."

Ilona's smile returned. "You'll talk to Magda's father with me?"

"Yes. Together we'll convince him."

Ilona wrapped her arms around him. "Thank you, Andrei. Thank you for being my friend and my ally."

The voivode looked haggard as Vlad rode toward him, thinner than he remembered. His father's eyes flickered away from him to search the faces of the other mounted men in Vlad's party. When the prince dismounted and bowed, his father didn't even greet him.

"Mircea . . . ," the voivode said instead, his voice thick and shaky. "Where is he? At the camp with the family?"

"Mircea's dead."

Finally, Vlad's father looked at him, but the voivode's eyes were glazed and he seemed to be gazing right through Vlad.

"Dead?"

"Yes."

The voivode closed his eyes, and didn't open them again for several long moments.

"Did you find my son's murderers?"

My son. As if Mircea were the voivode's *only* son.

Certainly the only son who mattered.

"I found them," Vlad said. "I executed them."

"Good . . . Good . . ."

The voivode stared into space. Even the stoic, straight-faced janissaries flanking him showed signs of awkward discomfort as the voivode's silence stretched out longer and longer.

"There are others to be punished," Vlad said. "Hunyadi, the Dăneşti clan, the boyars who support them."

The voivode stared blankly at Vlad, then blinked and nodded. "Yes . . . Mircea must be avenged. Hunyadi and the House of Dăneşti must pay for what they have done."

"I've prepared an army," Vlad said. "I've collected several hundred more soldiers to add to your forces. Over the last few weeks, I've convinced most of the southern boyars to ride with us to take back Târgoviște. All they've been waiting for is your return and your command to attack."

Something reminiscent of the intimidating man Vlad knew flashed through the voivode's eyes. "Attack? Yes, we will attack. By sunset tomorrow, Wallachia's soil will be red with Transylvanian blood."

The voivode straightened his shoulders and turned to an Ottoman soldier who stood a few respectful paces behind him. "Colonel," he said. "Take command of Prince Vlad's forces. You will spearhead the attack against Hunyadi's southernmost positions."

"No."

The voivode turned toward Vlad in surprise.

"*I* will command my forces," Vlad said. "*I* will lead them into battle."

A scowl darkened the voivode's face, but Vlad squared his own shoulders and glared back. He was now the crown prince. He had as much right to lead an army as Mircea ever did.

"You dare to challenge me?" the voivode growled.

Vlad fought the urge to back down; he hadn't done the things he did only to give away his glory now.

"If I must."

The voivode studied him a moment. Finally, a slow, thin smile crossed his lips.

"Very well, then. If you die in battle, there are others who can take your place."

"I won't die in battle. Anyone who dares to challenge me will die. The world will know my name and tremble."

His brazen boast pleased the voivode, he could see it in his father's eyes.

"Come to my tent," his father said. "Help me plan János Hunyadi's demise."

CHAPTER TWENTY-EIGHT

"Over there," Andrei whispered. "Do you see it? On that branch?"

"Where?" Ilona asked.

"There. Do you have one of those in your sketchbook?"

Ilona followed Andrei's pointing finger, spotted the bird, and bounced excitedly on her toes. "Not yet. Quick! Hold the ink for me!"

The orange-throated bird hopped to a lower branch.

"What is it?" Andrei asked.

"A *méhevő*. A bee-eater."

"Bee-eater? Too bad for the monks. They have an apiary."

"I doubt they'll need to worry," Ilona said. "There are plenty of wild bees in the fields and woods. I doubt that this little fellow will have much effect on the monastery's hives."

She shifted her eyes from the bee-eater to her open book, sketching quickly so she wouldn't forget the bird's plumage. Her subjects rarely stayed put for long, so she'd trained herself to form shapes and patterns on the paper as fast as she could. The bee-eater was no exception to that rule; she'd barely managed to capture its long, thin beak and banded wings before it darted after a small black bee.

"See? Just as I told you. Plenty of wild bees to keep it happy."

Andrei glanced over her shoulder. "How do you draw so fast and still make it look so . . . so perfect?"

Ilona blushed. "It's not perfect. It would be perfect if I could reproduce the colors. The greens, the reds, the blues . . . it's such a beautiful bird. I wish we could find its colony. Bee-eaters burrow into the banks along rivers. If we could find that, I could get a better look."

"Good luck getting Magda and Gizela to stay focused that long." Andrei laughed. "Where are they anyway? They were right behind us just a few minutes ago."

"Probably picking flowers," Ilona said with an exasperated sigh. "Poor Magda! She watches Gizela while we study birds."

Something moved in the trees on the slope above them, but it wasn't a bird.

"A stag," Andrei whispered, unslinging the crossbow he carried during their woodland expeditions. "A plump one! The cook will be able to carve some juicy roasts out of it."

Andrei rested the crossbow's stock over his shoulder and curled his finger around the tickler, but Ilona looked into the stag's wide brown eyes and couldn't bring herself to passively watch it die.

"Wait!" She pushed the crossbow down.

The stag startled, bounded over a rotting stump, and disappeared up the wooded hillside.

"No roast venison tonight," Andrei said.

"I know. I'm sorry."

"It's all right. We can't kill anything here anyway."

"Why not?"

He pointed up the hill to a place where a white stone wall interrupted the spaces between the trees' hanging branches. "The Mănăstirea Dealu."

They had inadvertently wandered off Magda's father's property. Technically that was a violation of the White Knight's orders, but Hunyadi wasn't here to enforce it. They should be all right if they turned back before anyone saw them.

"Do you think the monks will mind if we climb up to look at their monastery?" Andrei asked.

"I don't know. I don't see why they would care. Father Mihai knows us."

"I wonder if he knows Magda's nephew."

Andrei had become unusually interested in Călțuna and her son since learning of their existence. He only brought it up around Ilona, but lately he had been mentioning them enough to make Ilona wonder. One of these days she would have to confront him about it, but for now she wanted to enjoy the sunshine and the warmth of his hand. Together they climbed the hill.

The monastery wasn't much to look at. Just a rock wall, a few huts, and a tiny wooden church. Mircea the Elder had given the monks the hilltop, and the voivode's brother, Alexandru, gave them two villages to support themselves. Despite the villages, the monks had little in the way of food and other resources. Magda's father helped out by bringing them a wagonload of provisions once a week.

The boyar referred to his donations as "loving his neighbor

as himself." In return for his generosity, Father Mihai conducted services at the Racovița chapel every Sunday.

Ilona's father would have never thought to send food to monks. Not even if it earned him favors from heaven.

"I just remembered," Ilona said, "about the owls that are supposed to be nesting somewhere around here. I'd really like to sketch them while I have a chance."

Andrei nodded, but he didn't seem to be listening to her. He was staring at the wooden church.

"I'll be right back," he said. "I need to see something."

Ilona looked at him, bewildered. "Andrei? Where are you going?"

Andrei ventured out of the trees. He walked to the church and pressed his ear against the door. Ilona followed, casting nervous glances at the other buildings. "Andrei!" she whispered.

He still wasn't listening to her. As if in a trance, he cracked the door open just enough to peer in with one squinting eye. Ilona moved to peek over his shoulder and saw the kneeling men inside.

Light from the church's stained-glass windows cast red, yellow, and blue patterns over the monks' bowed heads. One of the heads was youngish-looking. The young monk looked up a moment, and Ilona shivered. The voivode's features were clearly chiseled across the young monk's profile.

Ilona stepped back. When Andrei didn't, she grabbed his arm and pulled him away. Andrei finally looked at her.

"What's going on?" Ilona demanded. "Why did you do that?"

"I . . . I needed to see something."

"See what? That monk who looks like the voivode?"

Andrei hesitated a moment before nodding. Then he glanced at the church's door, took Ilona's hand, and hurried back to the hill's wooded slope. When they were safely in the trees, Ilona pulled him to a stop and made him face her.

"What's going on?" she asked again.

"He's the voivode's son," Andrei said quietly. "A fourth son. I wasn't sure before, but now I am."

Ilona shook her head, confused.

Andrei stared into space, pondering out loud. "It makes sense that he would be here. Here where Boyar Racoviţă can watch over him. Here where he can—"

With a glance at Ilona, Andrei abruptly stopped speaking.

"There's something you're not telling me," she said. "What is it? Tell me. Now."

Andrei shook his head. "It's nothing. Just suspicions. I have no proof. At least not enough."

"Proof of what?"

Andrei shook his head again.

"He's Magda's nephew," Ilona said. "Isn't he? And . . . and he's also the voivode's son."

Andrei nodded. "VC." He rubbed his temples and took a deep breath. "Vlad Călugărul. Vlad the Monk."

Andrei looked at Ilona a few moments, then came to some kind of a decision. He opened the bag that hung from his belt and removed two items: a small block of wax and a crumpled piece of parchment. He handed the parchment to Ilona.

"I found it at Codru Conac. It was in the workshop. I think it's a list of boyars and the Wallachian heirs they support."

He pointed at the first column. "VD," he said. "Vlad Dracul."

He pointed to the second column. "BD. Basarab of the House of Dănești."

Ilona placed her finger on the third column before Andrei could. "VC," she whispered. "Vlad Călugărul. But why would a list like this be at Codru Conac?"

Andrei handed her the wax block. Ilona could see someone had pressed a key into the block, leaving its impression behind.

"I don't understand . . ."

"It's a copy of the key to the voivode's bedchamber," Andrei explained. "The assassin who tried to kill him had a carved replica of the key."

"You found both of these in the workshop?"

Andrei nodded.

"But who would put them there? Who would need—"

Ice crept up her spine.

"My father . . . ," she said. "Magda's father . . . But you can't possibly think . . . There's no way they would ever . . ."

Bits and pieces of things Ilona had either heard or seen clicked into place in her mind. The wood carvings in Boyar Racovița's studio. The painting of the little boy on Călțuna's lap. Magda's comment about her father spending so much time with Ilona's at Codru Conac. Almost every evening. Even though Ilona hadn't been aware of it.

"They were plotting to overthrow Vlad's father," Ilona whispered, "while at the same time pretending to be his greatest supporters."

Andrei said nothing, only stared at his feet.

"My father has been playing rithmomachy at both ends of the board," she continued. "Doing everything he can to secure power for himself regardless of who ends up on the throne."

Andrei nodded.

"And sacrificing his own daughter in the process," Ilona whispered, "if that's what it required to get what he wanted."

Her head swam. She staggered, and Andrei caught her arm.

"I'm all right," she said. She shook her head and straightened her back. "There's one thing I don't understand, though. How did they get a wax mold of the voivode's key?"

"My guess is that it came from Călțuna," Andrei said. "A maid at the Curtea Domnească told Vlad and me that the voivode once had a mistress. If it was Călțuna, she would have had ample opportunity to make the mold while she was still in his favor."

"And her father—Magda's father—then carved a replica."

It was difficult to imagine Magda's gentle, smiling father plotting with hers to engineer the voivode's demise. And there was still one part of the puzzle that didn't make sense.

"I overheard my father speaking with one of his soldiers. I thought the assassin was allied with the House of Dănești."

"That's what the assassin claimed," Andrei said, "but he could have lied. Or the boyar and your father could have delivered the key to the House of Dănești's allies. Like you said . . . Your father was playing rithmomachy at both ends of the board. Once the voivode was dead—regardless of who murdered him—the boyar council would meet to select a new prince, and your father could then put forth Vlad the Monk's claim to the throne. A divided council probably would have seen it as a good compromise."

Ilona shuddered. There were so many questions swimming through her head—but those questions would have to wait because Magda and Gizela were climbing the hill toward them.

"Look what I've made!" Gizela called out in a singsong voice. "A garland for the Sânziene festival!"

"It's beautiful!" Ilona said, clapping her hands while doing her best to hide the disquiet that now troubled her soul. "But what about Magda? Where are her flowers?"

"She wants to make hers later. She was helping me with mine."

Magda nodded and smiled, but her smile faltered when she looked up the hill and saw where they were. "We've walked a long way," she said. "Don't you think we should head back?"

"Yes," Ilona said. "I think we definitely should head back. Before your parents start to worry."

She cast a glance at Andrei, and he met her eyes. They had much to discuss.

Every time Ilona began to think her worries might be done, new trouble fell over her.

CHAPTER TWENTY-NINE

Autumn 1443

THE DEEP-THROATED BELLS OF THE MĂNĂSTIREA DEALU RANG out a warning across the countryside.

Vlad stood in his stirrups to get a clearer look at Cântecul Lebedei. Far behind him, smoke rose from the Curtea Domnească. Before Hunyadi's lackey, Basarab II, fled with the White Knight's surprised soldiers, the Dănescu prince risked a few extra moments to set Târgoviște aflame.

When the voivode launched his attack, it swept northward with a vengeance. Vlad liked to think Hunyadi's forces crumbled as quickly as they did because his fearsome reputation preceded him. The voivode and his Ottoman allies didn't hurt, but Vlad now wished he had demanded more from the southern boyars and launched his own attack earlier.

He had waited too long to see Ilona again. Now, at the head of an army, he would return to her in glory. He was certain he would find her at Racoviță's manor. If Racoviță himself hadn't taken her there, Andrei surely would have.

Andrei.

Vlad no longer knew whether his cousin could be trusted. Ever since Radu made that stupid comment about the possibility of Ilona falling for Andrei, it had become a frequent visitor in Vlad's mind.

When he saw them, he would know if Andrei had betrayed him.

And that moment of reckoning was coming soon.

"Are we going to proceed, Your Highness?"

Vlad turned his head to look at Captain Lutz. With a nod, he settled back into his saddle and spurred Invictus forward.

The moment was coming very soon indeed.

"Why are the bells ringing?" Gizela asked, wide-eyed. "Why are all the peasants running to the manor?"

Ilona held her close and smoothed her hair back. "I don't know, madárka, but Magda's father will protect us. Everything will be all right."

Virghiliu Racoviță's voice boomed across the grounds like a cannon. "Arm yourselves with pitchforks! Scythes! Hammers! Whatever you can use to kill and defend!"

These weren't words Gizela needed to hear. She was already frightened enough.

Virghiliu Racoviță's fierce demeanor, at the very least, seemed to bolster the peasants' courage. Men separated themselves from their families to quickly gather around their beloved boyar.

"Women and small children inside the manor!" Magda's father commanded. "Men and any boy large enough to lift a weapon will come with me!"

Andrei looked at Ilona and shifted as if to leave, but she grabbed his arm.

"No!" she said. "Come with me to the manor!"

He looked at Magda's father and the other men. "They need me."

"*I* need you."

He was torn, but so was she. She couldn't take the risk that the unthinkable might happen and she would never see him again.

"What's happening?" she asked. "Who's coming?"

"I don't know," Andrei said.

One of Boyar Racoviţă's hired soldiers hurried past, pausing to hand Andrei one of the crossbows he was carrying.

It wasn't supposed to work like this. They were supposed to have advance warning of an impending attack. When they woke up this morning, there were rumors that something was going on in the south, but no indication that a war was headed their direction. It was Codru Conac all over again, only this time it was Transylvanians running northward.

"Andrei!" Magda's father had seen them. "Send Ilona and Gizela to the house and come help me."

Ilona looked at Andrei again. "Get me a weapon," she said.

"You need to go inside. Where it's safe."

"And what if whoever's coming gets inside and I have nothing to defend myself with?"

Andrei handed her his crossbow and the quiver that had come with it.

"Stay safe," he said.

"I will."

He hesitated another moment before jogging reluctantly toward Magda's father, procuring another crossbow on the way.

Another commanding voice called out. "Ilona? What are you and Gizela doing out here? Come this way! Quick!" Lady Racoviță motioned to her, and Ilona gently pushed Gizela toward the manor.

"This way!" Magda's mother shouted, directing the peasant women now streaming through the manor doors. "That's right. This way!"

Magda's mother ushered the new arrivals inside as fast as she could herd them through. She smiled at the children, briefly clasped their mothers' hands, and uttered comforting words.

No bedraggled serf would have ever been allowed into Codru Conac. Ilona's father wouldn't have permitted it. And that was why Ilona loved this home and this family more than she had ever loved Anton Csáki.

"Hurry, madárka," Ilona said. "You'll be safe inside."

"You're not coming with me?"

"I need to help Andrei."

"No! Don't leave me!"

Ilona glanced back toward where she'd last seen Andrei, then looked down at Gizela.

"We'll find Magda," she said. "You'll be all right with her."

She ushered Gizela into the line of frightened people, and they inched toward the doors. When Magda's mother saw them again, she gestured them to her side.

"Help me get these frightened women and their poor terrified children into the great hall," she said. "Hopefully Father

Mihai will come down from the monastery to comfort them with a sermon from the Holy Scriptures."

Magda was waiting just inside the doorway. Ilona tried to explain that she needed Magda to watch Gizela, but it was too loud and confusing. Magda grasped their hands and pulled them with her as she directed the manor's pale, wide-eyed guests into the rapidly filling great hall.

Magda seemed to know this routine well—as if she had practiced it. She knew just what to say and just when to stoop to hug a tearful peasant child. She made sure all their guests were safely situated and comfortable before motioning for Ilona and Gizela to follow her to the kitchen.

There was no chance to escape the manor to be with Andrei. Everything was happening too quickly.

When they reached the kitchen, Magda's mother was already there, loudly directing the scullery servants to prepare a hasty meal.

"Full stomachs calm frightened minds," she explained. "Get as much food as possible into the hall as fast as you can."

The servants were too busy to be frightened. Ilona got the feeling that was Lady Racoviță's intention. But Ilona wasn't busy. She felt *useless*. She needed to be with Andrei, but also needed to protect Gizela.

Momentarily forgotten in the chaos, Ilona grabbed Gizela's hand and quietly led her upstairs.

"We'll wait here," she said, "until things have calmed down."

She went to the window; she was still holding the crossbow. Ilona placed it on a small decorative table. Gizela came to the window beside her and pointed.

"Târgoviște is on fire."

Ilona looked with her and saw smoke rising above the tree-tops.

"Come away from the window, madárka. We'll sit on the bed and play Mother's memorization game."

"Who did it? Who set the city on fire?"

"I don't know, but there's nothing to fear. We'll be safe here inside the manor."

Gizela stared at Ilona. Her little sister was older and wiser than she had been the last time this happened.

"We'll be fine," Ilona repeated. "Haven't I promised to always keep you safe?"

"Papa promised. Then he left us and didn't come back."

"But I will never do that."

"You will when you marry Mircea."

Ilona took a deep breath and forced herself to appear cheerful.

"I'll never marry Mircea. Now, let's see how well you remember Mother's game . . . *Neque accedunt lucernam, et ponunt eam sub modio . . .*"

"Neither do men light a candle," Gizela translated, "and put it under a bushel." She put a finger against her lip and thought a moment. "The Gospel of Matthew. Fifth chapter."

"Very good. I thought you might have forgotten your verses after all this time. Now try one on me."

"*Sollicita es, et turbaris erga plurima.*"

"Thou art careful and troubled about many things," Ilona answered, staring out the window. "Our Savior's words to Martha, but I don't remember which gospel it's from . . ."

"The Gospel of St. Luke," Gizela said, clapping. "Tenth chapter. I win!"

"You've always been very good at this game. My turn again. This time I'm going to choose something more difficult."

"I hear horses."

"What?"

Gizela stood and looked toward the window. "Horses. Lots of them."

"It's not horses, madárka. That's Magda's father and his men building barricades."

"No! I hear horses! Listen."

Ilona listened, and a prickling sensation crawled up her neck. A staccato rhythm vibrated the window frame and bounced the floorboards beneath her feet. Gizela dashed to the window as muffled shouts rang through its thick glass panes.

By the time Ilona joined her, Magda's father and his men were already dropping down behind their barricades, readying themselves for battle. Magda's father kept ten or twelve soldiers in his service, but that wouldn't be enough to stop so many horse-mounted men.

Timariots. Ottoman horse archers. They wore chain mail and pointed bronze helmets. Ilona wasn't sure if this was good or bad. It likely depended on who led them. She pulled Gizela against her. She wasn't sure if it was her own heartbeat or Gizela's that hammered through her velvet dress.

Boyar Racoviţă's men were armed with swords and bows, but mostly Ilona saw rakes, shovels, rusted pitchforks, and even tree branches in peasants' hands. The soldiers aimed crossbows at the incoming horsemen.

Andrei was stationed with them behind the foremost wagon. Someone had given him another crossbow.

"You stay right here," Ilona told Gizela. "Don't move."

She went to the room's balcony door and stepped outside. The incoming army would reach Andrei and Magda's father first.

Andrei and the boyar would be the first to fight and the first to die.

Ilona knelt, balancing Andrei's crossbow on the balcony's stone railing, and she took aim. The nearest horseman came almost within range of the crossbows before reining his horse in. He rode a big brown destrier with white fetlocks and a white blaze from its ears to its nose. He stood in his stirrups, calling out to the defenders, and, unlike many of the other horsemen, he was dressed in a Wallachian uniform.

"Vlad?"

His name left her lips in a startled breath. She nearly dropped the crossbow over the balcony's edge but quickly steadied it. He looked up and saw her.

"Vlad," she whispered. And then she turned and ran for the stairs.

"Prince Vlad!" Virghiliu Racoviță stepped forward, his arms spread wide in welcome. "I must say, it's a relief to see you healthy and well after such a lengthy absence."

If there was a strained quality to the boyar's welcome, Vlad didn't notice it. Maybe because he wasn't listening for it like Andrei was. Or maybe because, although he smiled at the boyar, his frowning eyes kept flickering toward Andrei.

"It's a relief to be back," Vlad said, giving his cousin one last glance before focusing his attention on the boyar. "It's good to again be among friends. To be among those who are loyal to the House of Drăculești."

Boyar Racoviță bowed. "Which I am. I and every member of this household. Which you can see has grown a bit while you were gone." He smiled and nodded toward Andrei. "Anton's daughters have been under my protection as well. I assume he will soon wish to be reunited with them."

"Anton Csáki volunteered to remain behind," Vlad said. "The sultan required a . . . guest . . . in exchange for his armies."

Boyar Racoviță's face dropped, and he looked worried. "Oh . . ."

"Grand Boyar Csáki's daughters will come with me and will now be under the voivode's protection."

"We're already under Boyar Racoviță's protection."

The quiet voice came from behind Andrei, startling both him and Vlad. They turned toward Ilona as she stepped out from behind one of Boyar Racoviță's hastily erected barricades. She was panting. She must have run from the manor to be here.

"Ilona . . ." The harsh edges Andrei had noticed on Vlad's face suddenly softened.

Ilona was still holding Andrei's crossbow—hugging it against herself as if that could protect her from the news Vlad was delivering.

Vlad began to cross the space that separated him from Ilona, and Andrei stiffened and stepped into his cousin's path.

"Welcome home, Vlad."

Vlad looked from Andrei to Ilona. He narrowed his eyes and looked at Andrei again.

"It's good to see you, cousin. I wasn't sure you would still be alive."

"I had a promise to keep. I couldn't die." Andrei removed

Mircea's signet from his finger and held it in his cupped palm. "Mircea will probably want this back."

"Mircea's dead." Vlad smiled coldly at Andrei and took the ring. "Everything that was once his is now mine."

Something as hard as steel and as cold as ice tightened inside Andrei's chest.

Vlad stepped forward to stand before Ilona. He stared at her a moment, then gently took the crossbow out of her hands.

"I thought about you," Vlad said. "I thought about you every day."

Ilona took a shaky breath. "I thought about you, too."

Vlad smiled. She smiled back, but hers came with more effort than Vlad's.

"We need to catch up on what happened while I was gone," Vlad said. "We'll have a lot of time for that while you're with me at the Curtea Domnească."

Ilona took a step back, but Vlad caught her hand. She glanced at Andrei, who was already moving toward her.

"How long before the voivode moves Ilona and Gizela to the Princely Court?" Andrei asked. "This is unexpected. It might be good to give them a day or two to prepare."

"They're coming with me now," Vlad said. "So are you."

This time the malice in Vlad's eyes wasn't veiled. Somehow he knew.

Andrei met Vlad's stare, but ice crackled through his veins.

"Considering the news Lady Ilona has just received about her father," Racoviță said, "I have to agree with Andrei. I think it would be prudent to—"

Vlad waved a hand and cut him off. "They're coming with me. Immediately."

"No. No we're not."

Vlad blinked at Ilona. Andrei and the boyar blinked, too.

"This is home to us," Ilona said. "Magda, Lady Racoviță, and Boyar Racoviță are like family."

Vlad clearly hadn't expected this. He'd probably assumed Ilona would be overjoyed to see him again. Instead her entire body was stiff with tension. Vlad didn't know Ilona like Andrei did; it was a mistake for him to believe he could make her decisions for her.

Vlad changed tactics. "We have no choice. The voivode commands it."

He turned to one of his men. "Captain Lutz, ready a pair of horses for Lady Ilona and Lady Gizela. Boyar Racoviță, I would much appreciate it if your servants would help the ladies pack."

The boyar nodded and bowed, but his attempt at maintaining a cheerful smile had vanished. He coughed and nervously hitched his thumbs behind his belt to straighten it.

"And one last thing," Vlad said. "I deliver a message from the voivode. He expects to see you and every other member of the boyar council in Târgoviște tomorrow evening for a special announcement."

Vlad again looked at Ilona. His gaze was possessive, and the hairs on the back of Andrei's neck prickled. His own worry was reflected on Ilona's face.

The voivode was back, Vlad was crown prince, and the cycle of events they thought they'd escaped had rotated back to a place where neither of them wanted to be.

CHAPTER THIRTY

THE CURTEA DOMNEASCĂ HAD BEEN STRIPPED OF EVERYTHING valuable: silverware, artwork, furniture. As a last act of defiance, Hunyadi's puppet prince, Basarab II, attempted to burn the palace to the ground on his way out. He destroyed much of the city, but failed to bring the palace down. Its walls were now streaked with soot, and the choking stench of smoke hung in the air.

Ilona examined her room. Except for a bed, it was as empty as a worm-eaten walnut. The bed, which had no trace of fire damage, had almost certainly been "donated" by the local population. On her way into the city, she had seen how these donations worked: The voivode's soldiers pounded on doors and ultimately kicked them in if the residents refused to answer. Whatever could be used to restock the palace was dragged into the street and loaded onto wagons.

The voivode wasn't interested in gaining popularity. He was satisfied to rule by fear.

"I apologize for the lack of furniture."

Ilona spun; Vlad stood in the doorway. There was a time not long ago when his green eyes and roguish grin made her stomach flutter. That time was gone. Now the sight of him made her heart tighten with anxiety.

Despite this, she forced herself to smile. She couldn't let him see how she was actually feeling. Not if she hoped to make her dangerous plan succeed.

"I was beginning to wonder if I would ever see you again," she said.

Vlad's grin widened. "I've only been gone an hour."

She blushed and shook her head. "No . . . You know what I mean. After the White Knight attacked . . . After he replaced your father with Basarab on Wallachia's throne . . ."

Vlad entered the room and strode to the window. Ilona's sketchbook rested on the sill. Andrei's carved swan sat beside it. He touched the sketchbook, and his features darkened when he noticed the swan. He set it on his palm and carelessly tossed it up and down.

"The House of the Dragon will always rise above its enemies," Vlad said. "I have risen above mine and will crush anyone who is foolish enough to stand in my way."

He turned away from the window, walked to Ilona, and gently stroked her cheek with the backs of his fingers. She tried not to shudder. Her mother had once told her a man's eyes were the window to his soul. There was no light in Vlad's eyes. Only darkness. He had changed while he was away.

"I knew I would be with you again," he said quietly. "I built an army to make it happen. And after my father makes tomorrow's announcement, you and I will never have to be separated again."

"Announcement?" Ilona said, heart pounding.

"Two announcements, actually. One involves disloyal boyars and any courtier who hasn't shown proper allegiance to the House of Drăculești."

"And what is it," Ilona asked, "that doesn't constitute 'proper allegiance'?"

"Speaking out against my father's return to power. Openly or secretly befriending Hunyadi and his puppet prince during their unjust occupation." His face grew red as he spoke. "Those who have chosen to plot against my father will pay a steep price. The sultan has requested five hundred healthy Wallachian boys. They are to be sent to Adrianople to convert to Islam and serve as his janissaries. Every disloyal boyar family will be required to provide the sultan with one or more of their sons or grandsons."

Ilona felt her face drop in dismay.

"It might seem harsh," Vlad said, "but it will build mutual confidence between the sultan and my father and discourage further disloyalty." He paused a moment, lowering his voice before he went on. "And it won't just be the boyars who help pay the costs of this war. In exchange for Murad's help, my father has also agreed to send two of his own sons to Adrianople. They will live as guests at Murad's court, remaining there as long as is necessary to ensure peace and friendship between Wallachia and the Ottoman Empire."

Ilona frowned. "I don't understand. You almost seem happy about this. With Mircea . . . dead . . . the voivode only has two sons—you and Radu."

Vlad smiled and shook his head. "You're mistaken. He has a foster son."

Ilona's blood turned cold.

"I'm not happy about it," Vlad said, but it was clear to Ilona that he was anything but sad. "It's inconvenient, but it's a necessity. And since Mircea is gone . . ." He shook his head again. "Well, the sultan understands that the crown prince must remain at Târgoviște. He's willing to accept Andrei in my stead."

Ilona hugged herself.

Vlad looked at Andrei's carved swan and curled his fingers around it.

Ilona could contain herself no longer. She grabbed Vlad's arm and made him look at her. "You can't let the voivode do this! Not to Andrei! Not to Radu! Not to *any* of those boys!"

Vlad shook his head. "It's out of my hands. I didn't make this new treaty, and I can do nothing to alter it. But I can keep *you* safe. With your father imprisoned at Adrianople, you need someone like me to protect you."

She could no longer pretend she was happy to see him.

"Gizela and I were safe at Cântecul Lebedei! We would be safe there still!"

"Not now. Not after what the voivode learned from your father."

Ilona froze.

"Virghiliu Racoviță is a traitor. He was behind the attempt on my father's life."

"My *father* told the voivode this?" Ilona asked.

"That and much more."

She didn't believe it. Anything her father said that incriminated Magda's father would have incriminated him as well. But maybe that was why he was imprisoned at Adrianople. That was the word Vlad used this time. *Imprisoned.* Maybe her father had been tortured into a confession. Maybe he had betrayed Magda's father to save his own life.

"Where's Andrei?" Ilona said. "I . . . I need to talk to him."

Vlad glowered. "Andrei isn't feeling well. He's asleep in his room."

She didn't believe him. Andrei showed no signs of sickness on the way to the Curtea Domnească other than the worry Ilona was also feeling. Vlad was purposely keeping them apart. Perhaps he believed separation would convince Ilona to choose him over Andrei. It was too late for that. Even if the voivode forced Ilona to marry Vlad, she would always love Andrei. Nothing Vlad or the voivode did could change that.

"You told me the voivode has two announcements," she said.

Vlad grinned. "Yes, but before I share that with you, we have other unfinished business. Your birthday. I never got to give you your gift."

He tossed Andrei's swan onto the bed, opened the bag at his belt, and retrieved something shiny. Smiling with child-like anticipation, he placed the object in Ilona's hand. A blue gemstone blinked up at her—a sapphire eye in a small brooch shaped like Andrei's swan.

"It's . . . beautiful."

"I chose it myself. Somehow I knew you would like it."

"Thank you, Vlad."

She raised the brooch to pin it to her gown, but Vlad stopped her.

"Allow me."

She didn't want to risk further antagonizing him, so she

handed him the piece of jewelry. He took his time, leaning in close. She felt his breath in her hair, and she shivered, but it wasn't a warm shiver like the ones she had experienced with him in the past.

When the brooch was in place, she touched it and stepped carefully away from him.

"You're no longer wearing Mircea's ring."

Ilona looked at her bare finger. "No . . . I . . ."

"It doesn't matter. I don't want you wearing his ring. By tomorrow evening—"

"Your dinner, my lady."

They turned in unison toward Raluca who had just stepped through the door.

"Oh, my apologies!" she said. "The door was open . . . I thought . . ."

"It's quite all right," Ilona said. "Please come in!"

It was an awkward moment for all three of them, and Ilona was grateful for it.

"About the announcement," Vlad said. "I'll return once you've had your dinner. I can discuss it with you then."

"Yes, please do!" She said it far too cheerfully, but Vlad nodded and smiled before turning to leave.

Raluca stared at the floor as Vlad walked past her. "I do apologize."

"No apology is necessary," Vlad muttered.

Ilona stared at the platter in Raluca's hands, waiting to speak until Vlad was out the door. "Will it now be the custom to have dinner in my room?" she asked.

Raluca glanced over her shoulder, making sure Vlad was out of earshot. "The great hall is currently in a state of disrepair."

The prince's receding footsteps echoed in their ears. "Until the palace staff has time to restore it, I will bring your meals to you."

Vlad's footsteps faded.

"And I will deliver any communication," Raluca said, dropping her voice to a whisper, "that you would like me to pass between Andrei and you."

Ilona's heart beat faster. "Is he all right?"

"He's being confined to his room."

"Why?"

"He thinks it's because Vlad doesn't want him anywhere near you until the voivode's announcement is made."

"An announcement of betrothal? This time to Vlad?"

Raluca watched her and nodded.

"I won't marry him."

"You won't have a choice."

Ilona scowled. "I've already chosen Andrei. I need your help. We both need your help."

Raluca glanced toward the door again, worry creasing her brow. "May I set this down?"

Ilona looked at the tray and glanced around for a nonexistent table before nodding toward the bed.

Raluca stooped but froze when she saw the figurine Vlad had so carelessly tossed onto the bedcovers.

"Lady Muşat's swan . . ."

Raluca set the tray down and turned back toward Ilona with the carved bird gently cradled in both hands. "Andrei gave this to you?"

Ilona nodded.

"He must love you. Very much." Raluca continued to stare

at the swan. "He's in danger, isn't he," she whispered. It wasn't really a question.

"Many people I care about are in danger."

"How can I help you, then?"

"I need to get out of this palace and out of Târgoviște. Tonight. With Andrei and Gizela. Is that even possible?"

Raluca frowned. "I've gotten Andrei out of a palace before. It will be dangerous, but I'll find a way."

"If we don't get out, Andrei will be sent to Adrianople, perhaps for the rest of his life." Ilona's throat tightened. "If you can only get one of us out . . . If it's a choice between saving him or me . . ."

"Let me stop you right there," Raluca said with a grim smile. "We're all getting out of here. You, your sister, Andrei, and me. I'll find a way."

She turned to leave but stopped at the door.

"Vlad used to be a good boy," she said. "I don't know what's happened to him. I saw what he did to those soldiers. I saw what was done to his brother, and I think it might have been him."

"I . . . don't understand," Ilona said. "What he did to the soldiers? What he did to his brother? What are you talking about?"

Raluca closed her eyes and shuddered. "He murdered his brother. He impaled enemy soldiers. He . . . showed no remorse."

A cold, invisible weight fell over Ilona. She gazed at her toes and hugged herself.

"If he ever rules Wallachia," Raluca whispered. "If that ever happens . . ." She paused and shook her head. "I fear we won't be the only ones who need to flee."

In his absence, Andrei's room had been stripped of all his earthly possessions. He didn't even have a bed. The room looked like—and now served as—a prison cell. But he wasn't as worried for himself as he was for Ilona and Gizela. He knew what life was like in the voivode's household, and there would be none of the joy the Csáki sisters had grown used to at Cântecul Lebedei. Life in the House of Drăculeşti was by nature tense and gloomy.

If there had at least been some warning that Vlad was coming, Andrei might have been able to save Ilona from his cousin. They could have run away to Transylvania like Ilona wanted. They could have gone to Alba Iulia and sought out her mother's family.

But not now. Now Andrei was useless to her. Two burly sentries stood outside his door, and even if he could somehow overcome the men, an alarm would be raised, and he wouldn't even make it down the hallway let alone have time to find and free Gizela and Ilona.

The one hopeful thing that happened since Vlad ordered his soldiers to escort Andrei to his room was Raluca's fortuitous decision to deliver his evening meal herself. If not for that, she wouldn't have known he was being treated like a prisoner. If not for her, he wouldn't have had a way to make an inquiry about Ilona's safety.

Andrei paced his cell again. Raluca still hadn't returned to let him know if Ilona was well. Hours had passed since she delivered his dinner and promised to personally deliver Ilona's as well. His isolation was so monotonous, he might not have known it had been hours rather than days if not for the passing of time outside his window. It was dark now. Most of the palace was probably sleeping. He likely wouldn't know anything about Ilona until morning.

A light knock echoed through the door. It was so soft, he wouldn't have heard it if he didn't stop pacing precisely when he did. He almost thought it was his imagination until the door creaked slightly open.

It opened wider, and Raluca peeked in.

"I thought you would never come back!" Andrei said in a relieved whisper.

She placed a finger against her lips. "I haven't come alone."

She gestured to someone behind her, and the door opened wider to admit Ilona and Gizela.

Andrei had to stop himself from crying out in joy. Ilona ran to his waiting arms. She gazed into his eyes, stroked the scar that lined his face. He held her for several moments before remembering there were supposed to be two soldiers guarding the door.

"How did you—"

Ilona followed his eyes. "Raluca knows an herbal mixture," she whispered, "but there's no time to discuss it. We need to leave."

Her entire body was trembling, her eyes darting to and from the door like a frightened animal's, and she was pale with fear. Despite this, determination was etched across her face.

And there was something different about her. Andrei held her at arm's length. She was dressed like a man.

"Raluca has a plan," she said. "Hurry!" She grasped Andrei's hands and pulled him toward the door.

In the hallway, both guards were slumped to the floor.

They weren't the voivode's usual Saxons, but rather the sultan's janissaries. Raluca's "herbal mixture" was clearly potent; the food she'd given them had fallen, half-eaten, where they'd once stood.

"Are they . . . dead?" Andrei asked, concerned.

"Just unconscious. Here . . ." Raluca handed him one of the sleeping janissaries' sabers. "Pray you don't have to use it."

He nodded and slipped the sword through his belt. Ilona hurriedly stooped to take a crossbow from the nearest janissary's limp fingers.

"There are no soldiers this way," Raluca whispered, pointing to the left. Andrei was glad to see she intended to take them in the direction that didn't lead past Vlad's room. "Follow me."

Gizela's eyes were wide, and she walked so close to Ilona that she nearly trod on her older sister's borrowed boots. Andrei grasped the younger girl's hand, giving her what he hoped would appear to be a comforting smile.

They moved in silence, Raluca stopping them at every corner to peek around and make sure the coast was clear. She was headed toward the scullery. It was a good idea because they were less likely to run into guards there, but it wouldn't protect them from the soldiers posted outside.

They stopped outside the scullery.

"In here," Raluca said, her voice urgent. "The flour barrel in the corner."

At first Andrei thought she intended to smuggle them out of Târgoviște in empty barrels, but apparently Ilona was aware of the true plan—she hastily removed the barrel's lid and pulled out four waiting objects: two sipahi helmets and two soldiers' cloaks.

"Put these on," Ilona commanded, handing Andrei one of

the helmets and one of the cloaks. He did as directed, but he was beginning to piece their plan together, and perspiration beaded on his forehead.

"What about Raluca and Gizela?" he asked.

Ilona pushed her hair up under her helmet while Raluca explained. "Gizela will never pass for a soldier. We have to get her out looking like herself. If we're stopped and questioned, I'll tell them I brought my daughter to the palace to help clean the burned rooms. We intended to stay through the night to get an early start in the morning, but she became unexpectedly ill and I've decided to take her home."

Andrei didn't like this plan. He didn't like it at all.

"That might work," he said, "unless we run into a soldier who knows us."

Raluca shook her head. "They won't recognize us. The voivode no longer trusts his own men. He's guarding himself and the Curtea Domnească with the sultan's soldiers."

That made Andrei feel a little better, but not much. He could only pray that the sultan's men would be less concerned about someone leaving the Curtea Domnească than someone coming in.

"Are we ready?" Raluca asked.

Andrei, Ilona, and Gizela nodded, and each of them took a deep breath. Gizela looked sick with fear. Hopefully it would be too dark for the janissaries to notice and grow suspicious.

The courtyard wasn't filled with soldiers like Andrei thought it would be but was crowded instead with supply wagons. The nearest one was filled with armor. That explained where Raluca got the helmets. She had taken a big risk to help them, but the biggest still loomed before them.

"You take the lead," Raluca whispered to Andrei.

He nodded. It made sense to keep Ilona behind him and draw more attention to himself. The janissaries might not notice Ilona was a woman if they were focusing on him.

He kept them close to the wagons, hugging the shadows, but the stretch of cobbled courtyard between the last wagon and the gate was open and awash with moonlight. His heart beat against his ribs and his pulse pounded in his ears. Andrei forced himself to breathe deeply and slowly as they approached the sleepy guard. The guard wasn't so sleepy, however, when he noticed them walking toward him.

The guard raised his crossbow and stepped into their path. *"Dur! Neden buradasınız?"*

He was speaking Turkish. Andrei had been tutored in Turkish, but his mind now froze.

"Kız çok hasta."

Ilona's voice echoed past him, speaking low like a boy.

The guard said something else—something about orders not to allow anyone to pass—and Ilona pointed at Gizela, explaining that she had permission from the voivode to be taken home because she was sick. At least that's what Andrei deduced she was saying—Ilona's Turkish was much better than his.

The guard looked uncertain but still didn't move out of their way. Andrei's fingers edged toward the saber at his belt. Any moment now the janissary was going to notice that he and Ilona *weren't* janissaries. If Andrei fought the guard, the women might be able to escape. He likely wouldn't.

Scowling now, the janissary came closer and leaned forward to scrutinize Gizela. Andrei's fingers wrapped around the saber's hilt . . . and at that precise moment, Gizela vomited on the janissary's boots.

The janissary cursed and staggered backward. He gestured angrily toward the gate, and Ilona thanked him and pushed Raluca and Gizela toward it. Andrei nodded at the guard as they walked past him.

He could see by the tension in his companions' shoulders that, like him, they were all fighting the urge to break into a run. But they walked as casually as possible. More soldiers were camped just outside the Curtea Domnească. Hundreds of them. A few who weren't sleeping cast curious glances in their direction. But no one stopped or questioned them, and they eventually reached the narrow streets that wound like rivers between the merchants' homes.

Gizela shivered. Andrei worried she was going to vomit again; they couldn't afford to draw any more attention than they already had. Ilona hugged herself while Raluca cast jittery glances toward the palace.

"We need horses," Andrei said. "We'll never escape otherwise. I'll go back to the stables and try to steal some. If I don't return quickly, do whatever you can to hide yourselves."

"No," Ilona said. "I'm going with you."

"Neither of you have to go," Raluca said. "We just have to get ourselves to the edge of the city."

They turned toward Raluca in bewilderment.

"I sent a message," she said. "Help will come." She didn't look entirely confident about her claim, but she didn't pause for discussion.

"Wait!" Andrei whispered, jogging to catch up with her. "Who's coming to help us?"

"There's no time to talk. Follow me."

Raluca continued up the dark street and, putting his faith in her, Andrei grasped Ilona's hand and followed.

Raluca's path was purposeful, and she chose each street with no hesitation. Andrei cast numerous glances over his shoulder, expecting at any time to hear hoofbeats or see janissaries raging after them like a flash flood, but the only thing pursuing them was the soft echoes of their own footfalls.

God was protecting them. How else could they have made it this far?

Precious minutes slipped by. When a search party came, they wouldn't be following on foot and they would move ten times as fast. Andrei hoped Raluca's friends were faster.

Gizela stumbled and fell to her knees. Ilona yanked Andrei to a stop.

"Madárka? Are you all right?"

Gizela didn't answer. She simply shivered and shook her head.

"We can't go on," Ilona said. "She needs to rest."

Andrei scooped Gizela into his arms. "We must go on. I'll carry her."

"Just a little farther to the edge of the city," Raluca said. "We'll soon be safe if we can make it there."

Somewhere far behind them, Andrei heard the sound of shouting voices.

"They're coming," he said. "Run!"

CHAPTER THIRTY-ONE

VLAD'S DREAM WAS ABOUT ILONA. SHE WAS DRESSED IN WHITE, and he was following her through the woods. More than once he called out to her, but she wouldn't come to him. She cast furtive glances at him before momentarily disappearing behind moss-covered trees. She was barefoot like a forest spirit, her feet barely touching the earth as she ran.

She seemed to have some urgent destination in mind. If she reached it, Vlad would never see her again. He wasn't sure how he knew this. It was simply a feeling, and it wrapped his soul in a dark blanket of fear.

He glimpsed her again. She was searching for something. Or someone . . .

Andrei.

Vlad's fear morphed into anger. He reached for his sword and charged after her.

He caught up with Ilona in a large clearing. Here the trees, the grass, and the ferns glowed with a soft white light. Ilona stood next to something. A body.

She stared a moment at Mircea's corpse before lifting her brown eyes to gaze at Vlad in revulsion and terror.

"I did it for you," Vlad said. "Everything I've done, I've done it for you."

He took an imploring step toward her, but she backed toward the shadows beyond the clearing.

"I did it for you!" Vlad cried, lunging forward to grab her.

His fingers closed around the hem of her skirt as he fell, but he wasn't holding fabric. Instead, feathers pricked his fingers. He looked up as Ilona, in the form of an ethereal swan, soared quickly away.

Vlad's eyes flew open. He sat up in his bed, clutching not feathers but the sweat-dampened blanket that covered him. He threw the blanket aside, swung himself to a seated position, and leaned over his knees, panting as he stared at the floor.

She was meant to be *his*. If not for Andrei, she would love *him*. Only he could protect her. Only he could make her the queen she deserved to be!

Vlad stood, hastily dressed himself, and stepped out of his bedchamber. On his way to Ilona's room, he passed Andrei's.

Andrei's guards lay crumpled on the floor. They weren't dead, but he couldn't wake them even by shaking them or slapping their faces.

Andrei wasn't in his room. Someone in the palace must have helped him escape. And if Andrei was gone . . .

Vlad clenched his fists and ran to Ilona's room, flinging the door open without knocking. Her room was empty, too. The bed hadn't been slept in, but something silver rested on the pillow.

The swan brooch Vlad had given her.

He clenched his teeth.

She had chosen Andrei over him.

The men waited for them beside the river, half hidden behind thick bushes and poplar trees. Ilona wouldn't have seen them except that a horse's nervous snort gave them away. Two or three tense seconds passed while the men decided if Ilona and her companions were enemies. Her group was pondering the same thing.

Finally, a broad-shouldered figure stepped out of the trees, opening his arms wide to greet them.

"Uncle Virghiliu!" Gizela whispered.

Ilona's heart leaped, relief flooding through her.

"You escaped!" Magda's father said. He hurried toward them and enveloped each of them in a relieved hug. Seeing that their master recognized the newcomers, his men also came out of the shadows, leading the horses with them.

Magda's father turned to Raluca. "Yet again you have proved our salvation," he said.

Yet again? Ilona and Andrei looked at each other, both of them wearing puzzled frowns.

"I promised Andrei's mother I would protect him," Raluca said. "I'm still trying to keep that vow."

Magda's father nodded, gazed toward the city for a moment, then gestured toward the horses. "Mount quickly. Follow me."

Ilona wanted to ride as far away from Târgoviște as fast as she could. She was more than willing to go wherever Magda's father wanted to take them.

Andrei helped Ilona into her saddle. There were enough horses for each of them, but Gizela was in no state to ride on her own. Andrei realized this, too, and an unspoken communication passed between him and Ilona. He nodded and placed Gizela on the saddle in front of her sister.

"Hurry!" Magda's father called out.

Andrei swung himself onto his own horse, Umbră, and they quickly brought their mounts to a full gallop. Gizela swayed, and Ilona held her sister tight against her. This was made more difficult because of the crossbow in Ilona's hand and the sharp-cornered sketchbook hidden beneath her shirt.

"Is the voivode going to kill us?"

Ilona leaned her face into her sister's hair. "The voivode will never catch us. Magda's father will keep us safe."

Gizela relaxed and some of her shivers subsided. Ilona stoically resisted the urge to look over her shoulder to make sure her promise was true.

The landscape around them was shrouded in so much darkness that Ilona couldn't be sure which direction they were headed. She didn't think, however, that Magda's father was riding toward Cântecul Lebedei. He was following the Ialomiţa instead.

As comforting as familiar surroundings would have been, Ilona realized it was probably better that he was delivering them elsewhere. The first place Vlad and the voivode would think to search for them was at Boyar Racoviţă's manor.

She considered this a moment. The boyar was taking an awful risk—by helping them, he could endanger his entire family. That was too much for Ilona and Andrei to ask, yet they weren't the ones who asked. Raluca called on Magda's father for help, and he answered.

Raluca's involvement awakened so many questions. What was her connection to the boyar? What had she done for him before? And how did she get her message to him? Ilona could only hope there would be more than enough time to ask these questions later.

There was no conversation for the duration of the ride, but also no sign of imminent pursuit. Eventually, Ilona relaxed enough to succumb to the hypnotic sway of the galloping horse's body, exhaustion overcoming her.

She was feeling light-headed and numb by the time an unfamiliar manor rose out of the darkness before them. Magda's father rode as far as its outbuildings, raised a hand, and brought their company to a halt.

"Wait here," he said, "while I announce our arrival."

He continued through the darkness and Ilona stroked Gizela's hair. Her sister was asleep. This night's ordeal had taken everything out of her. It had taken almost everything out of Ilona, too.

"Where do you think we are?" Ilona asked Andrei.

He looked pale, and not because of the moonlight. "This is Dragoş Golescu's manor."

Electric fear sparked up Ilona's spine. "Why would he bring us *here?*"

"Because the grand boyar can get us out of Wallachia. All of us. Boyar Racoviţă's family included."

Ilona and Andrei both turned toward Raluca. "What?" they said in unison.

"Virghiliu can't very well help you and hope to avoid the voivode's wrath," Raluca explained. "He also has other considerations. Other lives to protect."

"Vlad the Monk," Andrei said.

Raluca's eyes widened in surprise. "You know about him?"

"About him. About his claim to the throne . . . About the key."

Footsteps interrupted their conversation, gravel crunching under booted feet.

"Now, isn't this a strange sight," a low, drawling voice said from the darkness. "Four fugitives from the House of Drăculeşti seeking asylum at *my* manor."

Ilona lifted her crossbow. Golescu's guards drew their swords. Andrei quickly pushed the crossbow down.

"There's much you don't understand," Magda's father said. "Dismount and come inside. Even now we don't have much time."

Ilona and Andrei exchanged wary glances.

"It's all right," Magda's father said. "Please. Come."

They didn't have much choice. Regardless of how they felt about Golescu, he was less of a threat at the moment than Vlad Dracula and the voivode.

Andrei dismounted first, took Ilona's groggy sister into his arms, and Ilona slipped out of her saddle. Dangerous times called for dangerous allies. At least that's what Ilona hoped Dragoş Golescu had become.

Vlad followed the voivode into Racoviţa's manor. Torches still flickered on the walls, but its inhabitants were gone.

"Search every room," the voivode ordered.

The janissaries' commander nodded and waved to his men. Sabers drawn, they swarmed into the building like angry ants.

Vlad gripped his own blade, agitated. They were too late.

The janissaries would find no one here. Racoviță and his family—and Ilona and Andrei with them—were probably already halfway to the border. His only hope now was that the soldiers encamped there would nab them and bring them back.

"I should ride to the north," Vlad said. "They probably took wagons. It will slow them down. I—"

"They are of no consequence," the voivode said.

"But they defied you. They—"

"I have too many soldiers at the border," the voivode snarled. "If you're going to be a voivode someday, you need to start thinking like one! They'll be stopped before they can cross into Transylvania. They'll be brought to me and I will execute them."

The voivode shoved Vlad to one side and stopped an entering janissary. "Gather up a handful of troops and take them to search the monastery on the hill. Find out if any of the monks left with Racoviță. Beat the information out of them if you have to."

The soldier looked uncomfortable about this but nodded. Vlad stared. Why would a monk—any monk—flee with Racoviță?

It didn't matter. The only thing that mattered was that Andrei had betrayed him, and Ilona was with him.

Vlad fought to control his anger so he could think more clearly. If he was Racoviță, where would he go?

Not toward Transylvania. The voivode was right; they would be captured too quickly.

But there was another path out of Wallachia.

Vlad gazed at his father and thought a moment longer before turning to slip back outside.

He grabbed a soldier. "You. Come with me. And you three. Bring horses and at least a dozen more men."

He would capture Racoviță on his own, and, when he did, he would put a sword through the boyar.

And another through Andrei.

They huddled together in Golescu's great hall. A fire blazed at the hearth, but they shivered anyway. Ilona looked at each of her companions: Boyar Racoviță and his family. Vlad the Monk. A handful of the boyar's soldiers. Raluca, Andrei, and Gizela. They all looked tense and frightened. They couldn't, however, feel as frightened as she did. Dragoș Golescu, after all, had once sent an assassin to kill her.

Golescu unfurled a map across the banquet table, searched a moment, and placed his thumb against the parchment.

"Here," he said. "My allies can get you across here. At Focșani. But you must leave for the border tonight."

Ilona shook her head. "No!" she cried out. "We can't go there, that's Moldavia. Andrei won't be safe!"

Golescu glared at her. "This is a conversation for men. We don't need your opinions, girl."

She almost lifted her crossbow and put an arrow through him right then, but Andrei placed a warning hand on her arm and shook his head. Golescu's remark angered him, too, but they both knew that antagonizing the grand boyar at a crucial time like this would do more harm than good.

"To keep everyone else safe," Andrei said, "I'm willing to take the risk."

"A wise choice," Golescu said, "since you have few other choices remaining to you."

He pointed at the map again. "This road is guarded by the sultan's janissaries. This one is being watched by the voivode's Saxon mercenaries. Dracul also has men at Moldavia's border, but they're spread thin. At the moment he's more worried about a counterattack from Transylvania than any incursions from the northeast."

"Why are you helping us?" Andrei asked.

Golescu looked at him and flashed a cunning smile before answering. "Virghiliu and I don't always see eye to eye, but there's one thing the entire boyar council can agree upon: Vlad Dracul isn't fit to rule Wallachia. Anything I can do to embarrass or weaken him serves my agenda. Your successful escape will be a great embarrassment to him."

Golescu now returned his attention to Magda's father. "You're giving up everything you have for these children."

"I have assets in Transylvania," Racoviță said. "We'll be all right once we get there. Some things, Dragoș, are more important than wealth or power."

Golescu snorted. "You never cease to amuse me, Racoviță. We can only hope that Dracul's reign is short so that you can return to reclaim your property."

"I'll do my part in exile to assure that happens."

"And I'll take the information that was delivered by your spy and prepare the boyars for the voivode's surprise announcement," Golescu said, then glanced at Raluca. "You've been of great use to us. It's a shame you'll no longer be at the Curtea Domnească to pass us information."

In unison, Ilona and Andrei turned to gape at Raluca.

"I'm sure the boyars will find another spy," Raluca said. "The voivode has no shortage of enemies."

Golescu chuckled and turned to Magda's father. "I don't mean to be an ungracious host, but you need to be on your way. One of my best men will ride with you to the border and introduce you to the people who can help you with the next step of your journey."

The two boyars clasped hands.

"Thank you, Dragoş," Magda's father said.

Golescu nodded. "I still owe you for warning me about Dracul's latest twisted plans."

Magda's father took Lady Racoviţă's hand and motioned for everyone to follow him to the door.

"May God be with us," Magda whispered.

Ilona wholeheartedly seconded that prayer.

CHAPTER THIRTY-TWO

It took Vlad and his commandeered soldiers two days to reach Moldavia's border. The voivode was going to be furious with him, but that fury would quickly abate if Vlad returned with the fugitives.

He was certain they were headed for Moldavia. A day ago, a peasant claimed to have witnessed a small group on horseback crossing through his master's fields. This morning, another peasant reported hearing horses clopping through nearby woodlands. Vlad was on the right track, but he was running out of time.

The border was near and the sun was setting. He needed to take another gamble. It was impossible to know exactly where they would attempt to leave Wallachia, but he thought he had a good idea. They would need food, and they would need rest. If Vlad were them, he would be heading for Focșani, just across the Milcov River, a half hour's ride to the east.

He would stop them before they reached the river. He would take them alive if he could . . . All of them but Andrei. If the others surrendered peacefully, they could have mercy, but as long as Andrei lived, Ilona could never completely give her heart to Vlad.

Andrei had to die.

Andrei stared into the darkness, sweating. Boyar Racoviță and Golescu's man had been gone for several hours. It was well past midnight now, and the longer it took for them to make contact with Golescu's allies, the more anxious Andrei became.

"You look worried."

Andrei turned. It still disconcerted him that the boyar's grandson shared Vlad's name and features. It was also disconcerting to see a monk—a man of God—gripping a sword.

"I'm a little worried," Andrei admitted, nodding. "I know that Vlad—the other Vlad—doesn't give up once he sets his mind on something. He wants Ilona, and he'll do whatever it takes to get her back."

"From what I've seen," the monk said, "she wants you, not him."

Andrei felt his face grow warm. "Maybe. I hope. But none of that will matter to Vlad. The only thing he wants more than Ilona is Wallachia's throne. Sometimes I think he would kill his own mother for that."

"He killed his brother for it," the monk said. "Or so some have been saying."

Andrei nodded. "I don't want to believe it, but more and more I think it might be true."

Something snapped in the woods.

Andrei jerked his head toward the sound, and Vlad the Monk looked, too. After several moments of silence, both started to relax.

"Probably a fox or a stoat," the monk said. "Nothing to worry about."

Andrei nodded, waiting for his heart to return to its normal rhythm. The only sound now was the slow breathing of the others who were asleep.

One of their horses pawed at the dirt and more twigs snapped. The monk was right. Nothing out of the ordinary. Andrei was simply on edge.

"What about you?" Andrei asked. "Do you want Wallachia's throne?"

The monk stared at his feet and didn't answer.

"I'm sorry. That was a personal question."

"Others want it for me," the monk replied. "My grandfather wants it for me. I think he believes it will make me safe. But everything I've seen convinces me that Wallachia's throne ensures nothing but blood and misery. I think I would much rather spend my life in a monastery."

The monk scanned the woods for a moment, then asked, "And how about you? I've been told that you, too, could lay claim to a throne."

Andrei shook his head. "Blood and misery. I'm not interested in thrones." He smiled. "But I'm also not interested in monasteries."

Vlad the Monk laughed, and when he laughed, he looked and sounded nothing like Vlad Dracula or the voivode. For once, Andrei saw the Racoviță blood in him. His laugh was deep and friendly like his grandfather's.

"I've been wondering about something ever since we left Golescu's manor," Andrei said. "It's another awkward question, but why wasn't Golescu worried about letting you escape? Aren't you a potential threat to his own plans?"

The monk smiled. "That's a valid question. And like you, I can only make guesses. My best guess is this: I'm a minor threat. The House of Dănești is far more powerful and has far more backing than a displaced boyar and an impoverished monk could ever hope to have." The monk laughed a mirthless laugh. "Boyar politics are complicated," he said. "Golescu might be helping me escape the voivode tonight, but that doesn't mean he won't send an assassin after me in the morning. There's no safety in being the voivode's son. Only endless danger."

Andrei considered the monk's words and nodded. Wallachia's bloodlines and its politics were a mess. He would be glad to get as far away from it as he could.

"Will your mother be safe?" he asked after a moment.

"She isn't a threat to the voivode or to the boyars like I am, and I think the voivode still loves her. *She* chose to seclude herself in a monastery. *She* brought their relationship to an end. She saw the cruelty in my father and realized that loving him was a mistake."

"But not before making a copy of his key."

Andrei didn't know why he said it. Maybe because he still had questions about how it was obtained and how it got into the House of Dănești's hands.

"Key?" The monk shook his head. "My mother had nothing to do with that key. My grandfather received the mold from Raluca and passed a copy along to others who could do something with it. But how do you know about the key?"

It took a moment for Andrei to process the monk's question. He was still startled to learn it was Raluca who obtained it. He blinked and shook his head. "The key? I found the mold at Codru Conac."

Andrei opened his belt pouch, removed the wax, and handed it to the monk. He examined it, then said, "It was risky for the cneajna to make this."

Andrei's mouth dropped open. Vasilisa? That didn't make sense. What reason did she have to want the voivode dead?

Unless she knew he was unfaithful to her. Or perhaps to protect Radu, just like Boyar Racoviță wished to protect his grandson from the voivode.

To protect him from a cruel warlord whose children were dispensable.

The monk turned the wax block in his hand and stared at it. "I disagreed with any plan to assassinate the voivode," he said. "'Thou shalt not kill.' Even giving the key to Golescu could be enough to put us under God's condemnation."

Something again snapped in the woods. This time both Andrei and the monk raised their swords.

"Wake the soldiers," the monk whispered. "We're not alone."

Vlad edged closer, hoping to catch pieces of the muffled conversation. He was sure this was Racoviță's party, but with no campfire to illuminate their faces, he couldn't be a hundred percent certain.

A little closer . . . A little closer . . . He picked out a few words. *Assassinate . . . condemnation . . .*

A twig snapped. Vlad cursed under his breath. He thought

janissaries were supposed to be supreme among the sultan's soldiers, but they had now given away their presence not once but twice.

Someone in the camp called out in alarm. Racoviţă's groggy soldiers scrambled to their feet. The element of surprise was lost.

"Get them!" Vlad barked.

The janissaries sprang forward. Hopefully, they would obey his order not to harm the women. If anything happened to Ilona, he would kill the man whose sword did it.

In the darkness it was difficult to discern his own men from Racoviţă's. He needed to end this conflict fast. The greatest advantage of this darkness was that when he killed Andrei, he could claim that one of his soldiers was responsible for it. Ilona's heart would be free to love Vlad, and she would never have to know the painful truth.

Swords clanged. Men shouted. Someone grunted and fell face forward to the earth.

The man wearing the monk's habit was skilled with a blade. He took on two janissaries at once and cut both of them down in a matter of seconds. Apparently Wallachia's monks needed to be better instructed in the biblical injunction "thou shalt not kill."

Vlad would have dealt with the monk himself, but he didn't have time. He knocked a soldier's blade to one side, slashed the man's arm, and scanned the trees for Andrei.

There!

The silhouette alone was enough to identify him. Vlad knew Andrei by his fighting style. Cautious. Always defensive. He set his jaw and charged toward Andrei.

If he'd been a fraction of a second faster, he could have

dispatched Andrei while his cousin was defending against one of the janissaries, but Andrei was better than Vlad wished to give him credit for. The janissary went down, and Andrei spun to ward off Vlad's attack.

Thrust. Block. Swipe. Clang.

Andrei must have been practicing in Vlad's absence, but he was still too predictable. Vlad watched for the signature block he had so often taken advantage of to disarm his cousin.

"I don't want to fight you, Vlad," Andrei hissed through clenched teeth, saving most of his breath for the fight.

"If you were loyal to me," Vlad growled, "you wouldn't have to."

Andrei slashed at Vlad's arm. What a fool! He passed on a chance to cut Vlad down in favor of merely disabling him. It would be a costly mistake because Vlad wasn't going to give him the same opening twice.

"You're like a brother, Vlad!"

"I *killed* my brother!"

Their sabers rang as Andrei blocked a nearly fatal strike.

"I did the world a service by getting rid of Mircea," Vlad snarled. "And now you'll die, too."

Andrei made his predictable block. Vlad struck and flicked his wrist, and the saber flew out of Andrei's hand.

Andrei staggered back, eyes wide, but he wasn't watching Vlad—he was looking over Vlad's shoulder.

Vlad spun and thrust at the soldier behind him, pushing the tip of his blade into the man's abdomen.

"*No!*" Andrei cried.

For several seconds, time slowed down. Vlad stared at the figure on the earth and suddenly saw what he hadn't seen before.

The soldier wasn't a man at all.

She was a woman.

Ilona.

She couldn't breathe.

She felt blood under her shirt, but it was only a scratch.

The sketchbook prevented Vlad's sword from impaling her, but the sword thrust had knocked the wind out of her.

In unison, Vlad and Andrei lunged toward her, stumbling over each other in their haste to reach her. Vlad swung his sword at Andrei, but Andrei caught his wrist, and both fell to the earth, grappling for the weapon.

Ilona tried to cough out their names, but she couldn't even draw enough breath to do that. One of them was going to die if she didn't stop them. She had to find another way to get their attention.

Andrei punched Vlad in the nose. Vlad freed his sword arm, and Andrei twisted away. On his feet again, Vlad stabbed at Andrei, but he missed and struck dirt.

When she fell, the crossbow had fallen with her. Ilona's stomach muscles finally stopped spasming, and her fingers scrabbled through the dirt. She grabbed the bow and rolled to her knees. She raised the weapon and aimed.

Andrei scrambled backward as Vlad snarled and went in for a killing blow.

Ilona squeezed the crossbow's tickler, and the bolt flew. She was aiming for the tree between and slightly past Vlad and Andrei, but when it struck Vlad's saber, that was even better.

With a ringing clang, the sword spun wildly out of his hand. Vlad and Andrei froze, then turned slowly toward her.

"Vlad, stop!" Ilona gasped.

He stared at her, speechless.

"He's your cousin," she said. "He's your *friend*."

Vlad looked at Andrei, unsure for a moment, but hate quickly twisted his face again. "He's a traitor! A kidnapper!"

"He didn't kidnap me. I left willingly."

Swords clanged behind her, and Ilona flinched. Vlad the Monk and three of Boyar Racoviţă's best soldiers stood in a tight circle around Gizela, Magda, and Lady Racoviţă, as ten janissaries pressed in on them.

Ilona turned back to Vlad. "Call off your men, Vlad. Please!"

Vlad's features hardened. "You're coming with me. I'm the only one who can protect you. I'm the only one who can promise you happiness. You can come willingly or as a prisoner, but you're coming with me either way."

Ilona shakily got to her feet. "No. *I'll* decide what's best for me, not you. I care about you, Vlad, but not in the way you want me to. I'll never love you like that."

Light shone through the trees as lanterns bobbed toward them.

"Over there!" a voice shouted. Magda's father. "Quickly!"

Andrei snatched Vlad's saber out of the leaves and brandished it above his head. "You're outnumbered, Vlad."

Vlad took a threatening step toward his cousin.

"I don't want you to kill you, Vlad," Andrei pleaded. "But you're going to leave me with no other choice."

It might have been the anguish in Andrei's voice, but more likely, it was the deadly earnestness on his face.

Vlad finally backed down.

"Retreat!" he called to the janissaries. He cast another glance at Ilona; then his gaze lingered on Andrei.

"This isn't over."

Vlad disappeared into the darkness as Boyar Racoviță and at least twenty other men charged madly through the trees.

Andrei stumbled to Ilona and hugged her close.

Finally, they were *free*.

CHAPTER THIRTY-THREE

THE VOIVODE'S INFORMANTS SAID ANDREI AND ILONA WERE IN Sighişoara. Racoviţă had property there. They might think they were safe—they might think they could outwait the House of Drăculeşti—but the Dracul clan would rule forever. One day Vlad would find Andrei and the others who took Ilona from him, and he would destroy them.

But the Ottoman Empire had saved them for the moment.

The voivode wasn't here to see his sons off, but Vasilisa hovered over Radu, weeping and covering his forehead with kisses. The company of janissaries who had been tasked with escorting Vlad and Radu to Murad's court watched the disgusting display uncomfortably.

Vlad turned his eyes away from the cneajna and her darling princeling and bounced the wax block in his hand. He'd stumbled over it in the woods after he told his soldiers to retreat—it still bore the impression of his boot. It also bore a second shape:

the mangled impression of a key. He traced it, and the simple act of touching it stoked his rage.

Spies and traitors! This couldn't go unpunished, but where Andrei was concerned, it would be a delicate matter. Vlad couldn't kill Andrei outright. That would only make Andrei's memory burn more brightly in Ilona's heart. No. Vlad absolutely couldn't have that.

Before Vlad's cousin died, Ilona must despise Andrei so thoroughly she would never want to lay eyes on him again. Vlad would accomplish that first; then Andrei could die. He could suffer like a wriggling worm skewered into sun-baked earth.

One day Vlad would escape the sultan's court, and, when he did, he would travel to Sighişoara for revenge.

Death wouldn't be pleasant when it came for Andrei Muşat.

She had almost forgotten how beautiful Sighişoara was. The memory of its steep streets, colorful buildings, and tree-carpeted hills had almost faded. When they arrived, she felt for several days as if she was floating in a dream.

Andrei and Magda spent those few days walking around in wide-eyed wonder. "It's so beautiful!" Magda exclaimed. "I've never been anywhere so bright."

It was definitely bright. That was one of the things Ilona had most missed about her former home—the pinks, the yellows, the greens, the oranges . . . Everywhere she turned, her eyes were assaulted with color.

She loved it even more because Andrei was here with her. As they slipped out the city gate, she squeezed his hand, and he turned and grinned at her.

"What's this important place you're taking me to?" he asked.

"You'll see" was all she would say.

They followed a dirt path to a quiet, wooded area, and Ilona ducked beneath a low-hanging tree limb, pulling Andrei onto a lesser-used path that cut through the trees. The forest floor was carpeted with orange and yellow leaves. The trees above them were ablaze with autumn colors.

It took a few minutes, but they eventually reached Ilona's intended destination. Musical chirping filled the clearing.

Andrei laughed. "I should have known it would have something to do with birds."

"My mother and I used to come here. It's where I first learned to identify them."

Ilona pursed her lips and made a warbling noise. Somewhere in the trees, a bird answered.

"How do you do that?" Andrei asked. "Imitate their calls so well?"

Ilona shrugged. "I don't know. I listen. I experiment."

Andrei attempted to make the same call, but failed to approximate the sound.

"You're holding your lips wrong," Ilona said, "and you need to move your tongue quickly up and down."

Andrei tried again. Ilona shook her head, reached out, and touched his lips.

"Rounder. And curve your tongue like you would to say the first sound in the word *iubesc*."

"As in *te iubesc*?"

She blushed, realizing what word she had chosen. "Yes," she answered. "As in 'I love *you*.'"

"I do."

"You do what?"

Now it was Andrei who was blushing. "I do love you," he said.

Somehow they were standing very close to each other even though Ilona didn't remember stepping forward. Their fingers were twined together. A warm shiver vibrated through Ilona's body.

"You have my permission," she whispered.

"What?"

"My permission."

Realizing what she was saying, Andrei grinned.

She closed her eyes. Their lips met. Andrei's kiss was cautious, questioning. Ilona answered the unspoken question by melting into him.

When they stepped apart, she felt dizzy and short of breath. "I was wondering when you were going to get around to that," she breathed.

"I should have gotten around to it sooner."

She smiled. "Yes, you should have."

Their laughter startled many of the birds into flight.

"And I think," she said, "you should get around to it again."

Acknowledgments

I owe a huge thanks to my incredibly talented editor, Emily Settle, who has coached me and cheered me on through the daunting process of preparing a novel for publication. I'll ever be grateful for her candid honesty and wonderful ability to see story potential far beyond anything my own limited vision can see. Thank you also to Linda Minton for her careful copyediting and thorough fact-checking and further thanks to Jean Feiwel, Lauren, Holly, Kat, and the rest of the Swoon Reads team for giving *Heart of the Impaler* its chance to be published. This has been the fulfillment of a long-pursued dream.

Thank you to Lynne Harter for supporting me through multiple drafts of multiple writing projects. Her beta-reading skills are unmatched. I've developed into a better writer because of her astute insights. Thank you also to Kaleigh Harter and Becky C. for their input during early drafts of this novel. Their thoughtful comments made a much-needed difference in the ongoing development of this story idea.

I'd be remiss if I didn't include Marlene Stringer in the list of those who have encouraged, supported, and guided me along the long path to publication. Thank you for your patient efforts and for all you did to help get me here.

Thank you to Kathleen Breitenfeld for *Impaler*'s stunning cover and to Michelle Gengaro-Kokmen for this novel's atmospheric book design.

I'm also grateful for the kind writers of the Swoon Squad. They celebrated with me and were swift to welcome me when the thrilling announcement was made that *Impaler* would be published. Among these authors, I need to give a special thank-you to Samantha Hastings for her sage advice and cheerful encouragement. I couldn't have asked for a better Swoon mentor!

Last but not least, I am eternally indebted to my wife, who believes I can accomplish more than I allow myself to believe. I am who I am because of her.

Author's Note

Dracula—the REAL Dracula—wasn't a vampire, but in his day he built a reputation as bloodthirsty as any vampire's. The Ottomans called him *Kazîglu Bey*, meaning "Impaler Lord," a name he earned because of his fondness for skewering his enemies on sharpened wooden stakes.

Vlad Dracula III was a proud descendant of Basarab the Founder, first monarch of an independent Wallachia, a small principality now part of modern Romania. Basarab's descendants, including Dracula, ruled their ancestral home for approximately two centuries. Holding on to power, however, was a complicated matter. Aspiring princes faced many slippery obstacles along the road to the throne. One of these was a huge disagreement within the House of Basarab itself.

After the death of Basarab's grandson, Radu I, Vlad's ancestors split themselves into two bitterly opposed camps. On the one side was the House of Dăneşti, the descendants of Radu's immediate successor, Dan I. On the other side were the progeny of Dan's half brother, Mircea the Great. Vlad's side of the family would come to be known as the House of Drăculeşti (House of the Dragon), and they would play a game of "musical thrones" with the Dăneşti clan as each side contested its right to rule.

Basarab's family wasn't alone in this competition. Christian monarchs to the north and Ottoman sultans to the south also had a personal stake in which descendant occupied the throne. Transylvania and Hungary pushed for an ally who could buffer them against the threat of an expanding Ottoman Empire. The Ottomans, for their part, desired a voivode who would pay tribute, provide young soldiers, and give their armies free passage into Europe. It was an impossible dilemma, either pitting the current Wallachian prince against his fellow Christians or forcing him to stand—sometimes alone—against one of the mightiest military forces in the world. Young Vlad, like his predecessors, was caught in the middle of it.

One Transylvanian leader would play a significant role in Vlad Dracula's life. Referred to by Pope Pius II as "Christ's Champion" and affectionately dubbed "the White Knight" by his many admirers, János Hunyadi was at first a Drăculeşti ally but became their enemy when Vlad's father signed his treaty with the Ottomans. This treaty would be disastrous for Vlad's father, and it set off a fateful chain of events that ultimately sealed Vlad's destiny as the future "Impaler Lord." *Heart of the Impaler*, although fiction, attempts to portray some of these events.

A significant difference between actual history and a key event in this novel is that Vlad didn't murder his brother Mircea. While Vlad and Radu were away at the sultan's court, Mircea was buried alive by the local boyars. The chronology of events in this novel also had to be altered to fit several years' worth of events into a shorter span of time. This being said, the story remains true to actual history whenever possible.

Ilona and Andrei are fictional characters, but their family names were real. The House of Muşat ruled Moldavia, and the House of Csáki held power, for a time, in Transylvania. János Hunyadi, Murad the Great, members of Vlad's immediate family, and Vlad the Monk (and his mother) were living, breathing people. For readers who would like to learn more about these characters and Vlad Dracula's fascinating history, the following books are highly recommended: *Vlad the Impaler: The Real Count Dracula* by Enid A. Goldberg and Norman Itzkowitz, and *Dracula: Prince of Many Faces* by Radu R. Florescu and Raymond T. McNally.

GLOSSARY OF TERMS

FOR THOSE READERS INTERESTED IN THE CORRECT PRONUNCIations of the languages used in this novel, a close approximation has been provided in brackets. Pronounce the bracketed letters as you would in English, giving emphasis to syllables printed in capital letters and pronouncing any "ah" like the "a" in the word "car," "a" like the "a" in the word "cat," "igh" as the vowel sound in "night," and "zh" like the "s" in "measure."

Ajută-mă [ah-ZHOO-tuh-muh] (Romanian) Help me

Bine! Cum vrei tu! [BEE-neh coom VRAY too] (Romanian) Fine! Whatever you want!

boyar [boh-YAHR] the English term used for a Romanian or Russian lord or nobleman

bun venit [boon ven-EET] (Romanian) welcome

Bună dimineața [BOO-nuh dee-mee-NYA-tsah] (Romanian) Good morning

Bună ziua [BOO-nuh ZEE-wah] (Romanian) Hello / Good
day

călugăr [kah-LOO-gar] (Romanian) monk

Cântecul Lebedei [KUN-teh-koo leh-BEH-day] (Romanian)
Swan Song

charger an all-around term for a medieval horse

cneajna [cnee-AHJ-nah] a Slavic title meaning princess or
duchess

Codru Conac [KOH-droo koh-NAHK] (Romanian) Forest
Manor

consumption the medieval term for tuberculosis

cu placere [ku PLA-tsce-re] (Romanian) with pleasure

Curtea Domnească [KOOR-tya dome-NYA-skuh]
(Romanian) Wallachia's "Princely Court," the voivode's
royal residence

dăunător [doo-nuh-TORE] (Romanian) pest

deochi [duh-OH-key] (Romanian) the evil eye

destrier [DES-tree-er] a highly trained, highly prized, and
very expensive type of medieval warhorse

doamna mea [DWOM-nuh MA] (Romanian) my lady

ducat a gold coin common throughout Medieval
Europe

Dur! Neden buradasınız? [dewr neh-DEN boor-uh-DUH-
sin-iz] (Turkish) Halt! Why are you here?

gambeson a padded, often quilted jacket worn under armor
or serving as armor in and of itself

garderobe a medieval term for the lavatory or toilet; also a
room for storing clothing or a private bedroom

Începe [un-CHEH-peh] (Romanian) Begin

Isten hozta [ISH-ten HOHZ-tah] (Hungarian) Welcome / (literally) God has brought you

Jó napot [yoh NAH-pote] (Hungarian) Good day / Good afternoon

Jó reggelt [yoh REHG-gehlt] (Hungarian) Good morning

kalpak [kahl-PAHK] (Turkish) a tall felt or sheepskin boyar hat

Kız çok hasta. [kuz choke HAHS-tah] (Turkish) The girl is very sick.

Kocs [COACH] a village in Hungary renowned for its carriages

Köszönöm [KUR-sur-nurm] (Hungarian) Thank you

La revedere [lah reh-veh-DAIR-ay] (Romanian) Goodbye

madárka [muh-DAHR-kuh] (Hungarian) little bird

méhevő [MEE-heh-VOO] (Hungarian) bee-eater

Minunat [mee-noo-NAHT] (Romanian) Splendid / Lovely / Wonderful / Great

Mulțumesc [mool-tsoo-MESK] (Romanian) Thank you

nagyon jó [NAH-gyo-eh yo] (Hungarian) wonderful or very good

neispravit [nay-spraw-VEET] (Romanian) dolt, dunderhead, dunce

Noapte bună [NWAHP-teh BOO-nuh] (Romanian) Good night

Olyan hülye [OHL-yawn HOOL-yeh] (Hungarian) So stupid

palfrey an expensive riding horse

Pe curând [peh cur-OOHND] (Romanian) See you soon

sală mare [SAWL-luh MAHR-ay] (Romanian) great hall

scovergi [sko-VER-gee] (Romanian) flat discs of fried dough, often eaten with jam, honey or cheese

Scuzaţi-mă [skoo-ZAHTS-muh] (Romanian) Excuse me

Slavă cerului [SLAW-vuh CHAIR-oo-looee] (Romanian)
Thank heavens

strigoi [STREE-go-ee] (Romanian) vampiric spirits that
live off the blood of the living, according to Romanian
folklore

szivesen [SEE-vesh-hen] (Hungarian) with pleasure

tâmpit [tum-PEET] (Romanian) imbecile, lunkhead, idiot,
coot

Te iubesc. [teh YOU-besk] (Romanian) I love you.

Vă rog [VAH rug] (Romanian) Please / For pity's sake

Vai de mine [vigh deh MEE-neh] (Romanian) Dear me /
Woe is me

vajda [VIGH-dah] (Hungarian) voivode, warlord

Viszontlátásra [VEE-sohnt-lah-tahsh-rah] (Hungarian)
Goodbye

voivode [VOY-vode] (Old Slavonic) a warlord, a Wallachian
prince

zevzec [zehv-ZEHK] (Romanian) rattle-head, addle-brain,
simpleton

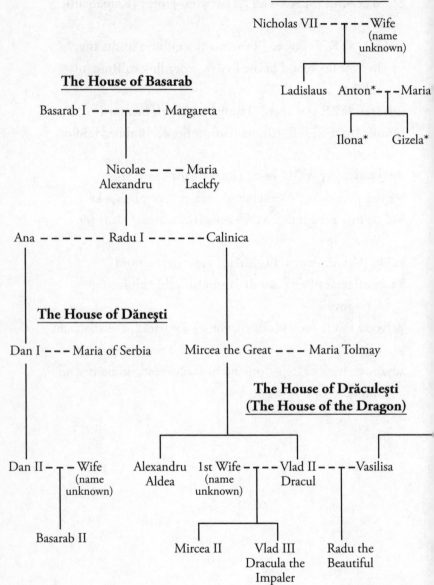

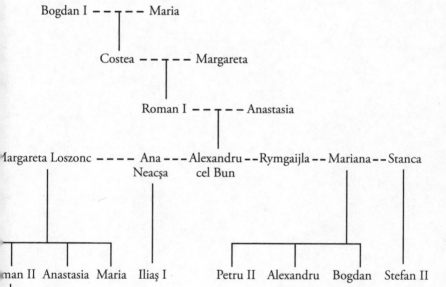

The House of Racoviță**

Virghiliu* – – ⊤ – – Sofia*

Călțuna   Magdalena

The House of Golescu**

Dragoș* – – – ⊤ – – Livia*

Daciana*

The House of Mușat

Bogdan I – – ⊤ – – Maria

Costea – – – ⊤ – – Margareta

Roman I – – – ⊤ – – Anastasia

...argareta Loszonc – – – – Ana – – – Alexandru – Rymgaijla – – Mariana – – Stanca
Neacșa   cel Bun

...man II Anastasia Maria   Iliaș I   Petru II Alexandru Bogdan Stefan II

...drei*

* fictional characters   ** The Houses of Racoviță and Golescu are actual
fifteenth-century Wallachian boyar families.

Check out more books chosen for publication by readers like you.

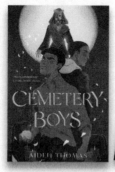